NOAH
AND THE
STORK

Penny
McCusker

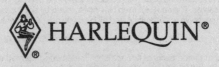

HARLEQUIN®

TORONTO • NEW YORK • LONDON
AMSTERDAM • PARIS • SYDNEY • HAMBURG
STOCKHOLM • ATHENS • TOKYO • MILAN • MADRID
PRAGUE • WARSAW • BUDAPEST • AUCKLAND

ISBN 0-373-75086-2

NOAH AND THE STORK

www.eHarlequin.com

Printed in U.S.A.

For my husband, Michael, and my kids, Mike,
Erin and Ian. Because you put up with me.

Books by Penny McCusker

HARLEQUIN AMERICAN ROMANCE
1063—MAD ABOUT MAX

Don't miss any of our special offers. Write to us at the
following address for information on our newest releases.

Harlequin Reader Service
U.S.: 3010 Walden Ave., P.O. Box 1325, Buffalo, NY 14269
Canadian: P.O. Box 609, Fort Erie, Ont. L2A 5X3

Chapter One

Men were generally a pain in the neck, Janey Walters thought, but there were times when they came in handy. Like when your house needed a paint job, or your kitchen floor could use refinishing, or your car was being powered by what sounded like a drunk tap dancer with a thirst for motor oil.

Or when you woke in the middle of the night, alone and aching with needs that went way beyond physical, into realms best left to Hallmark and American Greetings. Whoever wrote those cards managed to say everything there was to say about love in a line or two. Janey didn't even like to think about the subject anymore. Thinking about it made her yearn, yearning made her hopeful, and hope, considering her track record with the opposite sex, was a waste of energy.

She set her paintbrush on top of the can and climbed to her feet. She'd been sitting on the front porch for the past hour, slapping paint on the railings, wondering if the petty violence of it might exorcise the sense of futility that had settled over her as of late. All she'd managed to do was polka-dot everything in the vicinity—the lawn and rosebushes, the porch floor and herself—which only made more work for her and did nothing to solve the real problems.

And boy, did she have problems. No more than any other single mom who lived in a house that was a century old, with barely enough money to keep up with what absolutely had to be fixed, never mind preventive maintenance. And thankfully, Jessie was a normal nine-year-old girl—at least she seemed well-adjusted, despite the fact that her father had never been, and probably never would be, a part of her life.

It only seemed worse to Janey now that her best friend had gotten married. But then, Sara had been waiting six years for Max to figure out he loved her, and Janey would never have wished for a different outcome. She and Sara still worked together, and talked nearly every day, so it wasn't as if anything had really changed in Janey's life. It just felt…emptier somehow.

She put both hands on the small of her aching back and stretched, letting her head fall back and breathing deeply, in and out, until she felt some of the frustration and loneliness begin to fade away.

"Now there's a sight for sore eyes."

Janey gasped, straightening so fast she all but gave herself whiplash. That voice… Heat moved through her, but the cold chill that snaked down her spine won hands down. It couldn't be him, she told herself. He couldn't simply show up at her house with no warning, no time to prepare.

"The best scenery in town was always on this street."

She peeked over her shoulder, and the snappy comebacks she was famous for deserted her. So did the unsnappy comebacks and all the questions she should've been asking. She couldn't have strung a coherent sentence together if the moment had come with subtitles. She was too busy staring at the man standing on the other side of her wrought-iron fence.

His voice had changed some; it was deeper, with a gravelly edge that seemed to rasp along her nerve endings. But there was no mistaking that face, not when it had haunted her memories—good and bad—for more than a decade. "Noah Bryant," Janey muttered, giving him a nice, slow once-over.

He was taller than she remembered, and had a solid, substantial look to him now. In high school he'd been lanky, slim but wide-shouldered with a bad-boy gleam in his sharp green eyes that made every female heart within range tumble just a little. Except hers, Janey recalled. Her heart had taken the whole long, irrevocable fall the first time she'd laid eyes on him. That would've been the fourth grade. And she'd stayed madly in love with him, right up to the moment he'd blasted out of town without so much as a backward glance.

Ten years ago, that had been. She hadn't seen him since, but all the times she'd imagined this scene, it had never gone down like this, with him in a suit that probably cost more than she made in a month, while she was decked out in the latest in janitor chic. She reached up to pull the bandanna from her head, then decided against it; flat hair would only complete the fashion statement. "You swore you'd never come back to Erskine."

And there was the grin that went along with the gleam. "Things change."

"Really? You never could keep your word."

His smile dimmed. "Still haven't forgiven me, I see."

"Don't be ridiculous." She pulled her bandanna off, after all, to brush at the droplets that had splashed onto her legs. Who was she trying to impress, anyway? A guy who'd claimed to love her a decade ago and then hightailed it out of town without even telling her why? "You haven't crossed my mind in years."

"Well, I've thought of you, Janey. You're the one pleasant memory I have of this place."

"Yeah, this is hell on earth," she said, peering up and down the quiet street. Hundred-year old houses with perfectly manicured lawns and gardens sat behind white-picket or wrought-iron fences. Most of them were businesses now, all but her house and Mrs. Halliwell's, across the street and a couple down. To him, Erskine, Montana, was tame, boring, forgettable. To Janey it was simply home. "No wonder you couldn't wait to get out of here."

"I've always regretted the way things ended between us."

Regret? He had no idea what that meant. She glanced over her shoulder even though she knew the front door was safely closed, and then she went down the stairs to be absolutely sure her voice wouldn't carry inside. "Yeah, well, they did end, so why are you here?" she asked, taking a stance on the front walk, one hip cocked, arms crossed, chin lifted. Noah seemed to get some amusement out of it, judging by his slight smile, but it made her feel stronger.

"I was passing through on business and when I saw you…"

All she had to do was look at him and he got the message. He wasn't stupid, just untrustworthy.

"I guess I should head out," he said, but instead of leaving, he had the audacity to step up to the fence and offer his hand.

Janey was going to take it, too. There was no way she'd back down from the challenge she saw in his eyes, no matter what it might cost her to actually put her hand in his. She took a step forward, then stopped short at the sound of her daughter's voice.

"Mom," Jessie called, racketing out the front door and down the steps, jumping the last three as had become her habit. She hit the ground and barreled into her mother— another new habit—practically knocking Janey off her feet. "Mrs. Devlin called. They're riding out to bring in the spring calves this weekend, and she asked if I want to go along. She said I could take the bus home with Joey tomorrow and spend the night, if it's okay with you."

"Mom?" Noah said, his jaw dropping. Not that he couldn't see her as a mom; he couldn't think of anyone who loved children more or would be better at raising them than Janey. It was only that, in his mind, she was still seventeen, still carefree and single, not a grown woman with a kid eight or nine years old....

Jessie turned around then and Noah found himself looking into a pair of green eyes, the kind of green eyes he'd seen every morning of his life, staring back at him from his own mirror. His gaze lifted, slowly, to meet Janey's, suspicion oozing into the tiny part of his brain that shock hadn't paralyzed.

Janey pulled the kid back against her, wrapping her arms around the girl's thin shoulders. The truth Noah saw on her face slid into uncertainty, then misery when he didn't speak. They stood that way for a moment, eyes locked, nerves strained, enough emotional baggage between them to make Sigmund Freud feel overworked.

The kid came to everyone's rescue. She glanced up at her mom, then confidently stepped out of the shelter of Janey's arms. She stopped halfway between the two adults, fixed Noah with a stare that was almost too direct to return, and said, "I'm Jessie. Are you my dad?"

NOAH FOUND HIMSELF still at the curb in front of Janey's house, sitting in his car with no clear idea how he'd gotten there except that raw fury had something to do with it. By the time he fought through the red haze blurring his vision, the dashboard clock told him a couple of hours had passed. The day was no more than a pale crescent over the mountains and lights were burning in Janey's windows. Homey, inviting lights that weren't meant to make him feel like an outsider. But he did. He always had, his entire life. Some people would say that nobody could make you feel inferior without your own permission, but when you were the kid of a dirt-poor farmer in cattle country, and you moved to a town like Erskine where the people knew each other so well they were like family, ostracism was the least of what you felt.

Janey had been the one person he'd counted on to always stand by him, whether they were a couple or just good friends, even if it meant bucking the opinion of the entire town. He'd come back to town believing that hadn't changed. But all these years she'd shut him out, making a home for herself and her daughter in this small, close-knit community. Without him.

It wasn't fair of him to see it that way but he didn't care. He needed to be angry, because without the strength of that emotion, he'd have to feel the hurt and betrayal—weak emotions that would make it impossible to face her again. And he had to face her again, if for no other reason than that she owed him an explanation about his daughter.

His half-grown daughter.

Noah wasn't sure how he felt about that. Except scared. And angry.

He let the injustice of the secret Janey had kept carry him to her front door, three inches of solid, sound-deadening oak with a nice, big dead bolt. He'd kick it in if he had to.

Janey opened it before he could even knock, stepping out on the porch and closing the door softly behind her. "I think it would be best if you didn't come in."

"You can't expect me to walk away."

"I'm not expecting you to walk away, Noah. Just give yourself some time to calm down."

"And what about Jessie? The kid's been wondering where I've been all her life, and the minute I show up you hustle her off like I'm some kind of maniac."

"If you'd seen the expression on your face, you'd have done the same."

"Okay, so I'm steamed. But it can't be good—"

"Don't you dare lecture me on what's good for Jessie. You haven't been around—"

"How was I supposed to know?"

"I called you when…when I found out I was pregnant. I left you a message." She stopped, wrapping her arms around herself.

Noah got the impression she was fighting back tears—but that was absurd. The Janey he remembered never cried.

"You didn't return my call," she finally finished.

"You should've kept calling."

"That was my responsibility, too? To hound you until guilt brought you back here when love couldn't? It's not bad enough that I had to tell my father and see the disappointment—" This time her voice did break.

Noah took a step forward, just one, before she took a step back and he remembered that all he should be feeling toward her was anger.

It didn't take her long to get herself together. Janey was nothing if not strong. "What would you have done?" she asked him. "Given up college, forgotten all your plans for a big career and settled here?"

"You didn't give me the chance."

"No, you didn't give *us* a chance, Noah. You walked out with no goodbye, no explanation and now you stand there and tell me I should've dragged you back out of responsibility when it was clear you didn't want me? You knew me better than that."

Yes, he did. Janey wouldn't have begged, but when she'd called him all those years ago, he'd let himself believe she was going to do exactly that. He'd told himself that she loved him enough to swallow her pride and ask him to come back. He'd never imagined she might have another reason for contacting him—his ego hadn't allowed it—so he hadn't contacted her. And he'd thought he was being so noble, that if he really loved her he'd let her go because that was best for her. "Janey—"

She held up a hand. "That's behind us now, and I'd rather not rehash it, if you don't mind."

"No," he said after a contemplative moment. There was no use rehashing it, and what could he have said? That there'd been regrets? That he'd often wished he'd made different choices, burned fewer bridges? What good would it do them now? "We have a daughter. That matters."

Hearing it put like that shocked her. Her expression didn't give her away, but she stiffened and even in the deepening gloom of the covered porch, he could tell all the color had washed out of her face. The last of his anger faded. He'd just discovered he had a daughter, but it must, Noah realized, have taken a great deal of courage for Janey to even open her front door, knowing that no matter how he reacted, she'd have to deal with it and then help Jessie do the same.

"We can stand out here," he said, slapping at a sudden sting on his neck, "or we can go inside."

"A few mosquito bites won't hurt us."

"Okay, but it's not only the mosquitoes. Someone's bound to see us, and the news will be all over town before you can say West Nile virus."

Her mouth curved in a ghost of a smile. "Gossip is the national sport around here, and I get my turn to be the star player, like everyone else. It's never really bothered me."

"Even if it means you'd be linked with me again?"

She shot him a look. He had a point, but she'd be damned if she admitted that the last thing she wanted was to hear her name and his in the same sentence. In any context. She'd had enough of that when she was seventeen. "It's not as if we have much choice. People are bound to find out you're back in town again."

He didn't reply, and although his expression was inscrutable, Janey didn't get a very positive feeling about what he was thinking. Or maybe, where Noah was concerned, it was best to be pessimistic. "If you're truly worried about Jessie, leaving now is about the worst thing you could do."

"I didn't leave, did I? I want to discuss this, but I don't see why we have to be eaten alive while we're doing it."

"Consider it planning your part in the food chain."

Noah did the why-me combination, heavy exhalation, eye roll, a little shake of his head. "You were always too stubborn for your own good." He closed the distance between them and reached for her.

"Don't touch me."

"Worse things have happened."

"True, but you were around then, too."

"Does that include Jessie?"

She went still, one hand creeping up to rub at her aching chest. "I've never considered her a bad thing."

He cupped her elbow and steered her up the front steps. "Just the fact that I'm her father."

Janey would've told him to go to hell, but she couldn't have dug a coherent sentence out of her brain with a bulldozer, let alone voice it. The touch of his fingers on her bare skin had scorched enough brain cells to leave her temporarily senile.

When he let go of her to open the door and her mental processes kicked back in, she realized this was about Jessie. The girl had been wondering about her father for nine years, and when she finally met him, he completely freaked out. Heaven only knew what was going through her daughter's mind, Janey thought, because she rarely did. If Noah disappeared now, though, Jessie was bound to take it personally. Janey had firsthand experience with that.

"I can't believe you still live here," Noah said, as he ushered her into the big old Victorian house that had been built by her great-great-grandparents.

She slipped into the front parlor, turned on a floor lamp with a fussy, glass-fringed shade and felt instantly comforted. She loved the cheerful tinkling sound it made, how it threw prisms of light into every corner of the room, the same way it had for as long as she could remember. "Where else would I live?"

"New York, L.A., London. There are some real cities out there in the world, Janey."

"I like it here. You're the one who couldn't wait to get out of Erskine."

He went quiet for a long moment. "I had my reasons."

"I knew you weren't happy here, Noah, but you never wanted to talk about it."

"It's still never."

She stepped back out of the parlor. "Is that why you're standing in the hallway?"

He stared at her for a second, mouth set in a grim line, eyes dark and intense.

"The front door's right behind you."

She could see he was considering it, and she knew before he spoke that he'd come to the same conclusion she had only moments before. This was about Jessie.

"Where is she?" Noah asked.

"Upstairs, in the tower room." Janey said, referring to the uppermost floor of the turreted part of the house. The room was ringed with windows and high enough to see over the other houses in this part of Erskine. Jessie seemed to find the view soothing, although all that would be visible at this time of evening was the sun setting behind the mountains. "It's where she goes whenever something's bothering her."

"So did you," Noah murmured with a half smile Janey couldn't bear to see. The look of pleasant nostalgia on his face was too painful to believe.

"What have you told her?" he asked.

"What's there to tell her? I had no idea where you were or what you were doing."

"So all I am is some guy you slept with ten years ago?"

"What do you want to hear, Noah?" She straightened, coming out into the hallway to confront him, her voice as tightly controlled as her temper. "That she used to ask who her father was, and where he was, and why her mom and dad weren't married like most of the other kids' parents—or at least divorced and splitting weekends and holidays?"

"Those are good questions, Janey, every one of them."

"And I had good answers for them, except she was too young to understand those answers. She doesn't know how it feels to be in love, to trust someone so completely…" Janey clenched her fists, refusing to let him see how much it had hurt. "I lived it and I don't even understand it."

"Janey—"

"Then she started asking the hard questions," she continued, talking right over him. "Like why didn't her dad want to spend any time with her, or at least meet her? And here's the really hard one, Noah. What's wrong with her? No matter how often I said it had nothing to do with her, I could tell she still thought it was her fault."

"Jeez, Janey." Noah ran a hand back through his hair, leaving it rumpled, a fitting counterpoint to the wild light in his eyes, eyes so like Jessie's it was painful to look into them.

Janey bit back the rest of the angry words clawing at the back of her throat. He'd earned her anger, but making him hurt, like she and Jessie had hurt, wouldn't solve anything. "Jessie stopped asking questions about you a long time ago. She's accepted the fact that her parents aren't together. It's not unusual, even in Erskine. It's just—" She caught her lower lip between her teeth and turned away. It didn't help; Noah could still read her mind, it seemed.

"You're wondering whether it's a good thing I'm here or not."

"Yeah, well, something about stuffing toothpaste back into the tube occurs to me."

"So, what happens now?"

She brought her eyes back to him. "Right now that depends on you."

"I don't know what to say."

"And I can't give you the words, Noah."

He jammed his hands in his pockets, seeming more uncertain by the second.

"If you can't do this, I'll find some way to explain it to her."

"What if I say the wrong thing?"

"At least it'll be you saying it. And you can always apologize. It's not like she thinks you're perfect or anything."

He held her gaze for a moment, then smiled wryly. "No, I don't imagine she does."

"I'll go get her." When Janey got to the tower room, however, she found Jessie curled up fast asleep on the old sofa that had been there forever. For the last four years her beloved stuffed bear had held a cherished place on the topmost shelf of her bedroom hutch. The fact that it was back in her arms tonight spoke volumes about the state of her heart and mind.

Janey brushed the hair from her daughter's brow, carefully so as not to wake her, and covered her with an old knitted blanket. Better she have as many hours of peace as she could, Janey figured, easing out of the room and down the creaky staircase. Noah would have to come back tomorrow.

But when she got downstairs, he was already gone.

Chapter Two

Janey had been upstairs longer than she intended, but she'd expected Noah to hang around. Of course, he'd never had much staying power....

"I'm in here," he called out.

And she'd become way too cynical, she realized as she followed his voice into the parlor. So he'd romanced her out of her virginity after their senior prom and then left town. All on the same night. So he'd ignored her attempts to tell him he had a child, then got angry with her when he found out by accident. Water under the bridge, all of it. She'd gotten herself through college, with the help of her parents, and even after she'd lost them, within months of each other, she'd made a life for herself and her daughter. There were times—okay, there were lots of times—when she'd wished there was a man around, not just to deal with a broken-down car or paint the porch, but because it would've been nice to share the emotional load once in a while. But she had friends, a whole town full of them, and she had Jessie. And if, every now and then, she woke in the night, unbelievably lonely, that was her choice, too.

There'd been opportunities over the years, but no one who'd... Hell, she might as well admit she compared every man she met to Noah. Or not to him, exactly, but to the way he'd made her feel all those years ago. Nothing since had even come close.

Until now. Noah was sitting in her father's favorite arm-chair, suit jacket unbuttoned, tie loosened, his head back and his eyes closed. She'd seen her father sit just like that, count-less evenings after countless days at his law office. A strong sense of rightness washed through her—which she had no trouble shaking off when their history flashed through her brain. Even if she still loved him, she'd be a fool to trust him again. And Janey Walters was nobody's fool.

"Don't get too comfortable," she said.

He opened his eyes and stared at her long enough to make her antsy before he lifted a brow in inquiry.

"She's sleeping."

Noah felt every muscle in his body relax—well, not every muscle. He should be taking this unexpected reprieve as an opportunity to get his thoughts in order, but how could he with Janey prowling the room like that? He could understand the nerves that kept her on her feet, but when she reached up to straighten a picture, all he could think about was how in-credible she was. Beautiful. Her face was more angular than he remembered, pared down by time and maturity so that her inner strength showed through. He'd always been a sucker for strong, self-sufficient women, and there was something about Janey, taking charge of her life in that ratty old bandanna and T-shirt. And the jeans…

He closed his eyes, hoping that if the denim was gone from his sight, he'd forget how it hugged her bottom and skimmed the swell of her hips. It didn't work. Closing his eyes was like giving his imagination a blank canvas, and Janey Walters was a model who would've done any of the old mas-ters proud. One look at her and he felt as if a freight train had slammed into his chest.

Or maybe that had more to do with finding out he had a daughter.

He opened his eyes again, caught her watching him, and nodded toward the chair across from his.

"I have paint all over me," Janey said.

"It's probably dry."

She said a word under her breath that sounded suspiciously like *damn,* which, in light of what followed, made perfect sense. She started for the door, saying, "I left the paint open and the paintbrush is probably rock-hard by now."

"It's just a paintbrush, Janey."

"It's not just a paintbrush when—" She broke off, shook her head.

That hesitation was unlike Janey, at least the Janey he used to know. She'd always been so in-your-face, so unafraid to put her opinions and feelings out there and dare anybody to take issue with them. In Erskine that went beyond courage.

But she had someone else to think of now. What she said and did would reflect directly on Jessie, and if he knew Janey, she'd go well out of her way to avoid causing her daughter any unhappiness. Not that the old Janey wasn't still in there somewhere. She might be more tightly controlled now, more guarded, but one look into his daughter's eyes, and there was no question where she'd gotten that straightforward approach to life. Janey had raised her alone—and done a hell of a job. But then, Noah had never doubted Janey would be a great mom. She'd always known what she wanted. And he'd always been afraid he couldn't give it to her. In the end, he hadn't. He'd let her down just like everyone had expected him to—*worse* than they'd expected.

But she'd hadn't exactly given him a chance to redeem himself.

"So, how much does Jessie know about me?" he asked.

"Not much." Janey sank into a chair after all. "If anyone in this town heard from you in the last ten years, they didn't mention it to me, and they wouldn't bring it up to Jessie."

"It's no surprise that everyone rallied around you, Janey. This was always more your place than mine."

"You cut the ties, Noah."

"Dad was still alive and living here, then."

"And you didn't want anything to do with him, either. I get that. So do us both a favor and don't try to make this whole thing my fault. Maybe I could've found a way to tell you sooner. If you'd bothered to call me ten years ago."

He rested his head against the chair again and reminded himself that she was right: holding on to his anger over the past would only make the present situation more difficult. He'd learned that the hard way, not coming back for his father's funeral because the man had never made room in his life for anyone but himself. Funny, Noah thought, how petty that kind of retribution felt after a decade had passed. Funny how you didn't want it to happen again. "So tell me about her."

"Her name is Jessica Marie Walters."

That brought his attention back to Janey. "Walters?"

"Walters."

It took him a minute, but he swallowed that, too. "What else?"

"If you call her Jessica, she won't answer you. The rest I think you should find out on your own."

"Come on, Janey, give me a break."

"If I tell you everything, the two of you won't have anything to talk about, and you were concerned about that."

"Okay." He shoved a hand through his hair. "Okay."

"You should go."

"Yeah." Noah stood and rolled his shoulders, looking around the room as if the walls were hiding the answer to the strange way he was feeling. He tucked a hand in his pocket and jingled his car keys.

"I'll call you tomorrow night. Where are you staying?"

"The Erskine Hotel, I guess."

"The hotel is being fumigated. Termites."

Not surprising for a town built almost entirely of wood that hadn't seen the inside of a tree for a couple centuries. What surprised him was that any of the decrepit old buildings were still standing. But that wasn't really the point.

The Tambour clock on the mantel chimed once for eight-thirty. Past closing time for a community that started its day before 6:00 a.m. The hotel was the only place in town that stayed open pretty much around the clock, and even then the dining room shut down by ten. "I'll have to drive to Plains City before I can find a place to stay. That's fifty miles."

"Then maybe you'd better get started."

"Can't. I was almost out of gas when I saw you and decided to stop. I probably won't make it twenty miles."

"At least that would be twenty miles away from here," Janey muttered. She refused to feel guilty. It wasn't her fault he'd run his car nearly out of gas when he knew all too well that the streets of Erskine were rolled up promptly at 8:00 p.m. It was one of the reasons he'd been in such a rush to get out of town. She was the other reason.

"Is Max Devlin still around? Maybe I can impose on him for the night."

"Yes. *No!* I mean, Max is still here. He came back after college, but you can't bother him. He just got married." To her best friend, who would insist on hearing the whole story and then dissecting it as if it were a science experiment. Janey loved Sara Devlin like a sister, but she had no intention of reliving the past. She'd done enough of that for one night, she thought, glancing over at Noah.

He was smiling. At her. That couldn't be good.

"Then I guess I'll have to stay here."

"Uhhh… she said, waiting for her brain to come up with another objection. Eventually she had to close her mouth. She already felt stupid; she didn't have to look it, too.

"What are you worried about?" he asked, easing back a step, his hands spread out, just as she'd seen every cop on every crime show do with every cornered criminal. *Look at me,* he was saying, *I'm harmless.*

Harmless, hah. The man was a walking weapon, from his to-die-for face to the tall, solid body that made her heart pound so hard she could imagine it jumping out of her chest and throwing itself at his feet, leaving behind a flat-haired corpse in paint-spattered clothes. The way he walked was enough to stall the air in her lungs so she could barely breathe, which was probably for the best since not breathing meant not smelling. She'd always been far too susceptible to a man who smelled really good, and Noah Bryant appeared to be a man who'd learned how to balance his cologne with just the right amount of, well, himself.

"You don't worry me," she said. No, she was worried about herself. "But you still have to leave."

"C'mon, Janey, it doesn't make sense—"

"You can't stay here."

"—for me to leave—"

"You can't stay here."

"—when I'll just have to come back to talk to Jessie. Besides, where am I going to go?"

"You didn't seem to have a problem figuring that out ten years ago."

"I'm beat, Janey," he said. "I promise it'll only be for one night."

She folded her arms and glared at him, trying to find it in herself to send him packing. But he really did seem to be exhausted, and if she kicked him out she'd only be up half the night worrying about him stranded in the middle of nowhere, sleeping in his car. *If* he didn't fall asleep at the wheel and end up in a ditch filled with water, upside down with both his doors jammed shut and his seat belt stuck....

"One night." She left the parlor and started up the stairs, adding over her shoulder, "Tomorrow you find somewhere else to stay."

Noah took his time getting to the top, smiling benignly.

"I mean it."

He pressed his lips together. His eyes were still sparkling at her, but without the grin she could pretend he was taking the whole thing seriously.

She opened the door to the first bedroom she came to and said, "You can sleep in here."

"Do you mind if I have a shower?" he asked.

"Bathroom's right next door." Janey held her hand out, palm up.

He stared at it, clearly puzzled.

"Unless you plan to borrow my clothes, too, you'll need your suitcase."

"I'll get it."

"No way. Mrs. Halliwell is home by now. I don't want her to see you walking into my house carrying a suitcase."

"Won't she wonder about my car?"

"I can explain that away. You, on the other hand…" She shook her head. "There's no explaining you."

"Does that mean she's not used to seeing men come into your house at night and leave the next morning?"

"Men? That's not a revolving door down there, you know."

"Okay, *man,* singular. You don't have a boyfriend who does sleepovers?"

"None of your business."

"It is if he's going to come storming in here to punch my lights out."

Now there was a mental picture worth smiling about. "Maybe you should reconsider staying here."

"I'll chance it," Noah said, "but I don't want some dumb-as-a-post cowboy taking out his anger on my car."

"Dumb because he's a cowboy or dumb because he's dating me?"

He gave her a once-over, a slow grin starting at his mouth and moving all the way to his eyes. "Okay, I take back the dumb part, but only if you'll let me put my car in your garage."

Janey would've let him do anything—just about—as long he stopped looking at her as if he wanted to repeat history. "Nobody will beat up your car."

"I didn't really think so," he said, "but it's supposed to rain tonight, so I'd still like to put it inside."

"Why?"

"You're kidding, right? Did you see it?"

"Yeah, it has four wheels, a couple of doors. I think it was red," she added hopefully, but he just kept staring at her as though she'd let down the team. "What's the big deal?"

"It's a Porsche."

"So? It's not made of gold, is it?"

"It ought to be, considering what I paid for it."

"Well. Your fancy ride will be bunking with a Beetle."

Noah thought about it for a minute. "What year is it?"

"I'm not sure. Seventy-something, I think."

He nodded in approval. "Vintage."

Janey knew he was half kidding, but it was the half-truthful part that had her so bemused. She looked him up and down, shaking her head. "Expensive suit, expensive car and you probably have a prestigious address and a trophy blonde to go with it all. You got everything you wanted, didn't you, Noah?"

He shrugged. Sure, he had all the status symbols, along with a nice fat bank account to support his fast-paced, exciting lifestyle. But it was funny how the simplest pleasures still mattered the most. "What I really want is a shower and a meal, both preferably hot," he said. "And a bed. Any kind, but I like soft."

"There's hot water and a soft bed, but if you want to eat

you're getting leftovers," Janey said, accepting his car keys when he held them out.

She was true to her word, too. Noah had just stepped out of the shower when he heard a knock. He cracked open the door and peeked out, but he could've saved himself the trouble of slinging a towel across his hips. His suitcase was sitting there; and the rest of the hallway was empty, but his disappointment lasted about as long as it took the cloud of shampoo-scented steam to evaporate. He threw his clothes on and let his nose lead him down the stairs and through the house, as if he were a cartoon character following a tantalizing aroma. "It looks like a kitchen but it smells like heaven."

Janey swung around, startled. Her gaze dropped to his bare feet, skimmed the jeans and long-sleeved T-shirt and ended up on his wet, slicked-back hair. She turned away from him. "It's chicken stew."

"Like your mom used to make?" Noah sat down at the end of the table, where she'd laid out cutlery and bread and butter. In answer, she set a steaming bowl in front of him. He spooned some up and stuck it in his mouth, sucking in air to keep from burning his tongue. It tasted so good his eyes practically crossed in ecstasy. "God, that's incredible," he said. "Where is your mom, anyway? She move to Florida or something?"

Janey didn't say anything for a minute, and Noah realized she was still standing behind him, so close he swore he felt the warmth of her breath on the nape of his neck. He would have smiled, if not for her response.

"Mom passed away not long after Dad," she finally said, moving to sit at the other end of the table.

"I'm sorry, Janey. I didn't know. I heard about your dad, of course. The obituary of a state representative, especially one who was so well-known and well-liked, makes the front page of all the papers." Noah picked up his spoon again, stifling a pang of envy over how close Janey and her dad had been. "I'll bet you miss him."

"Every day. He was the best." Janey propped her chin on her hand and watched him eat. "So, what kind of job pays for that fancy car?"

Noah froze with the spoon halfway to his mouth. "I'm, uh…sort of a scout," he said, taking his time with the next bite of food. It was impolite to talk with your mouth full.

"If you came for the state championships, you're too late."

"Yeah, that's what I heard. Is there any more?" he asked, handing her his empty bowl.

"Sure." Janey got up, but when she turned around Noah was on his feet, as well.

"On second thought," he said, "I'm really tired. If you don't mind, I'll just go to bed."

He was gone so fast she'd just refilled his bowl when she heard the faint sound of his bedroom door closing.

She emptied the bowl back into the pan, shaking her head at her own stupidity. The man walked out of her life with no explanation and no goodbye, leaving her brokenhearted and pregnant, and here she was, giving him a place to stay, parking his car—making him a meal, for crying out loud. And he hadn't even offered to do the dishes.

Yep, men were definitely pains in the neck, she thought, looking up at the ceiling in the general vicinity of his room. Except the ones who were a pain in the heart.

Chapter Three

Noah rolled over, ramming his big toe into the footboard for the… Well, it had happened so many times he'd lost count. It barely even hurt anymore. The bed was too short and too hard, but he wasn't really sleeping, anyway.

He was reflecting—not something he normally indulged in. It was as if Erskine had a magnetic barrier at the edge of town that repelled common sense and logic and coherent thought of every kind. One minute he'd been innocently driving along, then *wham!* he'd crossed the city limits, and before he knew it he was standing in front of Janey's house. He had no idea how he got from point A to point B—except that his brain didn't have anything to do with it. And what insanity propelled him to get out of the car and walk up to her gate, just because he felt…

He felt. Seeing Janey again had brought back so many memories and emotions—more than he was prepared for—and he didn't like it. This trip wasn't about facing his past, surprising as that had turned out to be. It wasn't about his future, either, at least not the future that might include getting to know a nine-year-old daughter. It was about the next move in his career. Forgetting that would be like dancing on a sea of ice. The first step might be okay, but sooner or later he'd wind up on his ass.

He could see exactly how it would go bad, too. First he'd get sidetracked by the fact that he had a daughter, and then Janey would start to look good—hell, who was he kidding, she'd looked good from the moment he'd laid eyes on her again. He'd already conned her into letting him spend the night. Next, he'd be taking deep, appreciative breaths of the fresh country air, snapping photos of the beautiful scenery and thinking this place wasn't as bad as he remembered, that maybe he should think twice about why he'd come back here.

He thought, all right. He thought about the city where he belonged. At 11:00 p.m. his night was only beginning. Even after a long day of wheeling and dealing, he'd have gone out on the town, fuelled by caffeine and restlessness, and air polluted with enough chemicals to keep him on his feet two days after he was dead. And there'd be people, crowds of people to lose himself in, and loud music and the bottom of a scotch bottle to get to. No high-school sweetheart, no long-lost daughter, no sea of ice daring him to see how long he could keep his feet under him.

The problem was, he had to take that first step. Career destruction aside, he couldn't just walk out the door now. And it amazed him.

Who'd have believed he could feel this instant and overwhelming…awe? He'd never even considered the possibility of marrying, or having children. There'd been any number of reasons—good reasons having to do with his dismal family history and his burning ambition. What hadn't occurred to him was how it would *feel*, being a father. It wasn't just a job; you didn't go into it with a résumé or work experience, or anything, but complete and utter fear. And when you started out with a half-grown kid who was probably harboring resentment, on-the-job-training had a whole new meaning….

The long day and sleepless hours finally caught up with him, and when he opened his eyes again, they felt as if they were filled with about a pound of sand apiece, mixed with something roughly the consistency of school paste. He thought he saw Jessie. He blinked a couple of times, but the picture didn't change. It was still Jessie, barely visible in the predawn light leaking in around the windowshades, wearing the same clothes as last night, jeans and T-shirt, both baggy on her spindly frame.

He'd avoided thinking of the conversation that was coming this morning. He wasn't a man who worried and agonized, who rehearsed. He was a fly-by-the-seat-of-his-pants kind of guy. More often than not, he went with his gut. The problem was, his gut wasn't up to this conversation at the moment, not without about a gallon of coffee in it.

He rolled over and closed his eyes.

She took it as an invitation.

"What are you doing here?"

Noah flopped onto his back, thought about pulling the pillow over his head, and settled for scrubbing his hands over his face. "The hotel is closed," he said in a voice that probably should've scared her off. No such luck. "I didn't have enough gas to get to Plains City."

Silence. She stood there staring at him, unblinking. It would have been unnerving if he'd cared about anything but sleep.

"The gas station is open now," she said the minute he closed his eyes again. "It opens at five, on account of the ranchers and farmers."

He groaned and rolled over again, and then it hit him. He twisted around to squint at the clock on the nightstand. "Jeez, it's not even six yet. Nobody in their right mind gets up this early— Oh, I forgot, this is Erskine. I've left normal behind."

Jessie glowered in a way that reminded him of…himself.

"I wasn't talking about you and your mom."

"Why not? You left us behind, too."

Noah let his eyes drift shut, but it had nothing to do with exhaustion this time. He still wanted to go back to sleep, badly, but it was impossible now.

He sat up, scooting back so he could lean against the headboard. "I haven't seen a sunrise since Hell Farm," he said, his private name for the hardscrabble farm his father had bought when Noah was ten and lost to the bank not long after he'd graduated from high school.

"You haven't seen this one yet," Jessie said. "What's Hell Farm?"

"Forget I said that."

"If you won't explain it to me, I guess I shouldn't bother asking you anything else."

"Is that what you're after? An explanation?"

She locked her hands behind her back and stared down at her toes, giving him a one-shoulder shrug.

Noah waited until she looked at him, then crossed his arms and let his eyebrows inch up.

Her cute little face was scrunched in a frown. "So, what've you got to say for yourself?"

He rubbed his jaw, mostly to hide the smile. He could just imagine Janey saying that whenever Jessie got into trouble—and if she was anything like her mother, she got into plenty of trouble. It was a sobering thought, considering the situation. "Well, first off, I didn't know about you."

"Mom said."

"When I left town, it was just the two of us."

"Didn't you like her anymore? If you sleep with someone, you should like them. Or use a condom."

If she'd wanted to shock him, she'd succeeded. His mouth was open, but nothing came out except a strangled sort of sigh.

"I learned that in school. In health class. Condoms prevent…some sort of diseases and unwanted pregnancies. That's me, right?" She raised her chin and met his gaze head-on.

She was all but daring him to lie to her. Or maybe she was daring him to tell her the truth. "Um… Your mom—"

"Mom tells me all the time that she wouldn't trade me for

anything in the world, and I believe her. She never lies—or hardly ever, and then she always has a good reason." Jessie frowned. "Even if she doesn't say what it is."

"I thought I heard voices."

They both looked over and saw Janey leaning in the doorway. Noah could've kissed her, and not simply because the sight of her did things to him he should have outgrown ten years ago—although that would be reason enough.

Her hair was tousled, her eyes sleepy. She crossed her arms under her breasts, which just about killed him. He would've preferred something lacy and revealing to the loose midthigh-length T-shirt she was wearing, but apparently his hormones weren't very discriminating. Janey in a gunny sack probably would've gotten him revved up.

A glance at Jessie was all it took to cool him down again.

"What are you doing in here?" Janey asked her daughter.

"Talking to him." Jessie crossed her arms in a miniature copy of her mother's stance that gave Noah a pang he didn't want to examine too closely.

"She's after an explanation," he supplied helpfully.

"You won't be getting one," Janey said to her. "Why doesn't matter anymore. Where we go from here does." She glanced at Noah, then quickly away. "First we all need to get dressed."

"I'm already dressed," Jessie pointed out.

"In yesterday's clothes. Go wash your face, brush your teeth and put on something clean." Janey shooed Jessie from the room, following her out into the hallway.

Noah called her back.

Janey took a minute to watch Jessie disappear into her room, feet dragging the whole way, before she turned back. She should've gone with Jessie—that was all she could think. Noah had swung his legs over the side of the bed, covers be damned, and now that Jessie was gone, it was just too easy to let her mind—and her eyes—stray. And really, it was his fault for sitting there all bare, except for a pair of blue boxers. Silk boxers. His legs were tanned and muscular, peppered with dark hair; so was his chest, but her gaze kept straying back to those boxers. Who'd ever have thought silk could be so clingy? Who'd ever have thought he'd be so—

Dangerous.

She'd walked behind his chair to put his dinner on the table last night and been caught by the scent of him, fresh from the shower. He'd used her shampoo and soap, but on him it had smelled different, the familiar fragrances tangled with some wild and unpredictable aroma that defied description. All she knew was what it did to her. And what it did to her was unacceptable.

She had no business being attracted to Noah Bryant after all these years and all the pain he'd caused her. Not to mention Jessie.

"You need to get dressed, too. If know my daughter, she'll be ready in record time and I don't think you want her to see you like that."

"Our daughter."

She held his eyes, despite the fact that her heart lurched over hearing him say that. "You're right, biologically speaking. I wonder if you can make it true in any of the ways that really count?"

"But you're afraid I can, and that you'll lose part of her to me."

"I'm surprised you care what I'm feeling, Noah."

"But you're not denying it."

Because she was very much afraid he was right. It wasn't that she didn't want Jessie to have a father, but it had been just the two of them for so long. The idea of having to send her daughter off to live with Noah on summer vacations made Janey want to throw up. And what holidays could she stand to miss with Jessie? Even Arbor Day seemed to hold a special meaning suddenly, and as for Christmas or Thanksgiving, what would be the point if she was alone?

"Jessie is all that matters," he said.

She hated him in that moment, hated him for coming back and turning her world upside down again, for leaving her ten years ago, for moving to town in the first place. Especially, she hated him for showing her what should've been her first concern. But the guilt was stronger. "She deserves to make up her own mind about you. And, believe me, she has a mind of her own."

Noah gave her a crooked smile. "Now why is that so easy to believe?"

"Because it's the truth."

He dropped his gaze, exhaled heavily. "You weren't kidding, were you? You didn't tell her anything about me—"

"There was nothing to tell."

"—and you didn't tell me anything about her," he finished. "You're going to make us get to know each other without bogging us down with your opinions." He looked up at her, and what she saw in his eyes was more eloquent than whatever he might have said.

"Get dressed," she said gruffly, refusing to let his respect and admiration mean anything to her. "You've got fifteen minutes."

That made him smile, full and wide and just as irreverently as when he'd been a kid and the black sheep of the entire town. "And if it takes me sixteen?"

She returned his smile, but there was no amusement in her eyes. "I've still got your keys."

"COME ON, Bryant," Janey yelled up the stairs. "Get it in gear."

From her seat at the kitchen table, Jessie heard Noah shout down, "I thought you were kidding about the fifteen minutes."

"I have to be out of here, like, now."

Noah's *okay* floated down the stairs, and her mom came back into the kitchen. She stopped in front of the sink and stood there a minute, staring off at nothing with a goofy expression on her face.

Jessie rolled her eyes, thinking, *jeez, adults are weird.* "Uh, Mom, do you want me to finish making my lunch?"

"No," Janey said, stepping to the counter by the fridge. "Turkey or peanut butter?"

"Peanut butter," Jessie said, although she couldn't care less.

She didn't like the way Noah Bryant looked at her mom, and she didn't like the way her mom looked at him. And she didn't want a father anymore.

Okay, maybe when she was a kid she'd wished for a father, even if he didn't live with them. Some of the kids in school had parents who were divorced and they got to see their fathers, and that was all she'd wanted. But fathers weren't always nice. The kids at school were always complaining about how their dads yelled at them and Davy Martin's dad had even spanked him!

It wasn't as if she thought Noah would do something like that, though; he didn't seem to be that kind of guy. But she didn't see any reason for him to stick around, either. Her life was fine the way it was. There was Clary—Deputy Sheriff Beeber—who took her fishing any time she wanted. Sure, it was partly because he liked her mom, the boy-girl icky sort of like, but they were friends, too, she and Clary. And there were the Devlins, who treated her as part of their family, even though they weren't really related. That wasn't so many people when you counted them up, but there was the whole town, too, Mrs. Halliwell, and the Shastas and just… everybody.

So what did she need a father for? Especially one who couldn't even be bothered to explain why he hadn't been around for her entire life. Well, she didn't want explanations anymore. She just wanted him to go away and stay away.

"So where is he?"

Her mom glanced back at her. "He'll be down in a few minutes."

"He's going to make us late."

"No, I'm not."

They both turned around. Janey stared at him as if she'd never seen a man wearing a dumb old black suit before. And he stared back.

Jessie flounced around in her chair and put on what her mom called her thundercloud face—which seemed to get the point across because her mom turned around again, loaded up the lunch box and snapped it shut, holding it out.

"C'mon, Jessie," she said. "Bring your bowl to the sink and let's get going."

"It's only six-thirty," Noah said.

"I teach government and history at Plains City High School in the mornings—" Janey washed the two cereal bowls and put them on the draining board "—which, if you'll recall, is fifty miles away."

He didn't take the hint. "What do you do in the afternoons?" he asked, leaning against the wall.

"I counsel at the high school two afternoons a week and teach art at Erskine Elementary the other three. And if that isn't enough for you, I'm also Mayor of Erskine."

"Sounds hectic."

"That's exactly why I'm trying to get rid of you. School starts at 7:30, which barely gives me time to drop Jessie off and get to Plains City before class."

"I guess I'm on my own for breakfast."

Her mom gave him a look that said he'd always been on his own for breakfast. And then she turned to Jessie and said, "Go get your stuff together, kiddo."

"You just want to get rid of me so you can talk about me."

Janey half turned, placing a hand on her hip, mother-daughter shorthand for "Don't make me say it again."

"Okay, okay." Her mom followed her out to the front entryway, watching her go upstairs. Jessie stopped on the landing, just out of sight, but not out of earshot.

"Are you going to be around later?" she heard her mom say.

"There are…matters I need to take care of."

"Matters?"

"I'm here on business, remember?"

See, Jessie reminded herself, he wasn't even here for her. She was glad she'd already decided she didn't want anything to do with him. She sneaked up the rest of the stairs, so they wouldn't know she'd been listening, grabbed her stuff and ran down with her backpack in one hand and her duffel in the other.

"You must have the entire library in those bags," Noah teased. "What are they teaching you kids these days?"

"I'm staying at the Devlin ranch. I'm helping with the spring roundup. We're camping out Saturday night." Jessie puffed up for a minute, before she remembered who she was talking to and that the last thing she wanted to do was impress him. "I'll be home Sunday morning. You'll be gone by then," she said, wincing when she caught the way her mom looked at her. So what, Jessie thought. Noah Bryant had been rude for ten years. He deserved to get some of it back. "I heard you tell Mom you were leaving town. Again."

Noah's smile faded. "I have some business to take care of, Jessie. I'll call you when I'm back in the area, and maybe we can…I don't know, talk or something."

Jessie stared at him the way she'd seen her mom do when she figured what she was hearing was B.S., then she dragged her stuff out to the car and waited to go to school. Just like it was a normal day.

She'd had lots of practice pretending her life was normal.

Chapter Four

"Really, Mr. Gardner, it's the best deal you're going to get—unless there's been a sharp increase in real estate here that I'm not aware of."

Gardner scratched his head, staring intently at the purchase agreement Noah had set in front of him. "I don't know, Mr. Bryant. It's a big decision, selling my place."

My place. Just like his old man, Noah thought. Hell Farm had been all about him. His dream. His life. He made all the decisions and dragged everyone else down with him.

Noah took a sip of coffee so weak it was probably the fourth pot brewed from the same grounds. Mrs. Gardner and her children were watching him as if he was the answer to their prayers. He knew he'd regret it, but he pulled the purchase agreement back, crossed out the amount and wrote another above it. Then he spun it around and slid it across the table.

Gardner took in the revised sum, his expression a mixture of greed and revulsion. "It's not about the money."

Not about the money? There was a reason cows outnumbered people in Montana, Noah figured. Most people were too smart to live in a state where day-to-day life was such a struggle.

No, that wasn't entirely fair. Some people were cut out for this kind of life. He wasn't.

And judging by the worn furnishings, the nearly empty

pantry shelves, the hopelessness on the faces of Mrs. Gardner and her children, neither was John Gardner: He was just too stubborn admit when he was licked—or desperate enough to take the risk of blowing the deal on the chance he could squeeze a few more dollars out of the sale. Noah recognized in the man's face what he'd trained himself not to see in his own mirror.

Work hadn't been going all that well lately. He'd lost some of the momentum that had carried him to the upper ranks of the business world so fast, and the sharks were beginning to circle. He needed a big killing to get back on top of his game, and this was it. He couldn't afford to blow it. He might even have said he was desperate *not* to blow it, but the difference between him and Gardner was that he wouldn't let desperation drive him. "If that isn't enough—"

"I thought you had to have this property," Gardner said, looking up at him with suddenly shrewd eyes.

"I'd prefer this property."

Gardner took a moment to consider the difference.

It was a moment too long. Noah rose. "Thanks for meeting with me," he said, reaching for the purchase agreement.

Mr. Gardner snatched it from him. "I ain't said no yet."

"You haven't said yes, either."

"It's not as easy as yes or no, son. Like this bit about keeping it a secret. Why is that, exactly?"

Noah had already explained it as best he could without revealing too much, but he swallowed his impatience. "Like I said before, Mr. Gardner. There's nothing illegal or unethical about this deal. We're not building something that's harmful to the environment."

"If there isn't anything cagey about this deal, why the need to keep it from other folks?"

"We prefer to make the announcement when and how it best suits our purposes." And because there was sure to be some opposition, and he didn't want it to become public knowledge until he had the foundation of the project already laid. "If it gets out before we release it, the deal will be off."

"At least that'll make the decision easier."

Noah sighed and sat down again. "Are you worried that people won't understand why you decided to sell?"

"It's not other folks I'm worried about, it's myself," Gardner said. "About all I got left's my pride."

And that was more important than his family's welfare? "I'd like to be able to set your mind at ease," Noah said, putting aside his anger and disgust, "but you're the only one who can do that."

"We've worked long and hard to get this far and it don't sit right just giving up."

Noah shrugged. "It makes no difference to me. If you don't sell, someone else will."

The man still hesitated.

"Mr. Gardner, I know how you feel."

"You got no idea—"

"Yes, I do." Noah tried to tell himself this was about business and nothing else, but it was too late for that. "I grew up on a farm like this," he said. "My father didn't have the money to buy cattle, so we worked, harder and harder every year, trying to get a decent cash crop in a state where winter lasts eight months of the year and spring and fall make up the other four." And the worse things got, the more often he'd felt the back of his old man's hand. Then after his mother died…

He'd gone a long way to forget those years. There was no point in remembering them now. "I know you want better for your family, Mr. Gardner. That's not going to happen as long as you stay here, and we both know it."

There was a moment of stunned silence, both of them taken aback by how much it mattered to Noah, and not just because he wanted the property.

"I know I'm being stubborn, son, but—"

"Do you think another chance like this is going to come along? Ever?"

Gardner took a deep breath, let it out. "When you put it that way…"

The farmer held out his hand. Noah shook it, but the relief he felt had nothing to do with getting the job done. "You should have a lawyer check that purchase agreement over before you sign it," he said.

"Hell, Bryant, you seem trustworthy."

Noah countersigned the paperwork, thinking a lot of people made the mistake of thinking he wasn't trustworthy, but one of the first lessons he'd learned was to look out for number one. The second lesson was that by the time somebody had stabbed him in the back, it was too late to do anything about it. Little by little he'd adopted an offensive strategy toward life—he never purposely hurt anyone, but if someone got in his way, he didn't waste his energy on regrets.

The Gardners, however, had nothing to worry about; the purchase agreement was aboveboard and soon they'd be on their way to a new life. It wouldn't take much to be an improvement over this one, Noah thought, as he stepped outside.

The main house was mostly gray, with white paint still clinging to the weathered wood in enough places to give it a strange mottled appearance. The barn listed badly to one side and the other outbuildings weren't much better, including one Noah would've sworn was an outhouse. The Gardners followed him, Mr. and Mrs. Gardner looking eerily like the couple in the painting *American Gothic* with Mr. Gardner clutching the purchase agreement instead of a pitchfork.

Noah climbed into his car and started it, savoring the smell of leather and his own aftershave, the coolness of the air-conditioning on his face and the comfort of the seat, with its built-in heat and lumbar support, beneath him. He felt more at ease—not because of the luxury that surrounded him, but because the world could do with one less place like this. Even if some of the people hereabouts lamented its loss, at least the Gardner children would benefit.

He bumped and jounced down the potholed driveway, along the slightly smoother two-mile stretch of dirt road that led to the main gravel road, and finally to the two-lane highway, a straight and unforgiving line of blacktop that stretched to the mountains behind him and the horizon in front. He heard the throaty purr of the Porsche's engine, felt the rumble of it through his seat and saw the landscape passing by the car windows, yet he felt like he was going nowhere.

Two weeks ago he'd known exactly who he was and where he was going, and his world had been what he made it. He'd been a man without a past, at least as far as anyone he knew in Los Angeles was concerned. His friends had learned not to ask him about his childhood; he only made jokes, or if they pushed him, gave answers that were vague at best. And the women he dated weren't really interested in the past—or the future, for that matter. He made very sure of that.

Now, here he was, stepping right back into the life he'd managed to escape. And he'd done it willingly, not to mention arrogantly, certain he could walk in his own footsteps without any consequences. Hah. How deluded had he been to think that? And he wasn't talking about the stroll he'd just taken through the worst moments of his childhood.

He was talking about the best moments. All of which revolved around Janey.

She'd saved him from everything, the travesty of his family, from closed minds and unsympathetic authority figures, from his own self-destructive tendencies. At a point in his life when he was the town outsider, when almost no one in Erskine accepted him, Janey had. It was that simple.

And when she'd needed him, where had he been? Where was he now? Still focused on his career, his future, his own wants.

Sure, he'd called her house twice in the two weeks since he'd discovered he had a daughter. Both times she and Jessie had been gone and he'd left messages, grateful they weren't there to ask questions while resenting the fact that he felt obliged to check in with her at all.

He gunned the engine, watched the speedometer notch up to seventy, a foolish speed to be traveling on a backcountry road where a cow or a slow-moving tractor could be over the next hill. He didn't slow down, even when he passed the turnoff for Erskine. He wasn't ready to go back there yet. Besides, Jessie didn't want him around, anyway; she'd made that perfectly clear.

Spring in Erskine. There was no better season, Janey decided, and no better place to spend it than her hometown.

Erskine didn't change from year to year, the same old buildings, the same mountains and pastures and hay meadows, but in the spring it always seemed…newer, fresher. People opened windows to let in the breeze off the mountains, a breeze so crisp and clean it slipped into corners and swept through shadows, and left them brighter somehow. The winter's accumulation of dirt and dead leaves had been banished from the doorways, window boxes had been filled with geraniums and impatiens, and planters hung from eaves, dripping with ivy and crowded with glossy-leaved begonias.

It was such a beautiful day that she'd left her car at home and walked to the school for her afternoon art classes. She really should have taken Jessie directly home after school; she had a hundred tasks to complete, grades to tally for final report cards, trim to paint. Phone messages to listen to…

She looked down at her daughter and decided there wasn't any rush to get home. Two weeks had passed since Noah had left with a promise that he'd be back. Two weeks and two phone messages, they still hadn't seen him. As the days continued to add up, facing the answering machine each evening had become a real challenge. If the message light was blinking, it meant Noah couldn't make it again. If there was no message, it was even worse.

No one else in town knew about Noah's visit, a kind of unspoken agreement between mother and daughter not to bring up a subject sure to inspire gossip they didn't want to hear and questions they couldn't answer. But Jessie wouldn't talk to her about Noah, either, and that worried Janey.

"Clary's truck is at the sheriff's office," Jessie said. "Can I go say hi?"

"Absolutely. Tell him hi for me, too."

"You could tell him yourself."

Janey considered doing just that, for all of ten seconds. The hope on Jessie's face held her back.

Deputy Sheriff Clarence Beeber was not only Jessie's fishing buddy and good friend, he was the closest thing she had to a father. But it wasn't any secret that he wanted to be her father for real one day. It was Janey who was taking her sweet time. And she let them think that, because, honestly, she didn't know what else to do.

She didn't want to string Clary along, but she'd always been afraid of what it might mean for Jessie if she told him outright that they'd never be more than friends. So Janey walked a fine line between not encouraging Clary, but not discouraging him so much it became uncomfortable for him to see Jessie. Walking that line was even more important now, when the last thing her daughter needed was more change in her life.

"I have about a million things to do, Jessie, but you go on ahead. Just be home for supper."

Jessie headed off, dragging her feet, nothing like her usual upbeat self. Janey knew Clary would cheer her up, though, and in the meantime, she'd go home and weed or wash windows. Whatever kept her hands occupied and her mind off Noah Bryant.

"Hey there, Janey," Earl Tilford called out as she turned the corner onto Main Street and passed the bakery.

Janey backpedaled a couple of steps and stuck her head in the wide-open doorway. "How's it going, Mr. Tilford?"

"I was about to ask you that. I heard Bryant's in town."

"Where did you hear that?"

"Came by way of the usual sources."

Which meant Dory Shasta, wife of Mike Shasta, owner of the Ersk Inn. If the Ersk Inn was the town watering hole, Dory Shasta was a prospector who spent all her spare time panning for little nuggets of information that she used to her best advantage. In Erskine, gossip was currency.

There was no telling how Dory had found out. Mrs. Halliwell might have seen Noah outside her house two weeks ago, or maybe somebody had recognized him when he gassed up on his way out of town. Or he was here now, which not only gave Janey a serious case of butterflies, it made more sense. No way would it have taken two weeks for such a juicy rumor to get around.

This kind of information ran through town like a bad case of the flu. That thought made Janey smile, since in both instances stuff was coming out of people's mouths that would've been better off kept inside. Not that she resented the gossip all that much, even when she was at the center of it. Some people might not appreciate having everyone know their business, but to Janey it felt like being part of a huge, caring family. Being alone in the world and responsible for a daughter was a little less scary in Erskine.

"You being our newly elected mayor and all," Earl said, "maybe you could make a law against ex-boyfriends who show up every decade or so and cause trouble. I'm sure Clary would be happy to enforce it."

Janey didn't quibble with Mr. Tilford's assumption that Noah was there to cause trouble. Intentional or not, trouble was what he brought. As for the rest of it, "I think I can handle Noah without throwing around my political weight," she said, tongue firmly tucked in cheek, "or calling in local law enforcement."

"Well, at the very least, a girl could use a cookie when she's facing an ordeal like this." Earl came out from behind the counter and offered her one of the huge cookies—loaded with nuts and chocolate chips—that he was famous for.

"Just the air in here is enough to put ten pounds on me," Janey protested, but she took the cookie, broke off a piece and slipped it into her mouth. She closed her eyes and let it melt on her tongue, sighing her approval. "Then again, this is worth a couple hundred extra sit-ups."

"Here's one for Jessie," he said, handing her a bakery bag and waving off her thanks. "Knowing you appreciate it is reward enough for getting up at 3:00 a.m. If I was twenty years younger—"

"You'd still marry Meggie and break my heart."

"You're right. And my girls would still grow up and leave town." Earl sighed, but the smile was back on his face by the time he ducked under the pass-through and straightened to look over the counter. "Dee's stationed in Germany these days, and Andie's a fancy pastry chef in one of them New York hotels. Meggie's working on her, but the harder she pushes Andie to come home for a visit, the more stubborn the girl gets. I think Meggie'd be smarter to back off, use that reverse psychology I always hear about, but—" he shrugged "—they're peas in a pod, one of them just as pigheaded as the other."

"My money's on Meg," Janey said with a smile. Literally.

There was a pool down at the Ersk Inn, and Janey had put down her five dollars like everyone else in town. "If Meg can get Andie to visit by the Fourth of July, I'll have more to thank you for than your cookies."

She left Earl laughing, stepping out into streaming sunshine and nearly colliding with Sam Tucker. Besides owning one of the biggest ranches around, Sam was also the town veterinarian. As if that wasn't enough, he was tall and handsome, with a body that belonged on a billboard—the kind that advertised boxers. Or briefs. When Sam was in town, girls sighed and went dreamy, mothers got that wedding glint in their eyes, and fathers made sure their shotguns were loaded with rock salt. Better to chase him off in the first place than deal with the broken heart he always left behind. Sam wasn't known for monogamy.

Janey had gone out with him once or twice, but she'd been in no danger. Her heart had already been broken before Sam came into the picture.

Sam dropped a kiss on her cheek and plucked the rest of the cookie out of her hand in one smooth motion. "You going to marry me, Janey?"

"Not today," she teased back, watching the rest of her cookie disappear in two huge bites. "Y'know, Earl sells those right in there."

Sam craned his head to peer in the open door of the bakery, then gave her the kind of grin he used to charm women out of more than baked goods. "I've got a perfectly fine kitchen of my own out at the ranch."

"Then maybe you should stop flirting with every girl in the state and marry one who can put that kitchen to use."

"I keep asking you, but you keep turning me down."

"You keep asking me because you know I'll turn you down," Janey said, setting off down the raised wooden walkway that was a holdover from pioneer days, when the streets were dirt, or mud, and concrete wasn't a fact of life yet.

Sam laughed, slinging an arm over her shoulder and falling into step with her. "It's just wrong for a woman to keep this kind of anatomy to herself." He made a big show of peering over his shoulder.

Janey elbowed him in the side. "Forget my anatomy."

"Your anatomy is unforgettable. Nobody fills out a pair of jeans the way you do." Sam faced forward again. "But I should've known it was hopeless when I heard Noah Bryant was back in town."

"When did you hear that?" she asked, knowing she hadn't managed to sound casual when Sam tightened his grip, turning it into a comforting one-armed hug.

"George Donaldson ran into him in Plains City around lunch today. Said Noah told him he'd be in town on business for a little while."

"C'mon, Sam, can you believe anything George says?"

"Why would he make it up?"

"Well, it's George," was the nicest explanation she could come up with.

"It's no secret George gets a kick out of winding other people up and then watching them walk into walls, but I don't think he's stupid enough to make up something like this," Sam said. "If Max didn't kick George's ass, then Noah would. The two of them never got along. I remember one time…"

Janey tuned him out. She didn't need Sam's version of history; she'd lived it. "Do you know if he's in town yet?"

That question earned her another hug. "I don't know. But here's Clary. I'll bet he knows."

"Knows what?"

Janey looked up just as Clarence Beeber stepped onto the boardwalk, Jessie at his side. His gaze dropped to Sam's arm, still draped over Janey's shoulder. Clary didn't say a word, but Sam took his arm back and put some distance between them.

Janey smiled and shook her head. Even if Sam's flirting

had been more than big talk, he would never have moved in on a woman Clary was interested in. The two had been best friends practically from the womb.

"What am I supposed to know?" Clary asked again.

"Just the latest gossip," Sam said, glancing at Jessie, all big ears and wide eyes, hanging on every word—spoken and unspoken.

Clary's face hardened, and Janey knew he'd heard about Noah's return already. Even if his expression hadn't given it away, there was no need to guess how he was taking it. Everything about Clary was starched, from his uniform to his personality, and once he made up his mind, there was no changing it. He had very definite ideas of right and wrong, the kind of ideas that could best be described as black and white. As far as he was concerned, Noah had screwed up, and no shades of gray, like youth or ignorance, could mitigate his crime. But Clary would never say as much in front of Jessie. He might apply the law as if it were set in stone, but he did it with compassion—when he felt compassion was warranted.

"I don't suppose there's any way you'd leave it alone altogether, Clary," Janey said.

Sam snorted. "You'd have more luck asking old man Winston's prize bull why he keeps charging with the barbed-wire fence."

"If you're done insulting me, Sam, you ought to go on out there and stitch him up again."

"That's where I was headed, before I decided to propose to Janey." Sam winked at her. "She turned me down, Clary. Maybe you should give it a try."

Clary went red from his collar to his hairline. Sam clapped him on the shoulder and sauntered off in the direction of the vet clinic, laughing the whole way.

"Sam's just giving you a hard time," Janey said, turning toward home because the longer she looked at Clary, the more embarrassed he seemed to get, and she didn't want to be responsible for his head bursting into flame.

He started walking with her, but he kept Jessie between them, the poor kid's head swiveling back and forth like a tennis court official's, even though no one was talking. Or maybe because no one was talking. They continued in silence for another block or so before Clary spoke. Janey didn't miss the fact that Jessie got him going with a nudge.

"Can I, uh, give you and Jessie a ride to the graduation party tomorrow?" he asked.

Since everyone in Erskine and Plains City knew everyone else, they'd decided years ago to have one party each year for the eighth graders graduating from Erskine Elementary and the seniors who'd survived Plains City High School. Sara and Max Devlin didn't have any actual graduates, but they had a nice, big ranch not too far from either town, and they'd offered to host.

"Jessie and I are going out to Sara's early to help them set up," Janey said.

"I think it would be a good idea if I drove the two of you." Clary looked over at her. "You know," he said, his eyes dropping to nine-year-old level, then back up. "Just in case."

"In case of what?" Jessie piped up.

"Just in case," Janey said to her daughter. "Do me a favor and go on home. I'll catch up with you in a few minutes."

"You're going to talk about me, aren't you?"

"I think we're going to talk about Noah," Janey said, giving in to the inevitable.

"That's still about me. I have a right—"

"You're nine years old. You don't have any rights."

"Janey!"

"Mom…" Jessie said at the same time, making that one word about three syllables long, and loading it with indignation.

"Jessie, you know there are occasions when you get sent

out of the room—or sent home, in this instance—so I can talk without having to worry about what I say. Sometimes that conversation will be about you, and sometimes it won't, but it's always going to be something I don't think you're ready to hear, and stamping your foot and scowling at me won't change that fact."

"That's not fair."

"No, sweetie," Jane said, brushing a hand over her daughter's hair. "It's not fair, but it's how things work, and I think you'd rather I was honest about that much, at least."

Jessie glanced over at Clary, and when she saw he wasn't going to intervene, she did as Janey asked, making it absolutely clear she was going under protest.

"Do you think that was the best way to handle her?"

"She's not stupid, Clary. And if you weren't so determined to talk about this, I wouldn't have to handle her at all."

"You're right." Clary pinched the bridge of his nose. "I should've waited until you had a chance to tell her that her father's back in town."

"She met him two weeks ago," Janey said without thinking, then caught the look on his face. "Jessie didn't tell you."

"Neither did you."

"I'm sorry, Clary. It's difficult enough without the whole town asking questions—not that Jessie or I thought you'd spread it around. I guess neither of us really wanted to talk about it. But I should have told you."

"I'm sure you had a lot on your mind, Janey. Don't worry about it," Clary said. But his expression told a different story. He was hurt; maybe he hadn't officially asked her out, but everyone in town knew how he felt, and it was not only understandable for a man who'd buried his wife at his young age to take his time jumping into another relationship, it was expected in a town like Erskine.

He wouldn't admit it, but he wanted an explanation, and

after what she'd held back already, she felt she owed it to him. Not that there was all that much to tell. "He showed up two weeks ago, out of the blue, and before I could get rid of him, Jessie came out of the house. Noah took one look at her and just seemed to…know."

"It's the eyes," Clary said grudgingly.

"Yeah," Janey agreed. It was more than that, but the rest of the similarities were subtler, deeper, and she was the only person in town who knew Noah well enough to pick up on them. "Anyway, he said he was here on business, and that he'd be back this way when he was done."

"And you haven't seen him."

"He's back now."

"So I hear, but you haven't seen him."

"It can't be easy for him, either, Clary, discovering he has a nine-year-old daughter."

"It didn't have to be a surprise, Janey."

"I know."

"And yet here you are, defending him."

"Yeah," she said with a humorless smile. "But here's the thing. Being angry with him won't make this easier on any of us, especially Jessie."

"You're right." Clary flipped off his Stetson and rotated it in his hands as he always did when he was agitated. "It's just… With his track record, I'd hate to see her get her hopes up."

"Trust me, she's not going into this with false hopes." Janey smiled for real this time, remembering the way Jessie had seen Noah off that morning two weeks ago. "And she's not going to make it easy on him, either."

"She's your daughter," Clary said, his face folded into its usual sober lines. "Don't think you have to go through this alone, Janey. If you need anything…"

"You'll be the first one I call, but Clary—" she put her hand on his arm and he stopped, turning to look at her "—I know how you feel."

"I know." His face went red again, and there was so much hope shining in his eyes it was almost painful to see.

"Just for the next little while, I have to concentrate on Jessie."

"Sure. I understand."

"Thanks," she said, giving his arm a squeeze.

Clary opened his mouth to speak, but something over her shoulder caught his attention. "Does Bryant drive a red Porsche?" he asked.

Janey turned around and squinted in the same direction, barely making out a bit of red behind the rusted-out hulk of Arliss Cunningham's truck parked a ways down on the opposite side of the street. "You can tell from here that's a Porsche? Must be a guy thing."

He gave her a sheepish smile that hardly registered, since Janey was busy looking up and down the street. Sure enough, she saw a tall suit-clad form coming out of Keller's Market. Unfortunately, so did Clary. He took one step in that direction before Janey blocked him.

"Where are you going?"

"I just want to have a little talk with him."

"Is he doing something wrong? Something illegal," she qualified.

His expression was stony as he watched Noah change directions and come straight toward them. "I'm sure I can come up with something."

Chapter Five

Noah had been standing by the cash register in Keller's Market for what felt like hours, talking about the weather and the price of beef with Owen Keller, his mind wandering because Owen...well, Owen tended to be a putz, which Noah had forgotten until he ran into the market to get a Coke and Owen wouldn't stop talking. So, about the time Owen was claiming his astronomical profit margin had nothing to do with the fact that Keller's was the only market for fifty miles around, Noah glanced out the wide front window, searching for an excuse to bug out of there—politely, if at all possible. What he saw was Janey. With Sam Tucker.

Noah had never liked Sam Tucker all that much. He was too slick, always smiling and strutting around like this little backcountry town was New York City and he owned Fifth Avenue. Even from where Noah stood he could see there was manure on Sam's boots. He probably had dirt under his fingernails and smelled bad, too, but Janey didn't seem to mind when Sam draped his arm over her shoulders. She should've known better than to be taken in by a cheap-talking veterinarian who went through women faster than Niagara Falls made mist, but there she was, strolling slowly down the street with him, their heads bent together in conversation—until Sam peered over his shoulder, clearly scooping out her butt.

In two seconds flat, Noah was standing out on the board-walk, with no clue what he intended to say or do. But Sam was already walking away, and Janey had been joined by Jessie and a tall man who could only be described as square: a square jaw, square shoulders, square pleats down the front of his cop's shirt. The only thing that wasn't by the book was the way he looked at Janey.

Noah found himself walking over to them and saw Janey send Jessie off toward their house a minute or so before they spotted him. The big, bad sheriff stepped out from behind Janey and braced himself for a confrontation—and damn, Noah thought, if he wasn't happy to oblige the son-of-a-gun. Then Janey turned around and saw him. Even from a block away he could see the warning in her eyes. Whoever Janey chose to spend her time with was none of his business, she was saying, and she was right.

And it wasn't like she didn't already have enough reasons to be mad at him.

For a moment, Noah considered climbing into his car and driving off. But that would only postpone the inevitable. And he definitely wouldn't be doing himself, or Janey, any favors by avoiding her in front of the whole town.

Apparently, Janey felt the same way. She lifted her hand against the glare from the sun and waited for him to cross the street as if there was nothing in the world she'd rather do than say hello. He saw the waver in her smile, though, and saw her hands clench together at her waist before she dropped them to her sides.

"Hey, Janey," he said, casually joining her on the board-walk. "Pretty day, isn't it?"

"It was."

That stung—in a nostalgic sort of way. Janey had never been one to pull her punches. And he'd never been able to re-sist tweaking her back. He glanced over at the uniformed man beside her and swooped in to give her a peck on the cheek before she could avoid him.

She smiled, but there was a gleam in her eyes that explained itself when she introduced the cop standing next to her. "Do you remember Clary?"

He frowned, taking a longer look at the other man before it hit him. Janey wouldn't need to pay him back for that kiss; she had instant retribution standing right there. "Hey, Clary, long time no see."

Clary Beeber, never Noah's biggest fan, slid his hand back to rest on the nightstick in a loop at his left side. "It's Deputy Sheriff Beeber to you, Bryant."

Noah caught the just-give-me-a-reason look on the other man's face and eased back a step, then stuck his hands in his pockets, just in case.

"You remember what a crack-up Noah used to be in high school," Janey said, attempting to ease the tension.

"Yeah." Clary's expression grew even more sour. "Never did find out who filled my locker with shaving cream the morning after I broke the school record for the fifty-yard dash."

Noah held up both hands. "Wasn't my record," he said. "Two left feet."

Clary stared at him for a second, and when he realized he wasn't going to get a reaction, shifted his attention to Janey. His eyes warmed. So did his cheeks.

Cop with a crush, Noah thought, and nearly laughed before he considered what it would be like to spend a night in the Erskine jail.

"About the party tomorrow." Clary shot Noah a look, then took Janey by the elbow and steered her a little way down the boardwalk.

Noah didn't even try to pretend he wasn't eavesdropping, but he didn't need to hear the words to know that Clary, head down, rotating his hat in his hands, was asking Janey out.

Janey said something back. Her softer voice didn't carry to where Noah stood, but the way she rested her hand on Clary's arm spoke volumes. She'd turned him down.

Hallelujah was Noah's immediate reaction, although he managed to resist the overwhelming urge to shout it out loud and pump his fist in the air. And he only felt like that, because Clary was such a stick in the mud, completely wrong for Janey. Still, he couldn't help feeling sorry for the guy; even when Janey promised to save him a dance, in a voice loud enough for him to hear, Noah noticed she had Clary so torn up he nearly backed off the edge of the boardwalk thanking her. He salvaged some pride by sending Noah one last meaningful glare as he walked away.

"I think Deputy Sheriff Beeber was actually blushing," Noah said as she rejoined him. "You leave quite an impression."

The guilt on her face cleared up and she smiled a little, mockingly. "And you don't? Your name is still on the record board in the gym for the fifty-yard dash."

"Is it?"

"You got it back the day after the locker incident."

"Completely slipped my mind."

"And I'll bet you don't know anything about the case of shaving cream that went missing around then from the Five-And-Dime's loading dock? Which is practically right next door to Halliwell's—where you worked every weekend and every day after school."

Noah's mouth tilted up on one side. "Circumstantial."

"Around here that's enough to convict you."

He sighed. "Don't I know it."

She set off down the boardwalk, Noah walking by her side.

"So what's wrong with Clary?" he asked. "Aside from the fact that anybody who takes life that seriously can't be much fun?"

"There's nothing wrong with Clary."

"But you're not dating him, and it's not for lack of trying on his part."

Janey gave him a sideways glance. "Been checking up on me?" she asked.

"You know how people in this town are when it comes to sharing information."

"I'm surprised they can talk about anything but you."

"Unless I'm the one they're talking to," Noah said, "and then they can't seem to talk about anything but you. Mostly about how you moved on and made a perfectly good life for yourself and Jessie without me."

She smiled, and he knew why. The people of Erskine took care of their own. They didn't want him to think she'd been a hermit since he left town, but he didn't for one second think she'd been as socially active as people claimed. He wanted to hear it from her, though. He needed to hear it from her. "You haven't been lonely, I'm told, especially lately."

"Really?" Her eyes shone with so much amusement it brightened him just seeing it. "Anyone name names?"

"Sam Tucker."

She snorted softly.

"Well, it makes sense. He has that big spread outside town."

"So what?"

He knew he should let it go, but something wouldn't let him. "Isn't that what you always wanted? A man who's firmly planted here? A man who fits into your safe, comfortable world and doesn't ask you to take any chances?"

She stopped dead, staring at him for a moment.

"What?" he said, grimacing at the defensiveness in his tone. He'd forgotten she could do that to him with just a look.

"I'm not the reason you're here," she reminded him, "and I'm not about to let you turn me into the bad guy."

"What's that supposed to mean?"

"You're nervous about seeing Jessie again, and you thought

if you made me angry I'd chase you off. You were always better at running than talking."

"That's not fair, Janey." When she started to walk away he caught her arm. "I've been working the last two weeks—and I had my reasons ten years ago."

"You want to share them with me?"

Noah opened his mouth but nothing came out. Was there any point in telling her now what had sent him running from Erskine? What difference would it make in either of their lives?

"Exactly," she said as if she'd read his mind. "It's been behind us for ten years. Why drag it back out and dissect it now?"

"If it's behind us, why are you still angry?"

"All right, I'm angry." She jerked her arm out of his hand. "Does that make you happy? You dumped me and walked away after everything…" Her eyes, deep, dark pools of hurt, belied the defiant expression on her face. "I loved you and I thought you loved me."

"I did."

"Not enough." Noah started to object, but she held up both hands. "Why can't you just leave it alone?"

"Because there were good times, too," Noah said quietly. "A lot of good times."

She dropped her gaze from his, but she smiled—it was a sad, wistful smile, but it was still a smile. "And there's Jessie." She set off once again, turning the last corner that took them onto her street. "She's at home, by the way, probably wondering where the hell you've been for the last two weeks."

"I said I was working."

She huffed out a breath. "Brooding, you mean."

"Yeah," he admitted, "I did some of that, too."

"And what do you think Jessie was doing? If you're going to get to know her, Noah, it has to be on her terms. And you need to be sure you want this, because if you disappear again—"

"No. I mean, yes. I'm sure, Janey."

"Okay," she said, "good." She unlatched her front gate and—to his surprise—held it open for him.

He followed her up the walk and onto the wide front porch, settling into one of the bentwood rockers that had sat there every spring and summer for as long as he'd known Janey. "I know you're angry I took off, but I needed to figure some things out."

"You always liked to have a plan."

Noah made a noncommittal sound he knew she took as agreement, thinking, *a plan?* How did you make a plan for something like this? Especially when, as recently as two days ago, he hadn't even decided he was coming back.

But that had been a knee-jerk reaction to the Gardner farm and all it brought back about his own childhood. There'd never actually been any question about whether or not Jessie would be a part of his life—the question was how? And when? Would he be coming back here or would she be coming to visit him in Los Angeles? And what would that mean to both their lives? He needed to work it all out in his own mind— Janey was right about that. Jessie had already picked up on his uncertainty and she resented him for it. The next time he saw her, he needed to understand his own expectations so he could explain them coherently to her.

"You do have a plan?" Janey asked.

Noah took a deep breath and jumped in with both feet. "I wrapped up the business that brought me to this area. At least for now."

"But baseball's just getting going around here..." she said.

It took Noah a second to remember that she believed he was a sports scout—a misconception he felt mildly guilty for fostering. For a moment, he considered fessing up, but just as quickly decided against it. Since she was going to be mad at him, anyway, it didn't really matter if she was mad now or later. And later suited him a whole lot better. "I've seen everything I needed to see, so I decided to clear my calendar for the next couple of weeks—"

Jessie burst through the front door. "I started supper. You want to stay—" She looked over at her mother. "I heard voices out here and I thought…Clary was walking you home."

In the face of her daughter's accusatory tone, Janey was silent for a moment, thinking carefully. Another sign of how much she'd grown in the last decade. "We ran into Noah on the way," she said at last, "and Clary had some other things to do."

"No, he didn't. Clary's not here because he is." She sent Noah a poisonous glare, turned on her heel and flounced back inside, the screen door slapping shut behind her.

"I guess that means I'm not invited for supper," Noah said, knowing Jessie heard every word.

Janey got up and closed the inside door. She didn't take her seat again, leaning back against the front wall of the house instead, arms crossed. "So you're going to be around for the next two weeks," she said in a voice that questioned either his sanity or his arrogance for thinking that was all it would take.

Noah wasn't feeling so confident himself anymore, but he was a master at hiding his insecurities. "I want a place in Jessie's life. And if she wants a place in mine, I'm thinking we can work the rest of it out as we go along."

"It's not that simple, Noah. There are legalities—"

"Whoa," he said, the thought of anything permanent bringing him to his feet. "Why bring the court into this? Let's take just take it one day at a time."

Janey looked toward the closed door and the troubled little girl inside. Noah had good intentions where Jessie was concerned, but so far it was only talk, and talk, to Noah Bryant, came cheap. She'd learned that lesson the hard way. "If you really want to be a part of Jessie's life," she said, "you can start by going to the graduation party tomorrow."

"Uh…everyone in town will be there, right?"

"And a bunch of people from Plains City and around."

Noah went kind of pasty, probably unaware he'd begun to rock.

"If you can't handle it, that's okay. But you didn't used to be so timid."

He stopped rocking, sat forward. "Timid?"

"What would you call it?"

"I don't know. Cautious, maybe? I thought I could work my way back into Erskine society gradually."

"You never had a problem facing people before, Noah. You made an effort to get attention. It was the negative kind, but that was what you wanted."

"Yeah," he said, "but I was a teenager—a teenager with a bad attitude." And the last thing he wanted to do was remind everyone of that before they found out why he'd really come to town. "I've changed."

"Here's an opportunity to prove it." Janey straightened, pushing away from the wall. "You said you want to be a part of Jessie's life. Well, this town is a big part of her life, too, and if you're serious about Jessie, you'd better learn to coexist with the people here."

"That would be something new for me."

Janey gave him a sideways look. "Think you're up to it?"

"I have to be, don't I?" He climbed to his feet. "You sure there's no chance Jessie will change her mind and let me stay for supper?"

"And if you can get her to come around before dessert, you won't have to make an appearance at the party tomorrow. I don't know about the rest of you, but your ego has grown in the last ten years."

He shrugged. "It was worth a try."

"I think you should go," she said, reaching for the screen door.

"Y'know, you're always trying to get rid of me,"

"And yet you're still here."

"Get used to it." Noah grinned like old times, stuck his hands in his pockets and walked away.

But at least this time it was what she wanted. Right?

Chapter Six

If he'd had to label people, Noah would've said Janey had been his best friend in high school, but Max Devlin ran a close second.

He and Janey had shared everything: their deepest feelings, innermost thoughts, most precious dreams—everything. That night ten years ago, when they'd made love after their senior prom, had been the first time for them both. It had been the first time for a lot of other things, too. The first time he'd intentionally hurt her, the first time he'd lied to her, the first time he'd understood that if he didn't want to risk dragging her down with him, he'd have to move on with his life and put her out of his mind. Or at least try.

Max Devlin had been the one he'd gone to before he left town that night, the only one who knew how much it had torn him up to leave. Max had tried to find out why he was leaving and done his best to talk him into telling Janey, face-to-face, that he was going away. But Noah had believed it was better to leave Janey angry, that it would be easier for her to move on if she hated him. Stupid, he realized now, believing he could manipulate such a headstrong, stubborn woman, but stupid had been one of his best things back then. Maybe it still was.

He'd thought it would be so easy to come back to Erskine, the big hero bringing jobs and prosperity to his poor, backward hometown. And if he could find a way to make peace with his regrets, that would be gravy.

Instead, the woman who'd haunted him for the last decade, the woman he'd counted on being happily married, was instead the struggling, single mother of his nine-year-old daughter—who apparently wanted nothing to do with him. He had a feeling he wasn't going to get a warmer reception this time.

One thing he was sure of, though, was the kind of welcome he'd get from Max Devlin. Otherwise, he didn't think he'd have been able to show his face at a gathering that promised to offer a concentrated dose of Erskine cold shoulder.

The annual graduation party was well under way at the Devlins' ranch when Noah swung his Porsche into their long driveway. Instead of using the barn, they'd set up a wooden dance floor on a raised platform outside, well away from the cows, chickens and their byproducts. Streamers in the high school colors fluttered between poles at the four corners, and a white banner congratulated all the new graduates. Big Ed's Rhythm Method, the town's one and only resident band, pounded out a tune that could have been "The Tennessee Waltz" or "Purple Haze." Or something else entirely.

Old Glory flapped in a warm spring breeze, babies napped in strollers or on blankets spread in the shade, and tables groaned with cakes and pies, baked hams and casseroles whose secret recipes were guarded more carefully than most bank vaults. Mike Shasta held his traditional post as bartender, although there'd only be punch and soft drinks in deference to the children present. And nearly every citizen of Erskine and Plains City was there, eating dancing, celebrating. Gossiping.

Noah hung back, under a huge, old elm tree, searching the crowd until he found what he was looking for. Or rather whom. Jessie was off in a dusty part of the ranch yard where someone had set up a baseball diamond, and from what he could see, she played a mean shortstop. Which he was very happy to let her continue doing for the time being—especially when he got sidetracked by the sight of Janey, up on the dance floor, swaying in the arms of one of the itinerant cowboys who floated around, working at a different ranch each season. She smiled at some remark the cowboy made, naturally lifting her face to his. That was when the cowboy dove in.

Noah jerked forward, stopping when he saw how she neatly evaded the kiss, then soothed his cowboy's ego by whispering something in his ear that made him laugh.

Noah relaxed back into the shadows. It took another moment for his fists to unclench.

"At least you learned some self-control in the big city."

Noah swung around and found Max Devlin standing a little behind him, a cautious grin on his face. "I didn't learn it there," Noah said, offering his hand.

Max took it, then pulled him into a back-thumping hug, like the old days. It was just what Noah needed. "Thanks, Max, for… Thanks."

"Kind of a rough homecoming, huh?"

"Not exactly what I expected."

"What exactly did you expect?"

Noah cracked a half smile. "I don't know. Maybe I should be thankful I haven't been lynched."

"Nah. Tar and feathers. maybe, but there hasn't been a lynching around here for, oh, a hundred years or so."

"I'll bet Barney Fife over there wouldn't mind reviving the practice."

Clary stood at the side of the dance floor, dividing his dirty looks between the guy dancing with Janey, and Noah.

"Clary's all bark," Max said. "He has a thing for Janey."

"He's not the only one," Noah said, taking in the dance floor scene again.

"You can't blame a guy for trying, but Janey—" Max shook

his head a little "—she's left a trail of bruised hearts and wounded egos a mile long."

"You make it sound like that's bad."

"It's not as if her life's been easier for being alone, Noah. Maybe if she'd found someone…" He paused before continuing. "She wouldn't want me to say anything, but I don't want you to think you can waltz back into her life like nothing's changed."

"I'm not that stupid."

"No, you went off to college and got an expensive education."

"Which I worked my ass off for."

"Did you have a baby to take care of, too?"

Noah glanced up at the hard note that had crept into his friend's voice.

"Did you have to face her parents like she did?" Max went on. "Or hold your head up in a town full of people who were thinking God knows what when they were face-to-face with you, and saying it behind your back? You got to follow your dreams while she had to settle for a job that barely pays a living wage, let alone enough to raise a kid and keep that huge old monstrosity of a house."

It was the last part of what Max said that got to him. "Are you saying she's broke?"

"She doesn't drive a thirty-year-old Beetle because it's good in the snow."

"Her father was a lawyer. And a State Representative."

"A country lawyer doesn't make that much money. Neither does an honest politician, but that's beside the point. Didn't it ever occur to you that you're about a decade behind on child support?"

It hadn't, and he was ashamed to admit that. He'd been so wrapped up in what the discovery of a daughter would mean to his future that he hadn't stopped to think about how difficult the past ten years must have been for Janey, financially if nothing else. "What do you think she'll say if I offer her money?"

"She'll be mad as hell, but she's a practical woman, Noah."

A practical woman who was raising his daughter, all alone. He was only now coming to appreciate that. "You're right," he said, "but I'm not about to mention child support to Janey yet. I don't want her to think I'm trying to buy her and Jessie off."

"Feeling a need to prove yourself?"

"Do you think that's possible?"

Max whistled under his breath. "I don't know, but Jessie's a good kid, Noah. You'd be a fool not to get to know her."

"I know that. It's just, with Janey…things are complicated."

"She can be really difficult if you get on her bad side."

"All her sides are bad where I'm concerned."

Max grinned full-out this time.

"What, you're not going to defend her?"

"Janey can take care of herself," Max said, then his grin faded away. "And if you hurt her, I'll kick your ass."

"When I asked you to look out for her ten years ago, I didn't mean you had to protect her from *me*."

Max turned, met his eyes. "You're the one who can do the most damage."

"Guess who's here," Sara said as Janey begged off the next dance and joined her on the lawn.

Janey followed her best friend's line of sight and saw Noah standing in the shade, well away from the crowd. Sara's husband, Max, was by his side, but although the two of them had been great friends once upon a time, Noah seemed to be in his own lonely world. He could've been any rancher or farmer, in his jeans and checked shirt, but there was an aura of isolation about him that set him miles apart from everyone else.

Suddenly she was eight years old again, feeling sorry for the new kid in town. He was standing alone on the school playground, jaw tight, face set in an expression that said he couldn't care less if anyone ever accepted him. It hadn't masked the shadow of hurt in his eyes, though.

She'd slipped her hand into his, all those years ago, and lost her heart. The impulse was still there, the need to comfort him so strong. But he wasn't that lost little boy anymore, and her heart was all edges and corners now—sharp, jagged corners.

"He hasn't taken his eyes off you," Sara said, nudging her with an elbow. "Except to look at Jessie, and when he does…" She sighed. "He goes all soft and he gets a little smile, the way Max does when he's watching Joey."

That shouldn't have made her feel warm and fuzzy, dammit. She was supposed to hate Noah, but, well, it was so hard to do.

"I gotta say," Sara continued, "he doesn't strike me as the unfeeling monster I've been hearing about all over town."

"Appearances are deceiving, Sara. The man oozes charm. He can get just about anyone to do just about anything, whether they want to or not."

"That sounds like firsthand knowledge."

"You think?" Janey said, the two of them gazing off to where Jessie was stepping up to home plate, digging her feet in the soft dirt for her turn at bat.

"I'll bet you won your share of battles," Sara said.

Janey only smiled. When she thought back to their high-school days, she was proud to remember that she'd held her own. She and Noah had argued a lot, but she'd won as often as she'd lost. Maybe that was why they'd been together so long; how could you respect someone you could walk all over? You certainly wouldn't want that in a life partner.

But then, Noah hadn't wanted her for a life partner. "I didn't win the big ones," she murmured.

"Maybe you can win this one," Sara said, "or at least Jessie can."

"You'd give the devil the benefit of the doubt, and apparently it runs in the family."

Janey nodded toward Max and Noah. Max had his arm slung around Noah's shoulders and the two of them laughing.

"Traitor," Janey muttered.

Sara was too busy watching her to take offense. The guys headed in their direction and Janey went from sullen and resentful to nervous and fidgety. And she began to glow. Her cheeks pinked up and her eyes gave off sparks that had nothing to do with anger.

Noah didn't even glance at Janey, though. Instead, he took Sara's hand and flashed her that thousand-watt smile. "You must be Sara." He kept her hand in his and leaned in just enough to flatter. "Max tells me you're originally from Boston. You'll have to tell me how you managed to get the people in this town to accept you."

"I married one of them."

Noah looked over at Janey and held her eyes for a long moment, then went back to Sara. "Somehow I don't think that's an option—unless you're willing to dump this hick and run away with me."

"Hey." Max shouldered Noah aside. "Get your own girl. This one's taken."

"He says that like it was his doing," Sara said. "It took me six years to convince Max he couldn't live without me."

Noah grinned. "Then he's not only stubborn, he's a fool."

"You were right, Janey," Sara said, "he's a charmer."

Noah lifted a brow. "What else did she say about me?"

"Just girl talk," Janey said. She loved Sara like a sister—a sister who was too sweet and naive to know when she shouldn't answer a question, especially from a man who'd only take advantage of all that sweetness.

"Must be an inside joke," Noah commiserated with Max.

"Girl talk is no joke," Max put in. "It's a very serious business."

Sara tugged on his ear playfully. "And don't you forget it."

"How could I, when it got you me? Or got me you," Max said.

"We've got each other," Sara said. "That's all that matters."

The look they shared was so deep, so intimate, that Janey felt as if she was intruding. Her eyes met Noah's; and the wistfulness she saw surprised her.

He couldn't have missed the longing she felt when she saw the love between Max and Sara. She wanted that for herself, wanted to find a man she could live with, laugh with and, yes, fight with, for the rest of her life. She'd been able to hold the loneliness at bay pretty well, but then Sara married Max, and Janey remembered how she'd had that kind of love once, and lost it. And maybe, she thought, once was all you got.

"Mom, Dad!" Joey, Max's son, raced up, so excited he couldn't stand still. "Big Ed's gonna let me play my trumpet in the next set."

"I've heard you play the trumpet," Sara said, reaching out to ruffle Joey's sandy hair. "I'm not sure it can be called actual music yet."

"I don't think you can call what Big Ed and his boys put out actual music, either," Max deadpanned.

That didn't curb Joey's enthusiasm. "C'mon!"

Max raised a hand in farewell as his son towed him off.

"It was…interesting to meet you, Noah," Sara said.

He shook her hand, his smile so warm and genuine Janey felt a slight burn of jealousy. "The pleasure was all mine."

Sara hesitated in front of Janey, looking as if she wanted to say something. But after a quick glance in Noah's direction, she gave Janey a hug, and set out after her family.

Janey turned to leave, as well, but Noah stepped out to block her.

"Everybody's watching," she hissed, trying to get around him.

"They're doing more than watching."

Janey surveyed the small knots of people scattered over the lawn. Every now and then they'd exchange a sentence or two, pretend to check out the potluck or tune in to Big Ed's efforts. But mostly, she knew, they were waiting to see what would happen between her and Noah.

"Why don't we dance?" he suggested. "Give them something to really talk about."

"Well, there's a glimpse of the old Noah, the boy who used to thumb his nose at everyone in town and do exactly what he wanted."

"Well, the old Noah wants to dance with the old Janey, the girl who dated that obnoxious kid just to prove she didn't give a damn what everyone else thought."

"That's not why I dated you."

"You sure? Wasn't a part of my charm that I was the troublemaker everyone warned you to stay away from?"

"If you believe that, it's a fortunate thing you left town when you did," she said, as calmly as if he hadn't just opened an old wound and then rubbed salt in it.

"Janey, wait." Noah grabbed her arm, wincing when he saw the pain on her face. Pain he'd put there. "I'm sorry. You always believed in me, even when everyone told me I was no good for you. I'm sorry. About everything."

"I'm not," she said, and walked away from him.

Noah raked a hand through his hair. Somehow he always managed to say the wrong thing, and while it would have been easy to just walk away he'd regret it—and he knew how that felt. "I wasn't talking about Jessie," he said when he'd caught up with Janey.

"I know." She changed directions to take them by the makeshift baseball diamond. "Jessie's playing softball."

And Janey, it seemed, was playing hardball, turning the tables on him. He'd gotten personal so she'd shut down—a complete role reversal from their relationship in high school. She'd always sensed when things were at their worst between him and his old man, and she'd always tried to help. More often than not she'd been snubbed or snapped at for her trouble, but she'd never thrown it in his face or held it against him or used it to get what she wanted once he'd worked his way through those dark moments. And he'd never, ever, questioned the fact that she'd be there the next time he needed her, even if he told her to go away.

He didn't like it, knowing he'd hurt her feelings and not being able to do anything about it. He liked it even less that he understood, finally, how much she must have loved him to put up with his roller-coaster moods. And that he'd destroyed something so nearly indestructible. "Janey, I—"

"Don't!" She shaded her eyes as she took in the softball game, her expression as placid as if that one anguished word hadn't all but exploded out of her.

Noah let it go, partly because he wasn't really sure what he wanted to say to her, but also because no matter what he said, it was bound to hurt her and he'd already hurt her enough.

"Jessie's over there," she said, pointing to the opposite side of the field. She set off in that direction, leaving Noah no choice but to follow.

"She's a pretty good shortstop," he said.

"And fielder, and batter." Janey managed a smile as the conversation took them back onto comfortable ground.

"So you're telling me she's a tomboy."

"Who loves to read and play video games—and she could argue the ears off a mule. That kid has a streak of stubbornness in her that defies explanation, and when she thinks she's right, she just won't give up."

"I wonder where she got that from?"

"I like to think she got it from my dad." She stopped on a

slight rise, where they'd have a good view of the field, and sank down on the grass. Noah sat beside her, but not too close. "There were times he'd take a stand on an issue, and in the beginning people would just laugh at him, or ignore him altogether. But he'd keep at it, somehow finding a way to make it matter, to make people care. And before anyone expected he'd have a big crowd backing him up, and the loudest voices would inevitably come from those same people who'd been his strongest opponents at the start. Jessie's a lot like that."

"So are you."

She didn't respond but he could see it pleased her to be compared with the man she'd idolized. A man Noah had never believed he could measure up to. "Your dad was a hell of a man, Janey. He'd be proud of you and Jessie."

"He was," she said simply.

"He didn't hold her against you, then." Of all the things he'd cost her, her relationship with her father would have been the worst.

"He loved Jessie to pieces. When he died…" She plucked a dandelion, then another, reaching farther for them than she had to while she blinked back tears. "I miss him so much sometimes I can't breathe, but when I wish him back it's for Jessie's sake. The two of them would've been inseparable. My mom—" she laughed softly "—she never could understand any of us."

"But she was the happiest woman I've ever known," Noah said quietly.

"She was. But she used to look at Dad and me like we were aliens, and whenever we tried to include her in one of our crusades, she'd say the sun was going to come up the next morning and the earth was still going to be spinning around it and whatever world crisis we were worrying over wasn't going to be solved by a country lawyer and his daughter. My dad would agree with her, but he always believed he could make a difference."

"So did you, Janey." She'd often talked about going into public service, and she hadn't meant teaching high-school government. Noah didn't ask her what had happened to derail her dreams. He already knew, and it added yet another weight to the load of guilt he was already carrying round.

"Don't look now," she said, "but either the softball game has gotten very popular, or you're attracting a crowd."

Noah was only too happy to have her change the subject, until he glanced around and realized that several people had settled on the grass near them. "I think *we're* attracting a crowd," he said.

"It's not me," Janey countered. "Word's gotten out that you're from California. Movie stars, swimming pools…"

Noah rolled his eyes, but sure enough, it was only a matter of minutes before someone worked up the gumption to approach him, and the first question made it a real struggle to keep a serious face.

"Hey, Noah," Molly Cunningham said, plopping down beside him and nudging him with an elbow as though they were still seniors at Plains City High School and class had just ended for the day.

"Hey, Molly," Noah said back to her.

"My mom was wondering if you know Harrison Ford."

"Or Sean Connery," Maisie Cunningham piped up from so close behind him that Noah jumped.

"Uh…no." He got to his feet, which put Maisie eye-to-eye with him. "If you want to ask me about actresses…"

Maisie hooted with laughter, giving him a bone-jarring thump on the shoulder. "You were always a troublemaker, Noah Bryant. It's nice to see you come back here and do the right thing by Jessie."

He tried to find Janey, but she was already gone and he was completely ringed in by people—those whose curiosity was stronger than their resentment of him. Most of the town's residents hung back: the same people who'd looked down on him ten years ago and who apparently still weren't ready to accept him. But they stood close enough, he noticed, to hear the questions fired at him, and the answers he gave back.

The sun was setting and the lightning bugs coming out before Noah managed to excuse himself. He quickly spotted Jessie, wearing an old pair of rubber boots and carrying a bucket, heading out to the pond with Joey Devlin and a half dozen other boys—going frogging, no doubt. Jessie saw him, too, but the expression on her face... He didn't have the heart to go up to her while all her friends were there. It would only have put her in an awkward position. She'd probably feel the need to prove that a man who'd never been interested in her existence meant nothing to her. And they already had enough to sort out without adding Jessie's pride in the mix.

"I have to admit this wasn't the best idea I've ever had."

Noah had to follow the sound of the voice, or he'd never have seen Janey sitting in the gloom a few feet away on Max's back porch.

"Getting to know Jessie at the party, I mean." She stood and came down the steps. "The people who weren't dragging tabloid details out of you were watching to see if you'd create some."

"And Jessie completely avoided me."

"That, too," Janey said.

"Wow, that's twice in two days you've agreed with me."

"I prefer to think of it as twice in two days that you've made sense." She glanced over at him. "Don't worry, I'm not expecting it to become a habit."

Noah laughed. "What would you say if I stopped by tomorrow afternoon and gave it another shot—and maybe I could spend some time with Jessie while I'm at it."

"Careful, you're coming dangerously close to making sense again."

"Was that a yes?"

"Actually, it was a no. It's Sunday. Jessie always has tea with Mrs. Halliwell on Sunday afternoon."

"Really?"

There in the shadow of the outbuildings, it was difficult for her to read his expression, but Janey felt the change in him. "You haven't seen her yet."

"No."

And Janey knew why. After his mom died, Mrs. Halliwell had been the closest thing to a mother Noah had had. "She would never be disappointed in you, Noah."

"But I left her behind, too."

There wasn't anything she could say to that, so she walked away before the urge to put her arms around him became too strong to resist. It wasn't her job to comfort him anymore.

Chapter Seven

Bright and early Monday morning, Janey walked into her sleeping daughter's bedroom—she didn't tiptoe, or try to avoid the squeaky floorboards or the stuff strewn everywhere. It was part of the ritual, making as much noise as she could so that when she smacked Jessie on the rump she was already awake. But today was different. Jessie didn't so much as stir.

She finally opened one eye and glared up at her mother for a second, grumbled something unintelligible and turned over onto her stomach.

"C'mon, Jessie, time to get up."

"School's out for the summer," she said, her voice muffled by the sheets she dragged over her head.

"Noah's coming here today."

There was a moment of…not just silence, but stillness, a moment during which Jessie seemed to be absorbing that bit of information. Then she rolled over and snored flamboyantly—a commentary that made Janey smile.

It took a real effort to make her voice stern enough to invoke the triple-name threat—"Jessica Marie Walters"—which was usually all she needed to let her daughter know she meant business.

Today, Jessie just continued snoring.

"Okay, you have two choices," Janey said. "You can talk to Noah, or we can clean this room."

Jessie's bedroom was the one room in the house that Janey purposely didn't touch. It was her daughter's personal space, and if she wanted to live in a cesspool, well, that was her prerogative, except for twice a year when Janey insisted they dig the place out in case there were strange things growing under the bed or in the corners.

It was testament to how much Jessie hated cleaning that she got up and stomped off toward the bathroom, so busy glaring at her mother she nearly walked into the door frame. Slamming doors wasn't allowed, but she made sure to shut it firmly behind herself.

"Be downstairs in fifteen minutes," Janey said as she walked by the bathroom. There wasn't an answer, and she didn't expect one. What she did expect was obedience.

She put out cereal and milk, and in exactly fifteen minutes, Jessie appeared in the kitchen, letting her pajamas speak for themselves.

Most kids would try to claim they were sick or scared; Jessie was more of an in-your-face type of kid. She took after her mother in that. "Go back upstairs and get dressed," Janey told her.

When Jessie crossed her arms, Janey put her hands on her hips and cocked one eyebrow in a you-know-you-won't-win look that had Jessie heaving a long-suffering sigh.

Grinning, Janey plucked a wooden spoon out of the holder by the sink and tapped her daughter on each shoulder. "I dub thee Jessie," she said ponderously, "Erskine, Montana's, queen of drama."

Jessie's smile was so restrained it brought tears to Janey's eyes. "Does he have to come over?" she asked.

And there, Janey thought, was the fear, all the more heart-wrenching because Jessie tried so hard not to show it. *No.*

Janey wanted to say. *Let's just send Noah packing and forget about him so we can go back to the way it was before. Because even if you didn't have a father, everything was pretty close to perfect.*

And while they were at it, maybe she could go back to the way it'd been before she remembered what it felt like to be in love—the kind of love that filled you up so much that when it was gone, the emptiness was deeper, the loneliness heavier. You could search for the rest of your life knowing you'd never find anything else that even came close, yet you couldn't bear to settle for less.

She knew Jessie still yearned for a father, regardless of what she said or how she acted. And Janey would do anything to spare her daughter the sadness she herself was feeling right now, she also knew she had to give Jessie—and Noah—a chance.

She sat down and pulled Jessie into a loose hug. The fact that the girl didn't protest was a pretty powerful sign of her unhappiness. "Let me ask you this," Janey said, brushing the hair out of her daughter's face so she could see her reaction. "What if I told you you didn't have to see your dad—Noah," she amended when Jessie immediately stiffened, not yet ready to hear him given that precious title. "What if I said you could leave the house before he gets here? And what if he didn't try to force the issue, either? Suppose he just went back to Los Angeles?"

Jessie's eyes filled with hurt and confusion. "Would he do that, do you think?"

Janey gave a slight shrug. "He has a life and a job back there, Jessie. He can't hang around Erskine forever waiting for you to warm up to him, can he? And if he leaves, and you don't get to ask him any questions, or spend any time with him, aren't you always going to wonder what he was like? And if maybe it was a mistake to make up your mind before you gave him a chance?"

"But you—"

"This isn't about me. What went wrong between Noah and me has nothing to do with you. We were just kids, we both made mistakes. You aren't mad at me for not telling him about you, are you?"

Jessie shook her head.

"Then you can't be mad at him for not showing up before now."

"Yes, I can." Jessie pulled free, returned to her chair and dropped into it. When Janey didn't react, she gave her bowl a shove that sent it skittering halfway across the table, then crossed her arms, scowling in defiance.

Janey recognized an act when she saw one, and even if there was real pain and resentment behind it she couldn't let Jessie get away with manipulating her. She waited, silent, and when Jessie snuck a glance over at her, Janey crossed her arms and nodded toward the stairs.

Jessie huffed out a breath, but she went, dragging her feet the whole way. She might've given in, but she wasn't going to make it easy on Noah.

MONDAY MORNING Noah awoke around eleven to discover that the world was a study in gray. Fine, gray drizzle fell soundlessly out of a gray sky, gray mountains loomed in the distance, even the green of the grass and trees seemed to be tinged with gray, and everything dripped.

The farmers and ranchers would be tickled to death—rain wasn't exactly a plentiful commodity—even if it was hell to work in. There was no way to stay dry and get your chores done at the same time, Noah remembered from his childhood. Everything stuck to you—hay, feed, your clothes—and there'd be mud everywhere. But there was one thing Noah had always loved about the rain, and it gave him an idea.

He took a quick shower and threw on jeans and an old

sweatshirt he'd brought along in case he got a chance to go running. An hour's drive from Plains City and a quick stop at Keller's Market later, he was pulling up in front of Janey's house, actually feeling he stood a chance of getting through to his daughter.

But when Jessie opened the door and he saw the hostility on her face, it took some of the spring out of his step. He followed her back to the kitchen, helping himself to a seat in the chair across the table from her. She wouldn't look at him, so he wordlessly appealed to Janey for help. Janey just lifted a shoulder, her expression saying, *I made her answer the door, the rest is up to you.*

He turned back to Jessie just in time to see her eyes shift away. The little manipulator, he thought, sitting there acting like she didn't care if he stayed or went, all the while waiting to see what he'd do. Oddly, it made him want to smile. She might've inherited the confrontational gene from her mother, but she'd gotten that sit-back-and-pick-your-moment thing from him. The way she decided which approach she was going to use, she must have figured out for herself. Smart kid.

"I'd like to take you fishing," Noah announced, jumping right in because that was the last thing she'd expect from him.

"It's the middle of the day," she said. "Where were you at dawn?"

"Sleeping. Where were you?"

She ignored that. "Everybody knows you're supposed to go fishing at dawn or sunset."

"Or when it's raining. That's the best time to fish. Everybody knows *that.*"

She sat back in her chair. "Clary takes me fishing."

It took everything Noah had not to react, especially the way he wanted to.

Thankfully, Janey stepped in before he was forced for him to come up with some response other than a four-letter word.

"Noah is taking you fishing today," she said to Jessie, "and if you're smart, you'll stop arguing now because you're not winning this one."

"But it's raining."

"Just barely," Janey replied. She came over to pick up Jessie's cereal bowl, pausing to give her daughter a long, level look. "I've seen you play outside all day in worse weather than this. Go upstairs and find your raincoat and then get your stuff together."

"Thanks," Noah said, once Jessie was safely out of the room.

"You were getting a little wild-eyed," Janey told him.

He felt a little wild-eyed—more than a little when he got right down to it. He kept telling himself he knew how to handle Jessie, but somehow she always put him on the defensive.

"What's in here?" Janey pried from his fingers the plastic market bags he'd forgotten he was still holding, opening them and lining up the assortment of items on the table. "Not bad, Bryant. Jessie actually likes this kind of juice—although I don't usually let her have it. Too much sugar."

"Owen Keller told me she liked it."

"Bribery, huh?"

Noah managed a weak smile that lasted about as long as it took Janey to pick up the six-pack of beer he'd included and walk it over to her refrigerator. "C'mon, Janey, be reasonable. I'm bound to get thirsty, what with all the talking Jessie and I will be doing."

Janey came back with a couple of apples and some bottled water. "It's not San Pellegrino," she said, "but it'll do the job."

"You're taking all the fun out of this for me."

"No, I'm taking all the worry out of it for me."

She crossed the kitchen, produced a small cooler and some ice packs and proceeded to pack the drinks and the apples, re-bagging the snacks he'd brought.

"Okay," he relented, mostly because he could see there was no changing her mind, "but I'm not letting you keep my beer."

"I don't drink beer."

"Yeah," he said, smiling in remembrance, "but you drink wine. And it doesn't take much for you to get very friendly."

Janey could feel herself blushing, but there was nothing she could do about it, any more than she could halt the memories that caused it. She hadn't slept with Noah on prom night because she'd been drunk, and if she *had* been drunk, he wouldn't have taken advantage of her. Whatever else Noah was, he wasn't that kind of person. She knew that because there'd been times when they'd gone out to where the kids parked and passed around a bottle of wine, and her inhibitions had lowered to the point where she'd all but jumped him in the bed of the ancient Ford pickup he'd driven back then. Noah had always been the one to keep a cool head at those moments. But when she was sober, he'd been all over her. And on prom night, she'd been all over him.

It was just that kind of remembering that sent the heat from her face to parts of her body that shouldn't have even been lukewarm when he was around. The way he was looking at her, as if he was taking the same walk down memory lane, didn't help.

Jessie saved the day, stomping down the stairs one by one—stomp, pause, stomp, pause—making a statement with every resounding footstep.

Noah got that slightly deranged look that made Janey wonder if she should let the two of them leave without her. He leaned back in his chair, crossing his arms and uncrossing them in an attempt to appear relaxed when he was anything but.

Janey took pity on him. She poured him a cup of coffee and set it on the table, dropping a bagel into the toaster because if she knew Noah, he hadn't eaten breakfast. It popped up just as Jessie entered the kitchen. Janey slathered some butter on the bagel and set it in front of him. He pushed it away, but she pushed it right back.

"Eat it," she said, trying not to let him see how much the situation amused her. "I have a feeling you're going to need your strength today."

Chapter Eight

Strength was the least of what Noah needed. There wasn't charm enough in the world to crack Jessie's attitude, his sense of humor seemed to have deserted him completely, and patience was definitely in short supply. A SUV would have helped, too. It took him a half-dozen tries to find a place to fish—not because the places he'd frequented as a kid were gone, but because whatever wasn't three-foot high brush was a quagmire of mud, neither of which the Porsche was up to navigating.

Jessie sighed more loudly each time, making sure he knew how dumb she thought he was. He finally asked her to direct him to a site, thinking she might enjoy telling him what to do. Not his best idea ever, but the Porsche-scratching field of brush she directed him to was no surprise—considering the Porsche-size mudhole at the last one and the Porsche-gutting ruts at the one before that. Still, he'd be damned if he gave up.

"Is there really a place to fish here?" he asked, which was a real accomplishment, since he'd locked his jaw so tight that in order to keep from yelling at her his head ached.

"Clary drives a Blazer," Jessie said. "He doesn't have any trouble getting back there."

"Neither will we." Noah climbed out of the car and fought to get their fishing poles from behind the seats. He'd bought two new poles in Keller's that were short enough to fit in the car. Jessie had given the half-size pole a disdainful once-over and handed him an expensive-looking state-of-the-art rod. He'd had to bend it almost to the breaking point to get in the car so she wouldn't have an immediate excuse to refuse the outing.

"The river's at least a mile from here," Jessie protested. "I'm not walking."

The kid was stubborn, and quick on her feet, seeing as how she kept coming up with new excuses for every situation. Problem was, he was smarter than her, not to mention really, really ticked off. "You can't walk a whole mile?" he asked mildly, opening the trunk and pulling out the cooler.

Jessie emerged from the car reluctantly. "I'll get soaking wet," she said in a sullen voice.

Noah looked at her raincoat, misted with the slight drizzle that was still falling.

She got the point, but it didn't faze her. "I'm talking about my shoes and jeans."

"You know, I didn't think of that." He set the cooler back in the trunk. "We can go shopping instead, or maybe do some other girl-type thing so you won't get your shoes wet."

Jessie gave him the kind of glare that should have reduced him to a smoking pile of sludge among the weeds, then grabbed her pole and headed off toward a line of trees in the near distance. Noah grabbed the cooler and tackle, picked up the other two poles and took off after her. They walked in silence, but there was a whole lot of communication going on, Jessie sending him occasional sidelong death stares that Noah pretended not to notice, but received loud and clear.

They crested a slight rise. From there they could see a smallish lake, more of a pond, really, sitting at the edge of a hay meadow a couple hundred yards away. Noah stopped for a second, taking in the slate-gray, wind-rippled water. The shoreline was heavy with cattails and fallen, rotting logs, great places for fish to hide. He almost said as much, but Jessie was already gone, climbing over the half-exposed roots of a huge old willow tree on the bank. All in all he was feeling pretty good about the day so far—if outwitting a nine-year-old was something to be proud of.

"This isn't so bad," he said as he joined her. "I'll bet there are some decent-size bass in there, maybe a bluegill or two."

"Clary says only amateurs fish off the bank. Too easy to get your hook caught. And besides, only the small fish come in close to shore."

Noah didn't see any boats around, so they had no choice but to fish from shore. He figured he wouldn't gain anything from pointing that out, though. "You want me to bait your hook for you?"

Jessie gave him an *oh, puh-lease* look, plucked an earthworm out of the little plastic dish and impaled the poor thing several times with the hook, leaving no doubt that she wished he was the one wriggling in agony. "Clary says you don't fish unless you bait your own hook."

Noah stared at her.

"Well, he does," she said belligerently, wiping her hand on her jeans for good measure. "And he's right. It's not fair to expect you to bait my hook just because I'm a girl."

What he'd actually been wondering was if he could ask her to bait his. Probably not, he decided, taking up a worm and doing a much poorer job than she'd done. Torturing worms just wasn't as much fun when you were his age. It had been a while—a long while—and the pole wasn't exactly top-quality, but he managed to cast out a respectable distance. "Huh?" he said to Jessie. "You gotta admit that's not bad."

She snorted, gave an expert flick of her wrist and dropped her hook about five feet short of his.

"That's pretty good, too," Noah said, "for a girl."

Jessie looked over at him, trying, he assumed, to figure out if he was joking or not. He made sure to keep an absolutely straight face, so she reeled in her line and cast out again, her hook plopping down precisely as far as his, but still a couple feet over.

"Now I'm impressed."

She didn't respond, just reeled in her line and cast it out to the same place as before.

"Can you show me how to do that?" Noah asked, even though he knew exactly what he was doing. He might be rusty at it, but he'd fished every spare moment he had when he was a kid. It had been one of the few times his old man had let him duck chores, since it had the beneficial side effect of putting a meal on the table.

"Amateur," Jessie muttered. She didn't look at him, or give any indication that she was going to say anything else, but he could see she was debating, and he knew he had her by the ego.

"It's not how, it's where," she finally said. "See which way the wind's blowing the water?" She pointed to a leaf that floated slowly by a few yards out where there was open water, passing him first, then her. "I'm downwind from you, so I need to make sure my hook ends up down-current from yours and not as far out."

"Which keeps you from getting tangled up in this amateur's line," he finished for her.

She almost smiled before she stopped herself. "Clary says you're not supposed to talk when you're fishing."

Pretty damn smart. She'd effectively shut him up. How was he going to win her over if he couldn't talk to her?

They sat like that for a while, silent except for the quiet whisper of the drizzle hitting the water and the occasional groan of her plastic raincoat as she shifted to work her reel. Jessie had an air of smugness about her—Noah could feel it and he began to stew. Getting outsmarted by a nine-year-old, even one with his genes, just didn't set well.

And then he caught a fish. It was silly, but he expected her to be a little impressed, especially when he got it to shore and held it up—a nice, fat ten-inch-long bass.

Jessie took a minute to look it over, sniffed and said, "Clary catches bigger fish in here all the time."

"I don't give a damn what Clary catches," Noah snapped, "or what he drives or what he thinks.

"Well, I do." She shot to her feet, reeling in her line with sharp, jerky motions. "Clary doesn't make me do stupid stuff like go fishing in the rain, because he lives here and we can just go another day when it's sunny— Oh, damn!" Her pole had become tangled in the shoreline weeds.

Noah let her fight with it for a moment, then put his hands over hers. She let go as if she'd been burned. "I'm not going anywhere," he said quietly as he worked the reel and tugged gently on the hook. "You can keep doing whatever your fertile little mind can think up to drive me away, but I'll keep coming back."

"For how long?" she asked, and he could hear the pain and fear in her voice.

She was only protecting herself, the same way he'd been protecting himself by disappearing for two weeks until he'd gotten used to the idea of her. How could he blame her for that?

The hook jerked free and he handed the pole back to her, holding on to it until she looked up at him. "I'll be around for as long as it takes, Jessie."

"I thought you had to go back to California in two weeks."

"That's true, but there are all sorts of ways to get from California to Montana. Or from Montana to California."

Her mouth dropped open, and she sat down, either excited or scared—or both—at the idea of traveling to Los Angeles. Then the wonder of it seemed to wear off and she remembered who he was. "I don't want to go to California," she said, reeling in her line the rest of the way.

"Not now," Noah allowed, "but maybe once we know each other better, you'll change your mind. And you don't have to come alone. Your mom could come, too, and if you don't want to stay at my house you could stay at a hotel." He didn't know where all that was coming from, and he had a pretty good idea Janey wouldn't go for it, but he didn't care because it was working.

Jessie was fighting to stay aloof, but he could already see it was going to be a losing battle. She might love this little town, but that didn't mean she wasn't curious about the rest of the world.

Still, he didn't want her to like him because of what he could give her. "I'm not here to replace any of your friends." Or Janey's, he reminded himself, thinking of Clary. "I don't want to change anything about your life that you don't want changed."

"Kind of too late, isn't it?" she said. He was relieved to see she was half smiling.

"Yeah, for both of us. But that doesn't mean we can't take this slow, get to know each other and decide where we're going from here."

"You wouldn't…" He could tell she wanted to say something, something he wasn't going to like. "Jason Hartfield said you could take my mom to court."

"Sue for custody, you mean?" The look in Jessie's unwavering eyes told him he'd be better off if he didn't try to sugarcoat it. "I could sue for joint custody, and if I win, a judge would force you to come stay with me sometimes. Summers, holidays."

"But summer's the best time here." She stood up and edged away, holding her pole crosswise in front of her as if it was a magical line of protection he couldn't cross. "I won't go. I don't care what anybody says."

"I promise you I will never do that, Jessie. I would never take you away from your mom."

"How do I know you'll keep your promise?"

"You don't," he said. "That's one of the things we have to figure out—when to trust each other."

"You don't trust me?" She dropped the pole and jammed her hands on her hips. "I didn't do anything to you."

"No, but you could." That was all he said; she was smart enough to figure the rest out on her own, and when she did, it was a like a light coming on in her face.

"Oh," she said. Her cheeks pinked up and she suddenly turned shy.

"I know we just met, Jessie, but finding out about you... I never expected to have kids."

"Why not?"

Noah shrugged, a little uncomfortable talking about this personal stuff with Jessie. On the other hand, it was getting through to her when nothing else had. "I thought I'd make a lousy dad."

"So far you're right."

He grinned. "Yeah, well, now I have a daughter, and I didn't realize how that was going to make me feel."

"And if I don't like you..."

"That would make me sad. And if I let you down, that would make me sad, too."

"Like you let my mom down, you mean, by going away and not coming back?"

Noah nodded. "Do you think she'll ever forgive me?"

"I don't know," Jessie said, sitting back down and nodding sagely. "Clary says she's a hardheaded woman."

THE SOUND OF VOICES brought Janey to her front door. She knew it had to be Jessie and Noah, but when she saw them coming up the walk, actually talking to each other, she still couldn't believe it.

"I caught three fish," Jessie said, climbing the steps.

Noah came up behind her, the cooler Janey had packed in his arms. "But I caught the biggest one." He slid the top off and tipped it forward so she could see a pile of slimy fish in place of the juice and snacks they'd left with. "And since we caught them, you have to clean them."

"No, I don't."

"You invited me for dinner," he said, "remember?"

They both looked at Jessie, who reached for the door handle as if she hadn't heard a word they'd said.

"Oh, no, you don't." Janey stepped in front of her. "You're covered in muck from head to toe. Go around to the back porch and take off those sneakers, and then go upstairs and change into something clean and dry. In the bathroom," she called after her daughter, who was already down the stairs and heading toward the back of the house.

"What about me?" Noah asked.

His shoes were muddy, as were his jeans all the way to his knees, but the mud looked mostly dry. "Just take off your shoes and scrape off as much of the dirt as you can."

She turned to go inside, but Noah called her back. "Are you sure I should stay? Jessie didn't say it was okay."

"She didn't say it wasn't," Janey pointed out.

"And what about you?"

"It's fine," she said, "but if you expect me to cook those fish, you're cleaning them."

Truth was, Janey wasn't sure how she felt. Noah staying for dinner was fine, and she wasn't foolish enough to believe he wouldn't win Jessie over, eventually. But to see her beginning to warm up to him... It kind of hurt, she realized. She'd had Jessie all to herself for so long, and even though she'd been prepared for this, the reality of it was a whole different thing.

She was the one who'd raised Jessie from a baby, the one

who'd walked the floor with her when she'd been teething. She'd kissed her scrapes and cried and blamed herself when Jessie learned that she didn't have a father. Not to mention the whole sixteen hours of labor she put in and the screaming pain of what was laughably called a natural delivery.

And now that she was a fairly self-sufficient, interesting, precocious and charming nine-year-old, Noah had to come along, wanting to step in and claim a place in her life, just like that.

By the time he showed up at the back door, dirt-free and handed her a newspaper with four cleaned-and-filleted fish, she was feeling pretty resentful. Watching him continue to worm his way into Jessie's good graces hardly helped her disposition.

"…and you have to admit I was right about fishing in the rain," he said as the meal wore on. "Although I didn't think we'd ever make it to a fishing hole." He proceeded to recount the story about the ordeal Jessie had put him and his precious Porsche through.

Jessie sank deeper in her chair as her sins mounted, every now and then looking at her mother as if she was waiting for the other shoe to drop. Janey didn't feel a need to admonish her, though, not when Noah was only using her guilt to further batter her defenses.

"But I got the last laugh," he concluded, "because I caught the biggest fish."

"You did not!" Jessie sat up in her chair. "I caught the biggest fish. The three biggest fish."

"Longer maybe, but mine was fatter."

"Can you prove it?"

He indicated the empty serving plate. "Not a lot left to judge by."

"Then I guess next time you'd better bring a camera."

Next time. Those two words echoed in a sudden silence. Jessie's cheeks reddened.

"If you're in town long enough for there to be a next time," she muttered, wadding up her paper napkin and throwing it on the table.

"Next time," Noah said, "I'll take you fishing my way. Deep-sea fishing. And there'll be a camera, trust me."

Jessie stopped halfway out of her chair, mouth open, eyes wide. "Deep sea? Like the Atlantic Ocean?"

Noah chuckled. "Geography's not your strong suit, is it?"

Jessie's gaze automatically cut to her mother.

"Maybe you should get out the atlas," Janey said, the words barely out of her mouth before her daughter was racing off into the den.

"I'm not trying to bribe her," Noah said. "Honest. She likes fishing so much, and there's nothing like deep-sea fishing."

"You were showing off."

"Yeah. I guess I was showing off a little, but I really think she'd get a kick out of it."

"She would." Janey took a moment to reconcile the sincerity on his face with what she was feeling, then decided it was too big a task. "I guess you've got her all figured out."

"She's not so different from her mother," Noah said.

"Yes, she is." She had a lot of Noah in her. Janey took to her feet, more than ready to call it a night.

Noah, however, seemed to have daylight to burn—and twilight, and nighttime. "That was one of the best meals I've ever had. You've got your mother's way around the kitchen, Janey."

"Goody for me. I'll add it to my résumé," she said, refusing to be sweet-talked out of her sour mood. She had to feel *something*, and irritation was safer than the rest of the emotions Noah inspired in her.

Her sarcasm only seemed to amuse him, though. "You should get a dishwasher," he said as she began to ferry dishes from the table to the sink, running hot water over them.

"Or you could help."

Noah cupped his hands behind his head and leaned back,

stretching his legs out, man-of-leisure style. "It's more fun to sit here and watch you," he said grinning at the dirty look she shot him.

Her face was flushed from the hot water, tendrils of hair she'd tried to tuck back curling around her cheeks and over her forehead. A wave of need hit him, so hard it knocked the grin from his face. And it wasn't just desire, either. There was something soothing about watching her perform a task like doing the dishes, a hominess he'd never realized he missed. In his house it had been a chore, his chore to be exact, as his father didn't hold with doing women's work. It was okay for his son, though, along with everything else the old man hadn't wanted to do himself. And that was a lot.

"You really have to stop staring."

Noah blinked a couple of times, then smiled as he came back to Janey's kitchen and her annoyed face. "Am I making you nervous?"

"This whole thing makes me nervous," she muttered. She turned back to the sink, scrubbing the dishes hard enough to take the glaze off them, mumbling under her breath and shaking her head every now and again. He knew exactly how she felt. He couldn't put it into words—they'd gone through such a range of emotions during their twenty-year history—but he understood Janey's confusion.

And the least he could do, he thought, was not add to it. He joined her at the sink, took the dishtowel off her shoulder and began to dry the dishes as she handed them to him. He'd hoped she'd feel more comfortable if he wasn't watching her. What he hadn't counted on was the way it would make *him* feel.

If just observing the chore made him nostalgic that was nothing compared to the way it felt with the two of them working side by side in an easy rhythm, as if they'd done this a thousand evenings after a thousand dinners, while their daughter watched TV in the other room. He could see what he'd missed, what his life might've been like if he'd stayed instead of running off, an immature kid scared of the depth of his own emotions.

Still, something infinitely worse could've happened if that immature kid had married and left other dreams unfulfilled. Noah had never believed in anything remotely metaphysical; he'd put all his faith in himself, in his abilities and his drive. But maybe he wasn't supposed to be here until now, when he finally recognized what was missing from his life.

His hand closed over the next dish, on top of hers, and they both froze, eyes locked. Noah remembered, suddenly, what it had felt like to hold her in his arms, skin to skin, that one night. How had he ever thought of anything but that? he wondered. How had he found the strength to walk away from her when he couldn't imagine not feeling this again for the rest of his life?

But he didn't have to find the strength this time because she was gone between one heartbeat and the next. He turned to find her dumping leftovers into storage bowls as if nothing had happened.

He put the dish down and walked up behind her, clasping her shoulders. The serving bowl she was holding clattered to the countertop. "I think we should talk about what just happened," he said, his grip firming when she tried to duck away from him. "Obviously there's still something going on between us."

"It's just sex."

"It's not." He whirled her around, blocked her in between himself and the counter, angry to hear her reduce this huge, consuming thing inside him to something he could've found in any bar in L.A. "This is a hell of a lot stronger than sex, Janey. You know it, and it's got you scared."

"Let me go," she said softly, a whisper of sound that cut through his emotions like no shout could have.

He dropped his hands to his sides, but she didn't walk away. Instead, she started mopping up the mess she'd made.

"Aren't you going to say anything?"

"What's there to say?"

"It's too soon, isn't it?"

"Too soon?" She laughed, a tight sound that conveyed irony and pain, but no humor. "Never's too soon."

"What if I said I don't believe that?"

She set the bowl down on the counter with a crack, turned to face him again, and although her voice never rose above conversational tones, the anger in it had him backing off a couple of steps. "You've been back barely forty-eight hours and you've got Jessie practically eating out of your hand. Isn't that enough?"

"I don't know."

She closed her eyes, but not before he saw the anguish in them. "What do you want from me, Noah?"

A minute ago that had been so clear. He'd wanted a family—Janey and Jessie, to be exact. He'd wanted the last ten years back, or more specifically, he'd wanted to write himself into their lives and them into his. And then he'd begun to doubt himself, the way he always doubted himself when it came to his feelings.

"And what about your life in Los Angeles, the career you wanted so badly?" she asked as if she'd taken the next step down his own thought path. "Are you just going to give up your job and move here, to a place you hate?" She flicked a glance at the doorway and lowered her voice. "Or do you expect us to pick up and move, take Jessie away from her friends and her school?"

"No, I don't want to take Jessie away from everything she knows." He waited until their eyes met. "But it might be better for you, Janey. You had dreams, too, and they weren't teaching high-school government and grade-school art."

"We aren't talking about me."

"No, we aren't." But they would, he vowed, another time. "This is about Jessie. You may have found out about her by accident, but you stayed in town because of her. Only her."

"You're right. I don't know what I was thinking," he said, but he knew what he'd been feeling, and he knew she'd been feeling it, too. "I'm not going to stand here and tell you that you're just some one-night stand who accidentally got pregnant and all you are to me now is the mother of my child. I loved you for a lot of years, Janey. I loved you the night I left town—"

"But it didn't stop you from leaving."

"And that's the problem, isn't it?"

She turned away, the gesture itself all the answer he needed. Unlike with Jessie, he'd done something to destroy Janey's trust; he couldn't just expect her to forget everything and take him back.

Even if he wanted her to.

"Don't worry about it," he said, mustering up a smile in the hopes it would help lighten the mood. "Call it temporary madness. From what I've seen, you have that effect on the men in this town."

"Then I guess it's a good thing you don't live in this town anymore."

"I do for at least the next two weeks," he said. "I didn't see the sense in commuting from the hotel in Plains City every day, so I rented a house on Bighorn Drive. I'm moving tomorrow."

"But…that's the street behind this one."

"And one house over."

He left her there, openmouthed, while he went to say goodbye to Jessie. But he wasn't fool enough to believe he'd had the last word.

Chapter Nine

Having Noah as a neighbor wasn't as bad as Janey had expected it to be—as long as she didn't actually think about him living a few hundred feet away. Or remember how he'd felt pressed up against her. Or pay any attention to gossip. So, everyone in town was talking about her and Jessie, and their situation. What else was new? She plodded down the stairs and out onto the front porch to retrieve the newspaper.

There was no way she and Jessie and Noah were ever going to be a family, no matter what the Erskine busybodies wanted to make of the fact that Noah was renting a house a mere stone's throw from hers. He wouldn't stay in town; he was making very sure Jessie didn't get her hopes up on that score. But he was doing everything in his power to win her over while he was around.

Janey shuffled back into the house and set the paper on the kitchen table while she filled the teakettle. They'd had dinner at Noah's last night: soggy frozen French fries and charred hamburgers. The man couldn't even barbecue, apparently. But he'd had no trouble with dessert, remembering the messy hot-fudge sundaes he and Jessie had put together. Jessie had stayed behind to help with the dishes and watch a movie with Noah, and in a moment of utter insanity, she'd suggested Jessie spend the night there—which was the reason Janey had slept poorly. It wasn't the first time Jessie had been away from home, but this was different. She felt as though Jessie was gaining a father and she was losing a daughter—not to mention her mind, if she kept thinking that way.

She turned off the gas and fixed herself a cup of tea, making a mental list of the maintenance she'd intended to take care of that summer, maintenance that had been put on hold because of Noah. Sitting at the table, she drew the newspaper toward her, planning to leaf through the ad section to see if any of the local do-it-yourself stores were having sales. She didn't make it past the front-page article. And Noah's prominence in it.

"Mom!"

Janey didn't know how long it was before she heard Jessie's voice and two pairs of footsteps clattering across the back porch, but her tea had grown cold.

"We were hoping we could bum breakfast from you," Noah said, as they came through the back door.

"Yeah," Jessie said, all cheerful and sunny, "I want pancakes."

Janey twisted around and knew she hadn't managed to hide her expression when they both went silent, their smiles fading. "When were you going to tell me about this?" she asked Noah, holding up the paper.

He studied her face another second or two, then came over and took it from her, scanning the front-page headline, Megamart Coming To Plains City, before he set the paper back down. "I wasn't expecting it to make the news this soon."

Janey stood slowly, taking her cup to the sink and dumping it out. She tried to make a new cup of tea, mainly to give herself something to do, but she had to give up. Her hands were shaking so badly she was afraid she'd scald herself with the hot water.

"You're angry I didn't tell you," Noah said from behind her. "It doesn't have anything to do with you and Jessie."

"Go upstairs, Jessie."

Jessie didn't argue, but she didn't leave the room, either.

"We'll talk later," Noah said to her. "Go on upstairs." And she did.

"Got all your ducks lined up, don't you?" Janey said as soon as Jessie was gone.

"What are you talking about?"

"You came here to ruin this town, and I have to give you credit. You didn't think you'd have to contend with a daughter, but you managed to get her on your side before she had to find out what a schmuck you are."

"Hold on." Noah looked about as puzzled as a man could look. "I'm not here to ruin Erskine, Janey. The store's going to be in Plains City."

"It's not going to be anywhere if I have anything to say about it."

Noah sank into a chair at the table, then got to his feet again, unable to sit. He'd known there'd be some opposition, but he hadn't expected it to come from Janey. "This will bring jobs to the area," he said to her. "That's something your dad always worked for."

"It'll also ruin the small businesses in this town, which is something my dad would've hated to see happen. I know how companies like Megamart work, Noah. You come into a community and build one of your huge stores stocked with merchandise bought at the kind of volume discount the merchants around here can only dream of. You undercut their prices and drive them out of business, and then you jack your prices back up because you don't have any competition left and you can charge anything you want."

"That's not entirely true, Janey, and even if one or two business go under, the Megamart will employ hundreds of people."

"At a living wage? The businessmen you're going to bankrupt are supporting families. Do you honestly think a job at minimum wage fifty miles away from here is a fair trade for what they stand to lose?"

He headed for the door. "I'm not going to discuss this with you while you're angry."

"That's it, just run away again."

Noah stopped, turned around. "You're right," he said, brushing past her and going upstairs.

He found Jessie in the tower room, her elbows on the windowsill and her chin in her hands, staring blankly outside.

"Jessie."

She didn't move.

Noah put his arm around her shoulders, hating how stiff and tense she was.

"Mom's mad at you," she said miserably.

"Yeah. I kept a secret from her—from both of you."

"About a store?"

It didn't surprise him that she'd been eavesdropping and he couldn't blame her. She had a right to know what was going on, a right to make up her own mind, and since he was the only rational parent at the moment, he'd rather she heard it from him.

He knelt down but didn't force her to look at him. "I work for Megamart Corporation, Jessie. Do you know what that is?"

"Sure." She glanced over at him. "They have commercials on TV. They're really big stores and they carry everything. Do you work in one?"

"Not exactly," he said, relaxing a bit as she did. "I work for the parent company—the headquarters. My job is to scout out locations for new stores."

"And you're building one here?"

"In Plains City, actually, but it'll be close enough for you to shop there."

Her face fell. "I don't think Mom will want to."

"No." Noah sat on the old couch, his heart lurching when she sat down beside him.

"Why does she think it's bad?"

"She's afraid the store's going to cause problems for the town."

"Oh." She thought about that a second, her expression growing serious. "Is it?"

"I don't know." Noah dropped his head back, contemplating the ceiling. "I guess it might take business away from some of the stores in Erskine, but it won't make a difference in your life." He met her eyes. "I promise you that, Jessie."

"But Mom's so mad. That makes a difference."

"I can't do anything about that at the moment. She'll calm down," he said. "And once she does, she'll see reason."

Jessie seemed to be reassured, but when he got downstairs, he found Janey in the front yard, weeding maniacally with her headphones on. No matter what he did, she wouldn't talk to him. He gave up after ten minutes or so, trudging through her back yard and jumping the fence into his. There was a sick feeling in the pit of his stomach, but he believed what he'd told Jessie. Janey was only angry because he hadn't told her the truth about why he was there. She'd get over that, and if she didn't he'd find a way to talk her make her come around.

Besides, Janey had to accept that Megamart was building a store in her community. There wasn't really anything she could do about it.

IF ERSKINE COULD BE SAID to have a rush hour, it would be Saturday evening, when folks from all over came into town for dinner at the hotel or the diner, or to fill up on burgers and beer at the Ersk Inn while watching whatever game was playing on Mike Shasta's big screen. A traffic jam was unheard of, unless you counted the day Janey's friend Sara had accidentally tipped a ladder into the middle of Main Street last

November, leaving Ted Delancey dangling from the light pole he'd been decorating and causing a one-car pile-up. But that had been nothing. Ted had shimmied down the pole, and Maisie Cunningham's two beefy sons had pushed the car off to one side and cleared the broken ladder away, bringing things back to normal in no time.

So when Janey strolled down the boardwalk around five-thirty or so that Saturday, and nearly brought traffic to a complete halt, it was an event. Not that traffic was moving very fast to begin with, what with people leaning out of car windows to shout hello to friends or driving extra slow, hoping a parking space would open up along the boardwalk. But everyone, it seemed, had read the front page of the newspaper that morning. The larger drawbacks to having a Megamart right in their back yard seemed to have totally eluded the people of Erskine, but nobody had missed the implications for Janey's personal life. She'd expected there to be talk, but she'd never let the talk get to her before; she wasn't about to let it make her a prisoner in her own house on such a beautiful evening. She wasn't looking forward to the questions, but how could she expect Jessie to hold her head up if she didn't?

"Hey, Janey, where's Jessie tonight?"

Questions like that, she thought, pasting on a smile. Maisie Cunningham was staring over her shoulder from where she was walking up ahead with her husband, Arliss, the two of them waiting for an answer.

"Noah took her to dinner and a movie in Plains City."

There was a lull, and it felt to Janey as if everyone in town had sucked in their breath all at once.

"You're not mad about the store?" Maisie asked, slowing down so Janey could catch up with her. Arliss kept on going. He didn't like to get involved.

"The store would be bad for Erskine," Janey said evenly, "and Plains City."

She saw the elbow-nudging, the knowing looks exchanged by people within earshot, and knew they'd completely ignore any reasonable objections she could offer. They were much more interested in the entertaining possibility that her opposition had to do with her personal grudge against Noah. She had to try, anyway. She was her father's daughter, after all. "Do you people have any idea what a store like Megamart will do to the businesses here? You should want to stop it as much as I do."

"We're behind you, Janey," Mr. Tilford called out from his bakery doorway across the street.

"Good. Who wants to walk a picket line?"

The crowd faded away like smoke on a windy day. Everyone suddenly had something pressing to do in somewhere else in town. And Janey felt an urgent need for ice cream. She swung into the Five-And-Dime, heading straight for the soda counter at the side of the store. She got more than she bargained for; Sara was sitting there already, and the only thing Janey could've used more than calorie comfort was a friend.

"I saw the crowd outside and figured it was you," Sara said when Janey dropped onto the stool next to her. "I can't believe they didn't follow you in here."

"Must've had more important things to do," Janey said with a shrug she didn't come close to feeling. Sara seemed to buy it, though. Grateful for the reprieve, however short-lived, Janey picked up a plastic menu and pointed out her selection to the teenage girl working the soda counter. "Where are Max and Joey?"

"At the hardware store."

Janey couldn't help smiling at that, the kind of smile that came from knowing her world and loving it. For as long as she could remember, Erskine's male population had been congregating at the hardware store on Saturday nights to talk about their wheat crops and cattle herds.

If Megamart got its way, there was a good chance the hardware store wouldn't be there anymore. It would be history.

"So," Sara said as Janey's chocolate malt arrived. "Noah works for Megamart."

"Yep."

"And they're thinking about building a store in this area."

Janey nodded, taking a long pull at her straw. The cold was soothing, the taste of the chocolate instantly comforting.

"I haven't been to a Megamart since college. I practically furnished my dorm room from that place, everything's so cheap. It'll be fun to make the drive to Plains City to shop once in a while."

"Fun?" Janey swiveled around on her stool to stare incredulously at her best friend. "That place will ruin every small business in Plains City and Erskine."

"Hold on, Janey. It said in the paper that they haven't even finalized their plans yet. Why are you so upset?"

Because of Noah. He'd crashed back into her life as if he hadn't all but destroyed her ten years ago, and in a week he had Jessie eating out of his hand, and Janey couldn't stop thinking about how it had felt to feel his body pressed to hers, how good he looked and sounded and smelled—

He'd lied to her, she reminded herself, looked her right in the face and lied. Again. After so many years it shouldn't make a difference. It wasn't even personal. But he'd lied to Jessie, too, and *that* mattered.

"Janey?"

"They wouldn't have made the announcement unless they've already gotten the important phases of the plan locked down," she said, deliberately ignoring Sara's question.

"So why would they make it seem as if it's not a sure thing already?"

"Because they want to gauge public reaction before they sink the real capital into the project. They'd rather have a protest now than a boycott later, once they've put up a building and stocked the place. If we make enough trouble for them, they'll turn tail and run to cut their losses and protect their image."

"We? You know I'm with you a hundred percent, but I'm not sure this is so bad."

"Not sure!"

"Okay, Janey, I realize you take your civic duty seriously, but I've never seen you so worked up before." She glanced over her shoulder, lowering her voice. "It's Noah, isn't it? He came to town to build this store—"

"Maybe I am overreacting a bit." Janey swirled her straw around her glass to loosen up the thick shake, and to give herself someplace to look besides Sara's too-observant eyes. "But the local businesses can't compete with a Megamart. You said yourself everything's cheap there."

"I guess it might take business away from the Five-And-Dime and Halliwell's General Store."

"It won't be just them. According to the paper, this Megamart is supposed to be some sort of experimental version, tailored to the ranching and farming community. That means the hardware, the feed store—you name it, Megamart will eat into their business. And some of those places are barely surviving as it is. You lose those stores and pretty soon the hotel and diner will go, and all that'll be left is a lone gas station, a Main Street that's like a ghost town, and my house."

"Change always comes, Janey, and people always adapt. Erskine's been around a long time, and the people here are tougher than you give them credit for. I think you're overestimating the impact one store will have on this community."

And Sara was *under*estimating the impact one store could have, Janey wanted to say. Especially with Noah Bryant behind it. He'd hated Erskine since the moment his family had moved here, but she'd never believed he hated it enough to destroy the entire town and everyone who lived there. And that was exactly what he was doing. Plains City would receive all the tax revenue, but the store would pull a good share of its business from Erskine. At best, the town would have to citify itself to compete with the Megamart, get a couple of fast-food restaurants, maybe a movie theater to attract more people. Either way, Erskine would never be the same again, which was exactly what Noah wanted.

She couldn't explain that to Sara, though, not without having to explain a whole lot of other things she'd rather not talk about. "You're seeing the world through rose-colored glasses since you fell in love," she grumbled.

"I've been in love a long time," Sara reminded her. "It's Max who just fell in love. Maybe *you* should try it. I'll bet the Megamart will bring all sorts of interesting new men to town."

"Men?" The Megamart had already brought one too many, Janey couldn't avoid thinking.

"It never hurts to have a choice," Sara said with a teasing smile.

A choice, hah. Janey felt like a spider in the wind, hanging by a thread while the slightest breeze blew her whichever way it wanted. Most people—her included—lived their lives that way, just kind of wafting along, reacting to whatever fate threw at them. It wasn't really so bad unless a storm came. And a storm was coming; she didn't need to see clouds boiling over the mountains to know that, and to know she had to make a choice now, while she still had that luxury.

She could either take the steps to protect herself, her daughter and community, or she could ride out the storm, so to speak, let events unfold as they would and hope that if—or when—her thread snapped and she fell she wouldn't break anything. Like her heart.

It wasn't that difficult a decision to make.

"So what are you going to do about it?" Sara asked.

Janey propped her elbows on the counter and rested her chin in her hand. "Normally I'd go over to Plains City and talk to their mayor, but if I know Noah, he's already got that man convinced."

"Their mayor is no match for our mayor," Sara said. "I'd put my money on you and so would everyone else in this town, Janey. We knew what we were doing when we elected you."

"You elected me because the job mostly consists of listening to people complain about their neighbors, and after the last mayor got his big toe broken at the New Year's Eve party—which I might point out was Max's fault—nobody else wanted it."

"You got the job because you're the best one for it, Janey. You've been around politics all your life. How many times did you see your dad take a hopeless situation and present the facts in a way that couldn't be ignored…."

Janey lost the rest of what Sara was saying as an idea dawned on her. "Can you watch Jessie next Friday?" she asked.

Sara, who'd been cut off midsentence, looked at her blankly for a second, then said, "Sure. But what about Noah?"

"I have a feeling he'll be busy that night." Janey got up to go; she had some planning to do. But Sara stopped her with a hand on her arm.

"What just happened?" she asked.

"I think I found a silver lining," Janey said, though when she thought about it, she didn't really feel too elated.

After all, for every silver lining there was a dark cloud.

Chapter Ten

Noah pulled over onto the side of the road, midway between Plains City and Erskine. He turned the car off, and after a brief hesitation he killed the headlights. The pitch black of the moonless Montana night outside his windows seemed to suit his mood as well as his needs. He got out and paced up and down the gravel shoulder, his breath a steaming white cloud on the chill evening air.

Who did Janey think she was, coming to the Plains City Council meeting like that? Miss Mayor of Erskine? He snorted. No mayor he'd ever seen sashayed up to the lectern in a tight red sweater and slim black skirt that hugged every curve so faithfully even the old geezer at the farthest end of the table sat up and took notice. Noah had been pretty sure that old guy was either sleeping or dead until then—and Hell, if a dead man wasn't immune to Janey, how could he hope to be?

If he didn't figure out a way to resist her, though, *he* was dead. Or he could get fired, which would be even worse. Losing his job would be like losing his identity. If he *chose* to take another job or change careers, that would be different. But getting fired…

He couldn't afford to be angry, especially not with the one person who most wanted to see him in the unemployment line.

He closed his eyes and took several breaths. Eventually the

blood stopped pounding in his temples, and he calmed down enough to actually notice his surroundings. Then again, *surroundings* was probably not the best word. There was nothing for miles, just flat, empty land that rose gradually into the Rocky Mountains, barely visible as a jagged silhouette a shade darker than the wide bowl of night sky. Diamond-bright stars gave the night just the faintest sheen of silver that made everything around him appear to glow.

He'd always hated the emptiness of this country; it made him feel insignificant, unimportant. But tonight, there was something inspirational, something calming, about being in the middle of nowhere, alone with the stars. His Megamart goal seemed trivial against the backdrop of the entire universe. The pressure he felt to achieve it drained away and left him curiously at peace. Right up until the moment a light appeared down the road.

He watched as it separated into two lights—headlights—and reality crashed back down. The headlights looked like they belonged to a vintage Beetle. He stood next to his car and waited as the bug came closer. Sure enough, it was Janey. He saw her face clearly lit by the dashboard as she putt-putted by him, so close he had to flatten himself against the side of the Prosche to avoid being hit.

Noah tore his door open and laid on the horn, wincing as the sound shrieked through the silence.

She kept going.

He was about to chase her down when her brake lights fired. She backed up the car and jerked to a stop in front of his Porsche, opening the door. Temptation slammed into him. He would've preferred to get hit by the car; he had no business wanting a woman who was out to ruin him.

She slid her left leg out, an impossibly long leg that started at a foot clad in a black high heel and ended where her skirt had hiked up, about two inches south of his fantasies. "What's wrong?"

"For starters?" He stalked over and leaned one arm on the car roof, the other on her door. "You were going to drive right by me."

"I did drive right by you." A second leg joined the first and she scooted around, adjusting her skirt, much to his disappointment. "Um… Could you move, please?"

He stepped back, and when she unfolded that tall, voluptuous body he discovered he could be angry with her, after all. Furious, as a matter of fact, and if a little of that fury was directed at himself for being so attracted to her he figured it was just another tool he could use to get what he wanted. And what he wanted was to build the store that was going to put his career back on track, and then get the hell out of Erskine. Jessie could visit him in California.

But he wasn't thinking of Jessie. He wasn't thinking of anyone but Janey and what she was doing to him.

She sidled down to the end of her car and folded her arms under her breasts. "It's chilly out here," she said. "Can we get this over with so I can go home?"

"If you're in such a rush, why did you stop?"

"You obviously want to discuss what happened tonight. This seemed as good a place to do that as any."

And better than most, he thought. No witnesses, no gossip, no daughter to get caught in the middle of their disagreement, just the two of them clearing the air in private. "You ambushed me tonight."

"Ambushed!"

"Yeah, ambushed."

"I'm the mayor of Erskine and like it or not, what you're planning will have an effect on my town."

"Mayor, hell. What kind of mayor comes to a council meeting decked out like a…a…" His eyes swept over her skirt and sweater, settling somewhere near her neckline. "A walking distraction."

"You were distracted?"

He lifted his gaze, narrowing in on her smug little smile. "That's not the point."

"No, the point is that you weren't expecting any opposition at all. You brought your petition in complete secrecy, then strutted around Erskine as thought Jessie was the only reason you were in town."

"You knew I was in town on business."

"And when I asked you what kind of business?"

"I told you I was a scout, and if you took it the wrong way—"

The noise she made managed to convey complete and utter disgust. Ten years' worth.

"Part of my job is scouting new locations for stores," he said through clenched teeth.

"And the other part is lying to anyone who might find out too soon."

"I posted a notice in the paper just like I'm required to. And gave an interview."

"After you already bought the property and had the Plains City town council in your back pocket."

He bit off a curse. He should've known she'd figure that out. "Yeah, well, they didn't seem to be in my back pocket tonight, did they? I should be breaking ground Monday, but thanks to you, I have to wait six weeks in a state where the construction season isn't that much longer."

"I'm as surprised as you are," Janey said. "I mean, the Plains City Five aren't exactly known for their flexibility."

"Now there's an understatement."

Montana, with its seemingly endless winters, maddening solitude and everyday hardships, was a state, some said, where only the most stubborn, contrary and downright mean people could survive for a lifetime. The Plains City Five made a good case for the validity of that statement.

They ranged in age from seventy to ninety, and what medical conditions they didn't have, they faked whenever it suited their purposes. Hearing loss topped the list because it came in handy for so many situations. Bad eyesight and a propensity to catnap at critical moments also proved to be useful now and then, along with various levels of senility.

"I was sure when I walked into the Plains City town hall they'd already made up their minds, but I had to present my arguments, anyway," Janey said.

"Damn good arguments." Noah ran a hand through his hair and paced away, assuring himself there hadn't been a note of admiration in his voice. "Do you really believe the Megamart will damage Erskine that much?" *That I would?*

She sighed. "Maybe you believe the store will be a positive thing—"

"The store will bring you into the present. The nineteenth century was fun while it lasted, Janey, but now it's just old and quaint."

"And if we like the quaint, old feel of our town, that's too bad because you've decided you know what's best for us?"

"If it's so great, why do all the young people go away?"

"Gee, I don't know. College, maybe?"

"And when they've had a taste of big-city life, they don't come back."

"Not because they don't like the town."

"No, because there aren't any jobs for them here," Noah said when she refused to finish a thought that would only make his point. "The Megamart will bring jobs."

"Minimum-wage jobs."

"The store will have to be built first, which means construction jobs, and they pay considerably more than minimum wage."

"Construction jobs may pay more, but they're also temporary," Janey countered.

She felt her heartbeat quicken; not from nerves, or even the hormonal surge she could never quite suppress when she was around him. It was the debate she loved, the give and take of a lively argument. She was her father's daughter, after all. She'd taught teenagers about politics and civic duty all her adult life, but she finally felt as if she was doing something to help directly, and it felt *good*. "That's if your construction company even hires anyone from around here. More likely they'll bring their own people and put them up in trailers."

"Megamart Corporation will make it a condition of the contract that the builder hires local labor, to the extent it's available."

"A loophole if I ever heard one. And you can't make it a condition of the contract that the builder keeps his laborers from trifling with the local girls."

"I think it should be the responsibility of the parents to see that their girls are supervised properly so they aren't available for trifling with."

"If you think that's entirely up to the parents, you have a pretty convenient memory."

He had the audacity to grin. "My memory's just fine."

"Then maybe you don't care, because you'll be long gone before there are any consequences from the trifling."

Noah looked as if he'd been sucker punched.

"I'm sorry, that wasn't fair," Janey said. She was so ashamed of herself that tears burned behind her eyes. "I won't put this on a personal level again."

He nodded once, his gaze straying down to her mouth before they lifted to lock on hers. "Neither will I."

"What I'm saying," she continued, "is that you presented a nice rosy picture to the Plains City Five, but it didn't seem to me that anyone had considered the other side. He tried to speak but she talked right over him. "After the store's open, how many of the jobs will go to local residents?"

"As many as we can fill."

"But that doesn't include upper management, does it? There are probably employees in the corporation already in line to be manager of the next store that opens. I'll bet you already have some smart, slick guy all picked out. This being an experimental store—with you at its helm—I don't think you'd trust it to just anyone."

Noah smiled, but she could see she'd struck a sore spot. Score one for her.

"Who around here is qualified to manage a retail enterprise?" he countered.

"I can name you a dozen people who've nursed stores and businesses through good times and bad, and around these parts, even the good times are never that great."

"You're right, Janey, this new kind of store was my idea, and the first couple of years will be critical to its success. I do have the store manager picked out, but Megamart Corporation has a policy of promoting from within. As soon as we're able to fill the middle management positions with local residents, we'll transfer the implants back to other cities. Eventually even the store manager will be someone born and raised locally."

"That's if there's anyone left around here. Some of the businesses will fail. There'll be a loss in tax revenue."

"Which will be more than made up for by the Megamart."

"Erskine won't be getting any tax revenue from the Megamart, since it's situated entirely within the Plains City limits. We could easily lose enough revenue to make it necessary to shut down Erskine Elementary."

"I don't believe that'll happen," Noah said. "Like I tried to tell the council—"

"No offense, but your skewed rendition of the facts—"

"Skewed?"

"It's your job to get this approved. Of course you're going to show everything in the best possible light.

"Whether or not you're prepared to admit it," she went on, "Plains City and Erskine have always been sister cities. We have the grade school, they have the high school, and our economies are just as interrelated. What affects one affects the other, and you didn't take that into account in your proposal. That's why the Plains City town council tabled the vote until you conduct a study on the effects the new store will have on Erskine."

"And I'll do the study," Noah muttered, "but before you get to feeling too proud of yourself, it means I'll be in town until that permit is approved."

Janey started to say something, then snapped her mouth shut, taking a step away from him. The distance hardly helped; he couldn't smell her perfume anymore, but now he could see her. All of her.

"Didn't think of that while you were plotting your revenge, did you?" he said, tearing his gaze off her.

"Don't flatter yourself, Bryant. I'm doing this for Erskine—and for Plains City, if they'll just open their eyes and see what this monstrosity of yours will do to them."

"You're doing this because of what happened between us."

She laughed tightly. "Here's a news flash, hotshot, not everything in the world revolves around you. And as for the past, you're the one who's hung up on it. Why else would you pick Plains City, of all the small towns in the country, to build your precious store?"

"The past has nothing to do with it. Mine or ours."

"Then why did you lie to me about why you were in town?"

He stuck his hands in his pockets and looked away. "I'm sorry about that, Janey, but I couldn't tell you the truth until the company was ready to go public."

"You didn't tell me the truth because you knew I'd react this way."

"Because I left town ten years ago, after we slept together, and I didn't say goodbye."

Janey stared at him for a second, her jaw clenched. "We agreed not to make this personal."

"You're right," he said. "So this has nothing to do with my job. Or yours, Madam Mayor." And before he could think about what he was doing or why he was doing it, he hauled her up against him, slipped his other arm around her waist, and kissed her.

She fought him; he could've predicted she would. She beat ineffectively at his back, pulled his hair. He ignored it. She tried to knee him, but he stepped between her legs, backed her up against the side of her car and pressed into her until neither of them could move without feeling the other's raging pulse.

It took a moment, but he finally felt her relax in his arms, felt her lips part and heard a soft little murmur from the back of her throat. And with the first tentative touch of her tongue to his, he let her go.

"What was that all about?" she demanded, as breathless and shaky as he was, and now just as furious.

"You haven't needed me to explain anything to you yet," he said as he walked to his car. "Why start now?"

Chapter Eleven

The Ersk Inn sat around the corner from the town hall. It had been a saloon in its original incarnation, a speakeasy—or as close to one as Erskine could stand—during Prohibition, and had finally settled into a comfortable existence as the town watering hole. Big-screen TV, American beer on tap, burgers that qualified as all four food groups. The interior was always dim, sometimes smoky, often noisy and just as often companionably quiet.

As with most of the businesses in town, the Inn was family-owned; a Shasta had manned the same bar for well over a hundred years. The latest in the dynasty, Mike Shasta, was possessed of a willing ear and a selective memory, quick eyes and the hands to keep up, and the knack for knowing when to stop pulling the taps and start pouring the coffee. He rarely raised his voice and still managed to leave no doubt whatsoever that he was as fixed in his decisions as the establishment was in the town.

"I'm not filling out any forms and I'm not answering any questions."

Noah hooked a bar stool with his foot, eased down on it. "I'll have a beer."

Mike gave him a look and kept polishing a section of oak bar that was already so shiny it could've swapped places with the long mirror on the wall behind it.

Grinning, Noah dug some coins and a couple of dollar bills out of his pocket, change from the Coke he'd bought in the Five-And-Dime earlier that morning. Three things were important to Mike Shasta: his family, the inn and money. Not necessarily in that order. Noah made a little pile of green and silver on the bar and waited.

Mike glanced at the crumpled bills, then at Noah, his blunt fingers scrubbing through his grizzled crew cut. "Always were a smart aleck," he rasped, sounding as if he was chewing on gravel. He filled a pilsner glass and thunked it down in front of Noah, then punched a few keys on the old-fashioned cash register until a bell rang and $2.25 popped up. He ironed the bills with the heel of a hand that was as blunt as the rest of him, and slipped them in the drawer, along with a quarter, pocketing the rest of the change. "Heard you were back in town. Can't say I like the way you treated Janey Walters."

Noah pinched the bridge of his nose; it didn't do much for the headache throbbing behind his eyes, but he needed a moment. It seemed Janey wasn't the only one in town with a long memory. The Ersk Inn was the fifth business he'd visited that morning, Mike Shasta the fifth business owner who'd refused to talk to him, because of Janey and Jessie. "That was ten years ago. I was just a kid. I'm not trying to defend myself, but—"

"Defending yourself don't make it right, anyhow. You could save her some grief now, though."

"The Megamart isn't going to single-handedly ruin Erskine."

"Janey's against it," Mike said, a sentiment that summed up the position the entire town seemed to be taking. Janey was against the Megamart, and they were all behind Janey.

Here he was, canvassing for that ridiculous study she'd convinced the Plains City Town Council to ask for, and he was defeated before he'd even begun. Noah bit back the word he'd been about to say. Mike Shasta ran a family establishment. "Maybe Janey is against the store because of what happened between us ten years ago. Or has that possibility completely escaped everyone but me?"

Mike shrugged and went back to polishing glasses.

"Playing dumb is kind of redundant in this town," Noah muttered under his breath. It earned him another look from Mike, the kind of look that reminded him why the Ersk Inn didn't need a bouncer.

Noah slugged back half his beer, but it didn't wash the sour taste out of his mouth. His first impulse was to tell them all to go to hell, then head back to the city where people went out of their way to ignore each other. Part of his job, though, was public relations—positive public relations. He stood up, but before he could so much as turn around, someone mouthed off behind him.

"That's it, Bryant, take off. But don't stop at the door. Keep going until you can see Erskine in your rearview mirror."

Noah searched the dim recesses of the bar, and when he found the culprit, his jaw relaxed enough for his mouth to curve. "George Donaldson?" George had been that kid in high school who talked the talk, then fell on his face when it came to walking the walk. And then he swore someone tripped him.

Seeing George, just as loudmouthed and obnoxious as he'd been in high school, reminded Noah of how far he'd come himself. Too far to let the famous Erskine narrow-mindedness get to him.

"We don't need you around here, and neither does Janey," George said, stepping into the light, beer mug in hand.

"Let me guess, Janey still won't go out with you?"

"He's got you there, Donaldson."

Noah bet that if anyone but Mike Shasta had said that, George would've kept mouthing off. Instead he ambled to the counter and plunked down his empty mug. "Everybody knows Clary's set his cap for her," he muttered.

Mike worked the tap without looking down, busy staring

at George, making very clear that it was financial reasons prompting the refill and nothing else.

George wasn't fazed, but then maybe he'd gotten used to the eye rolls, head shakes and outright laughter that usually followed whatever he said. "Anybody here willing to poach on Clary?"

All eyes were on Noah. Spreading his hands, he said, "He wears a gun."

"Boy's got a point," Mike said around the laughter.

"Janey don't wear a gun," George said, "but I gotta wonder how long it'll be before she runs you and Megamart out of town. In fact, I'm willing to put money on it." He slapped a bill on the bar, which got him instant and undivided attention from everyone else in the place. George wasn't known for dipping into his wallet with any regularity. "How about we start a pool, Mike, right here, right now—" he patted his five-dollar bill "—and I get first stab at predicting how long it'll take this city slicker to repeat history. *Before* that store gets built."

"As long as I have a daughter here," Noah said, remembering how George operated and refusing to get all wound up, "you'll never be able to get rid of me completely. But while I'm away, you'll all have a nice, big Megamart in Plains City to remember me by."

"Janey says otherwise," George reiterated, "and we elected her mayor for a reason. My money's on her."

So, apparently, was everyone else's. Mike Shasta, CEO and artistic director of the Erskine betting pool, dug out a piece of white poster board, already graphed out in black marker, and half a dozen patrons strolled up to the bar, eager to invest their five dollars. Noah waited until they'd haggled over the hows and whens and what to call the pool, the one common denominator being the belief that Janey would send *him* packing this time around. He waited until everyone who wanted to ante up had picked a square before he stepped up himself and proffered the five-dollar bill he'd taken out of his wallet.

"Now why would we let you in on this?" George asked, snatching the bill out of Noah's hand. "I mean, you have some say as to when or if that store gets built, right?"

"Right." Sort of. He lived his life at the behest of the Megamart Corporation—and the vindictive nature of Janey Walters. "But I have a lot more at stake here than five dollars." He took a good long look at the poster board and saw that no one expected him to be there beyond the end of summer. "I'll tell you what. Anyone wins that pool, I'll double the take."

There was a moment of silence, and then it was George who elected himself spokesman.

"How do we know you'll pay off?"

This was met with eye rolls, head shakes and outright laughter. The earth was spinning around the sun again and George Donaldson was back to being comic relief. Noah's response was to pluck his five out of George's hand and tuck it back in his wallet. He then removed a fifty—the biggest bill he had—and placed it on the bar in front of Mike. "Here's my earnest money."

Silence followed him to the door, pandemonium erupting as it shut behind him. Noah paused to slip on his sunglasses, just long enough for word of the new betting pool to make it to the end of the block before he did—and since the end of the block was the Crimp 'N Cut Beauty Salon, it pretty much guaranteed the rest of the town would hear about it within the hour.

"Heard you were going to pay somebody off big-time before you leave town again," Rita Jenkins, who owned the Crimp 'N Cut, called out as he was about to cross the street, four women in black plastic capes and various stages of beautifying crowded into the doorway behind her.

"Only if the store doesn't get built."

Rita waved that off with a flip of her hand, Janey's involvement making that a foregone conclusion. "There's already side-betting over whether you and Janey will hook up before you leave."

Noah chucked her under the chin. "Janey who?" he said, winking and smiling at the other four, leaving five middle-aged women giggling and blushing like schoolgirls as he walked off.

Two more people stopped him on the next block, and he left both of them laughing, which made him wonder if he'd really been the outsider he'd always considered himself. He'd been a young, angry kid, seeing the town through a filter of unhappiness. He hadn't been able to laugh with the people of Erskine, so he'd felt they were laughing at him. Time and distance—not to mention confidence and success—let him see things in a different light.

The typical Erskinite worked hard, supported his country, drove a good old American pickup truck and buried his emotions beneath a hearty meal and sarcasm. Getting a supper invitation in this town was as good as a hug, and being teased, Noah realized, was the closest to acceptance he was likely to get.

That didn't mean they'd go so far as to welcome Megamart to their community.

He pushed through the bakery door, and before he'd even asked a question, Earl Tilford was giving him hell about the study. Same with Mr. Landry at the Feed And Seed. Before he made it to the center of town, he'd come to one solid conclusion. The business owners of Erskine would cooperate only when—if ever—Janey gave her okay.

First she saddled him with the stupid study, now she was preventing him from completing it—and he'd be damned if he wasn't enjoying the challenge.

"Well bless my soul, if it isn't Noah Bryant," Mrs. Halliwell said, when he walked into the General Store. "I was wondering when you'd cross my threshold." She came out from behind the counter and enveloped him in a hug that smelled of lavender and chocolate-chip cookies.

"I'm sorry I haven't been by before, Mrs. H. There's been so much going on— No, that's no excuse, I should have come by before—"

"Nonsense." She gave him another hug, this one brisk. "You've been busy, and I knew you'd come by. When you were ready."

When he was ready. Trust Mrs. H. to know him better than he knew himself, Noah mused. She'd always known just how to handle him, when to let him slide a little and when to clamp down. She still did. "You haven't changed a bit," he said, straddling one of the barrels in front of the counter, like he used to do when he worked for her way back when. "Neither has this place."

He took a deep breath, closing his eyes to better appreciate the rich scents layered on the warm air: spices and mothballs, potpourri and the hint of dry mustiness that came from the store's having been there, in that same wood-frame building, for more than a century.

Mrs. Halliwell still measured out bolts of fabric on the long wooden counter where they'd been measured forever, and barrels of dried beans and chicken feed flanked the door in positions they'd held so many years the floor underneath them shone with the original varnish while the rest of it was scuffed and faded with age.

Shelves lined the walls, made from hand-hewn boards and attached with nails forged in the blacksmith shop still functioning on the edge of town. Tables, themselves antiques, were piled high, the shelves stuffed with a hodgepodge of goods bought by generations of Halliwells—some of whom had possessed more optimism than foresight.

For its customers, the place was more an investment in time than money; if you couldn't find what you needed anywhere else in town, Halliwell's would have it, and at a reasonable price—if you had the patience to look for it.

"You always had the soul of a merchant," Mrs. Halliwell said, her voice adding to the nostalgia rather than disturbing it.

Noah smiled, and not just with his face. This smile went all the way to his heart. "Not really. I just liked being in here." Even that first time, he thought, when Mr. Halliwell had caught him trying to steal a pack of gum, a defiant nine-year-old with secondhand clothes and an attitude that was likely to get him a cell of his own one day. Instead of calling his father or the sheriff, John Halliwell had made him work it off by sweeping the boardwalk out front. Then Loretta Halliwell had given him cookies and milk. From then on, they'd treated him with a mixture of unwavering affection and uncompromising firmness that challenged him to live up to their expectations.

"You're the first person today who hasn't treated me like the enemy, unless…"

"I've heard," she said.

"And you're still willing to talk to me?"

"I know Janey believes this store will be bad for Erskine, but the two of you…" She sighed. "You were so much in love, but it was the kind of love that thrived on conflict."

"Yeah," he agreed, although truthfully, he'd forgotten that part of their relationship until Mrs. Halliwell brought it up. He and Janey had dated exclusively for three years in high school, but there'd been times they made the Hatfields and McCoys look like lovebirds.

"The people in this town have forgotten that for the moment, Noah, but they'll remember it soon enough. And when they do, they'll begin to wonder how much of this is about the store and how much because it's you building it. And then they'll begin to wonder when the two of you will pick up where you left off."

Noah shot to his feet. Rita Jenkins teasing him about Janey

NOVEL™

An Important Message from the Editors

Dear Reader,

If you'd enjoy reading novels about rediscovery and reconnection with what's important in women's lives, then let us send you two free Harlequin® Next™ novels. These books celebrate the "next" stage of a woman's life because there's a whole new world after marriage and motherhood.

By the way, you'll also get a surprise gift with your two free books! Please enjoy the free books and gift with our compliments...

Pam Powers

Peel off Seal and
Place Inside...

FREE GIFT SEAL

We'd like to send you two free books to introduce you to our brand-new series – Harlequin® NEXT™! These novels by acclaimed award-winning authors are filled with stories about rediscovery and reconnection with what's important in women's lives. These are relationship novels about women redefining their dreams.

THERE'S THE LIFE YOU PLANNED. AND THERE'S WHAT COMES NEXT.

Your two books have a combined cover price of $11.00 in the U.S. and $13.00 in Canada, but are yours **FREE!** We'll even send you a wonderful surprise gift. You can't lose!

FREE BONUS GIFT!

We'll send you a wonderful surprise gift, *absolutely FREE*, just for giving Harlequin NEXT books a try! Don't miss out — **MAIL THE REPLY CARD TODAY!**

Order online at www.TryNextNovels.com

THE EDITOR'S "THANK YOU" FREE GIFTS INCLUDE:

▶ Two BRAND-NEW Harlequin® Next™ Novels

▶ An exciting surprise gift

The Reader Service — Here's How It Works:

Accepting your 2 free books and gift places you under no obligation to buy anything. You may keep the books and gift and return the shipping statement marked "cancel." If you do not cancel, about a month later we'll send you 3 additional books and bill you just $3.99 each in the U.S., or $4.74 each in Canada, plus 25¢ shipping & handling per book and applicable taxes if any.* That's the complete price and — compared to cover prices of $5.50 each in the U.S. and $6.50 each in Canada — it's quite a bargain! You may cancel at any time, but if you choose to continue, every month we'll send you 3 more books, which you may either purchase at the discount price or return to us and cancel your subscription.

*Terms and prices subject to change without notice. Sales tax applicable in N.Y. Canadian residents will be charged applicable provincial taxes and GST.

If offer card is missing write to: The Reader Service, 3010 Walden Ave., P.O. Box 1867, Buffalo, NY 14240-1867

was one thing; Mrs. Halliwell had inside information. When she talked about him and Janey getting involved again, she made it sound like a real possibility. There might have been one or two episodes of madness, but he wasn't about to wholeheartedly embrace the insanity. "That's not true. I mean, there's Jessie, and if she's going to be part of my life, then Janey is going to have to be, too. But only as the mother of my daughter. There's nothing between us anymore, and there's never going to be."

"Are you sure about that, Noah? Are you sure it's business that brought you back to Erskine? Because there's Jessie to think of this time. Janey's a grown woman—whatever happens between the two of you now, she'll deal with it and move on. Jessie won't. She's just a little girl, for all she tries to seem tough. If you hurt her—"

"I'm not the one who's causing trouble."

"Now, you know better than that. Considering the way you left, you must've known coming back here was bound to cause trouble."

Noah sat back down, feeling as if all the fight had gone out of him—and some of it had. "You're right, as usual. I didn't really expect there to be this much uproar. But I didn't expect to find out I had a nine-year-old daughter, either. How was I supposed to prepare for that kind of complication? Should I walk away from my career, just because her mother doesn't agree with what I'm doing?" He looked up at the woman who'd been like a mother to him, desperately needing to see approval on her face, or at least sympathy.

"It's a dilemma," Mrs. Halliwell said. "But if you think the answer to it lies in this study you're doing, you're wrong, Noah. The answer lies with you and Janey. Solve that problem and the other will solve itself."

He knew she was right, but…"Janey isn't ready to see reason yet."

"No, and neither are you—I can tell." She smiled, staring off into the far distance. "Mr. Halliwell and I were a lot like you two, you know. We were married forty-seven years, and I still miss him—the fights as much as the loving."

Noah would've been grateful for the change of subject, if it had been any one but that. "I'm sorry I didn't come back for the funeral."

Mrs. Halliwell reached over and patted his hand. "I got your card, Noah, and your flowers."

"After everything the two of you did for me…" It wasn't enough, he finished silently when his voice failed him. He looked outside, the bright, clear day just a blur of color and light, like a scene through a rain-washed window. He blinked, and one of the blurs became Janey, headed down the street toward the General Store.

He cleared his throat and stood. "Do you mind if I come back later?"

"Go," Mrs. Halliwell said, her watery chuckle following him out the door.

He leaned against the wall just outside the General Store, in the shade of the covered boardwalk. He should've been angry with Janey, but watching her walk down the street was too much fun for him to work up a really good mad. There was a natural grace to her walk, a sashay that was fifty percent attitude, fifty percent blatant sexuality and one hundred percent woman. Her smile lit up her entire face, made the pretty features that were a blessing of birth into a face that glowed with beauty because of the heart and soul within.

She obviously wasn't suffering the same kind of sleepless nights he'd been having since his misguided decision to kiss her on the road between Plains City and Erskine. He still didn't know what had possessed him to jump her like that. Or rather, he did know—two weeks of seeing her day in and day out, of being reminded what she'd once meant to him and what she'd brought into his life. Two weeks of feeling frustrated that she could make him want things he'd given up on when he was a child. Two weeks of looking and not touching, of remembering that night ten years ago when he'd held her in his arms, and knowing he'd never feel anything like that again.

The worst part of it, though, was how simple it had been to tell himself that he'd kiss her to prove her personal feelings were more involved than she wanted to admit.

It hadn't worked—and that bothered him the most. That kiss had rocked his world, but here was Janey, strolling through town like her world hadn't even wobbled. But it hadn't, he realized. Whether or not the kiss had affected her, Janey had something he'd never had. Her life was built on an unshakeable foundation, this big, extended family of people who squabbled amongst themselves, who gossiped about each other and sometimes hurt each other's feelings. But when push came to shove, they'd fight to the death for one of their own.

A pang struck Noah—envy, he imagined. Erskine had always been Janey's world, and she'd never questioned her place in it. He'd lived in his house in Los Angeles for three years and couldn't even recognize his neighbors, let alone call any of them by name. And that was just fine with him. Back in L.A., he didn't have people sticking their noses in his business, or making comments and asking questions that made him examine his life and his feelings every five seconds.

"Hey, Janey," an elderly man called out from down the street. "I heard you gave Noah Bryant what for at the Plains City council meeting the other night."

Janey turned, smiling brightly. She seemed to thrive on the attention all of this had created, but then, she wasn't the one who'd failed. Yet.

"I did my best, Mr. Elliot." She crossed the street, her sun-dazzled eyes missing Noah where he stood in the shade. "The rest is up to you and everyone else in town," she said to the old man. "We just have to stick together and make Megamart understand they're not welcome here."

"Well, now, I don't see how we can make a big company like that change its mind, but your daddy sure would be proud of you," Mr. Elliot said. "He always fought for what was right, no matter the odds."

"Don't forget my father won some of those fights," Janey said and leaned forward to kiss his wrinkled cheek. "Thank you for reminding me of that—and for saying I'm like him. I can't think of a better compliment."

Neither could Noah. If he'd had a father like Janey's, a man whose approval meant something, graduating from college might've seemed like a big deal. Getting a good job, being fast-tracked, buying the house, the car—there might have been more satisfaction in passing those milestones if someone had been proud of him when he did. He was tired of it all, suddenly, tired of fighting his way up a mountain that didn't seem to offer anything but more obstacles.

Janey caught sight of him then, and he remembered why he continued to fight his way up that mountain. Because there wasn't anything else.

He walked toward her as if that was what he'd intended all along. Her smile trembled a bit at the edges, but she fluffed her fingers through her rich brown curls and brought her chin up, avoiding his eyes.

Nerves and guilt, Noah thought, and stifled a smile. "I hear you've been busy today," he said, managing to put a disgruntled note in his voice.

She murmured a goodbye to Mr. Elliot and stepped away from him. "Jessie's playing at a friend's house, so I've been wandering through town, talking to my friends and neighbors."

"I'm your neighbor now, too."

"Don't remind me."

Noah waited for her to catch up to him, then joined her in a slow stroll that didn't seem to be taking them anywhere in particular. "If you want to win this war, it'll take something bigger than bad-mouthing me all over town."

She slid him a sidelong glance. "I'm just a poor country bumpkin doing the best I can."

He grinned. Poor, country and bumpkin were three words he'd never have used in connection with Janey Walters. He'd always considered her one of the richest people he knew, if not in actual money, then in the ways that really counted: family, friends, a sense of her own worth. And although she lived in a small town, she had one of the sharpest minds he'd ever run across.

"Public opinion can be a pretty strong weapon," she said.

"And you're willing to use what happened ten years ago against me. That's dirty pool, Janey."

"And what was that kiss the other night?"

Noah's eyes met hers and then dropped to her mouth, stalling there for a moment. Seeing her lift a hand to her lips as if he'd touched them didn't help him get his suddenly raging pulse back under control. She turned to leave, and even though he knew it would be the best thing for both of them, he wasn't quite ready to let her go. He caught her by the elbow and felt a jolt that shook him to his toes.

Her mouth parted on a soft gasp, her gaze flying to his.

"He bothering you, Janey?"

They both jumped a little. Clary Beeber had pulled up next to the boardwalk while they'd been preoccupied.

He got out of the car and slid his nightstick into the loop on his uniform pants, staring at Noah's hand on her arm.

"Noah and I were just talking," Janey said, and when Noah didn't back off, she did.

Clary wasn't mollified. "Didn't look that way from where I was sitting. Maybe he needs to be reminded he's in a town where the local law enforcement knows everybody and takes it personally when one of his friends is mistreated." His smile became threatening as his eyes shifted to Noah. "If you press charges, Janey, you can get a restraining order to keep this clown away from you."

"I don't think that would be good for Jessie."

That only seemed to enrage Clary more. "I don't think *he's* good for Jessie. You ought to—"

"Let Jessie make up her own mind?" Janey said quietly, her eyes darkening with sympathy. "Noah is her father." When Clary started to turn away, she put a hand on his arm. "We need to give them enough room to figure out what they're going to mean to each other. That doesn't mean she won't need her friends, Clary, and you mean so much to her."

"I'll always be her friend," he said gruffly, glaring at Noah for a long, hard minute, "and yours, Janey. No matter what."

He set off down the boardwalk, toward the town square and his office.

"You've got him wrapped around your little finger, don't you? You've got this whole town dancing to your tune, and you don't care if it's bad for them."

"I don't *care?*" Janey spun around, swiping furiously at her cheeks. She pointed at Clary, then clenched her fist before Noah could see the shaking and mistake it for anything but anger. "There goes one of the best men I've ever known in my life—every bit as wonderful and loving and fair as my father, and do you care what your coming back here has done to him?"

"Maybe if he stopped stuttering and blushing around you for five seconds he could ask you out. If you'd actually go out with a man who'd bore you to death before the night was over."

"Don't make fun of him," she snapped. "Don't you dare. He's the closest thing to a father Jessie's had. He's spent time with her, he's there when she needs someone to talk to besides me, and he's never once asked anything from us other than friendship."

"It sounded like he was asking for more a minute ago."

"And I had to hurt him." Janey closed her eyes for a second, willing the tears back. "Has it occurred to you that since you've been in town he's stayed away from Jessie so the two of you could get to know each other without her feelings for him getting in the way? If he hadn't backed off—if he'd forced her to choose, Noah—who do you think would've won? A man who's been there all her life, a man who's her father in everything but name? Or a man who's her father in name only?"

"That's not fair, Janey."

She nodded slowly. "You didn't know about her, I understand that, and so does Jessie, but that doesn't change how she feels. What he means to her isn't going to disappear just because you're here now. Clary knows that, and he's trying to do what's right for Jessie. If you can stand there and tell me he's not paying a price for it, then you're not the Noah Bryant I loved."

He shoved his hands in his pockets and started pacing back and forth, looking so much like a repentant little boy that she would've laughed if she hadn't been so sad.

"You want me to go over to the jail and tell him I'm sorry?"

That did make her laugh, a little. "I don't think either of you would enjoy that, Noah. You should probably leave Clary to me."

His eyes narrowed, but she refused to read anything into it, and besides he seemed ready to drop the matter, too.

"I'll get that store built," he said. "With or without the blessing of this town."

"And I'll stop you no matter what it takes," she said and walked away, smiling at passersby as if she hadn't just sworn to make his professional life a living hell—no empty threat, considering what she'd done to his personal life. Noah stood there for a few seconds, long enough to notice how little her lemon-yellow tank top and snug khaki shorts left to his imagination. And to realize that the heat moving through him didn't have its origin in anger.

The desire that always seemed to simmer inside him when she was around boiled over suddenly—threatening to consume all thought and reason, leaving only impulse. And his impulse was to sweep her up in his arms and find a place where he could take what he'd wanted from her since the moment he'd seen her again.

And taking was exactly what it would be, Noah realized. Being with her wouldn't mean anything unless it was freely given.

Chapter Twelve

Noah's mouth was on hers again, an instant replay of their kiss a couple of nights ago. His arms were around her, their mouths fused as his thigh crept between hers to press against the dull, throbbing ache that had plagued her since he'd come back to town. The ache she shouldn't be feeling for him.

Janey lifted her hands to shove him away, but they curled into his shirt instead, then up into his hair to urge him closer. Only for a moment, she told herself, just long enough to sate the hunger that hummed along her nerves and backed up in her throat until she wanted to—

"Mom!"

The image of Noah popped suddenly, like a child's soap bubble. Janey's eyes flew open and slammed shut again when the morning sunlight stabbed through her brain like a railroad spike. She rolled over and covered her aching head with a pillow, not connecting her daughter's voice with the rude shout that had jolted her awake because she was just too tired. Sleep had been a rare commodity since Noah had returned, and even when she managed it, there were dreams and nightmares that disturbed her slumber and ultimately destroyed it.

She'd been doing a pretty good job of ignoring the feelings he'd reawakened in her. She'd even managed to convince herself that the kiss—that one kiss—had been nothing more than a weapon to Noah, another strategy in the war over his plans to build a Megamart outside Plains City. But that had been before yesterday, before she'd looked Noah in the eyes and faced the truth that was twined in and around everything else. She wanted him, he wanted her, and their argument over the store, instead of making it easier for her to keep her distance, was doing exactly the opposite. She'd always loved to argue and when she argued with Noah, he could get her so stirred up it was a toss-up whether she'd rather punch him or jump him—or punch him, then jump him.

"Noah's here."

Janey dragged the pillow off her head and blinked until she could focus on her daughter.

"Noah's here," Jessie repeated. "I'm going to Plains City with him, remember? He's downstairs."

Janey wanted to go down those stairs to see him—so badly she ached with it. "Okay," she said, deliberately staying where she was. "I'll see you later."

"You're not coming down to make sure I'm not being abducted by a complete stranger?"

There was more than surprise in Jessie's question; there was hurt, as well.

She hadn't even gotten up to hug her, Janey realized. She'd been so caught up in her own anxieties that she'd completely overlooked her daughter's. "I'm sorry," she said, throwing back the covers and swinging her feet over the side of the bed. She had to sit there a second while she fought a bout of sleep-deprived dizziness, then she hugged Jessie and sent her off again.

Jessie stopped at the bedroom door, clearly still unsettled, so Janey went to the head of the stairs and called down, "Noah, is that you?"

"It's me," he yelled back.

"I think it's safe for you to go, Jess."

But Jessie was still dragging her feet.

"I'm not going downstairs like this," Janey said to her.

"I know," Jessie said, "but I was thinking... Maybe you could get dressed and go with us."

Janey sighed, sitting on the top step and pulling Jessie down next to her. "You know that wouldn't be a good idea," she said, wrapping her arm around her daughter's shoulders and hugging her close.

Jessie didn't say anything, just stood up and went downstairs. She paused on the landing and looked back, and Janey could see how hurt she still was, and how angry.

"Do you want to talk about it?" she asked, her throat tight.

Jessie gave her a long, level, guilt-inducing stare. "I'm not the one who needs to talk."

THINGS WERE BAD AGAIN, like they'd been when her—when Noah first showed up. Jessie snuck a glance at him, but his eyes were glued to the road. He hadn't said a word since he'd picked her up, either, and even if her mom had been speaking to him he wouldn't have been able to get out of the house fast enough, just in case she changed her mind. It made Jessie feel all funny, like when she'd had too much junk food and needed to lie down until her stomach settled.

But resting wasn't going to solve this problem; she didn't know what would, and it made her want to scream bloody murder, as her mother would've said. Everything had been going fine before the stupid store, she thought resentfully. They weren't a normal family, but she had a mother and a father for the first time in her life, and they'd been trying to get along. Things had even been improving a little.

She should've known better than to hope for anything where her father was concerned. He was okay now that she'd gotten to know him, but he didn't live in Erskine and he wasn't ever going to be more than a part-time parent. And as for her mom, well, Jessie had been hoping forever that she'd marry Clary and he could be her dad—but she doubted that would happen, either.

"What movie do you want to see?" Noah asked, his voice so loud in the silence that it startled her.

She rubbed a hand over her stomach, glancing over at him again. He was still staring out the windshield; he didn't even give her a quick look and a smile like he usually did when they were driving and talking. "There's only ever one movie," she said.

"Something PG, right? That's how it was when I was a kid, but I thought maybe they'd gotten another screen since then."

An idea occurred to Jessie. It didn't solve any of the big problems, but at least it made her feel a bit better. "Do you think that'll change after the store gets built?"

"Do you want it to?"

Jessie shrugged, not sure how to answer that. She liked things the way they were. On the other hand, she wouldn't have minded more than one movie to pick from, or getting a paintball arcade, or maybe even a mall.

"Let me guess," Noah said, "you only want the stuff to change that you want to change."

Jessie heaved a sigh. She had a feeling there was a lecture coming. Noah had only known he was her father for a few weeks, but he'd already caught on to that part of parenthood. "And I can't have that, right?"

"I think you know the answer to that."

She nodded, folding one leg under her and turning to face him. "So Mom is right? Some stuff is going to change in a bad way?"

Noah pursed his lips, and she could see he was thinking about how to answer that question. "I'd like to tell you *no,* Jessie, but I can't. This is a small community—I have a pretty good idea what kinds of changes will happen as a result of the store, but I can't predict everything, and I can't guarantee you'll like all of them."

Jessie thought about that, weighing the stuff she wanted against the possibility that she wouldn't like some of what came with it. She didn't see a reason to take that kind of chance. "Could you call it off?" she asked Noah.

"Not without putting my a—uh, job on the line."

"But if you don't know everything that'll happen, and some of that stuff might be bad, then maybe you shouldn't do it."

"Is that you talking, or your mom?"

Jessie huffed out a breath, turning around to stare out the windshield.

"I'm sorry," Noah said after a moment. "You're not the kind of kid who lets other people do her thinking for her. But your mom… I'm not sure it's the store she's against—or not only the store. I think she's mad at me."

"I know she's mad at you," Jessie said. "And you're mad at her, and I get that it's not only about the store. What I don't get is why it's okay for you guys to be mad at each other all the time. Why don't you just apologize to each other and talk about the stupid store and stop making me crazy?" That last bit was something her mom had said to her before, in the same sort of half-yelling voice, and now Jessie understood why—because it felt good.

Noah didn't say anything; and after a couple of minutes, she realized he wasn't going to.

It ticked her off. How was he ever going to talk to her mom about the store if he couldn't even talk to *her* about it? "Maybe we should just go back," she said, because now she really felt like throwing up. "You probably have to work on that stupid study, anyway. That's all you ever do anymore."

"We're going to Plains City and we're seeing the damn movie. Your mom has enough to hold over my head already—there's no way I'm going to take you home and have to tell her we got into an argument." Noah looked over at her. "And we're not talking about the store. It has nothing to do with you, Jessie. That's between me and your mom."

The store had everything to do with her, she thought. It was the reason Noah had come back to Erskine, the reason he'd even found out about her. And it wasn't just between him and her mom; it affected everyone in town, and before this was over, Jessie had a feeling things would be even worse than they'd been before. She knew now how it felt to actually have a father; she didn't want to find out how it felt to lose one.

FOURTH OF JULY in Erskine was right out of a Norman Rockwell painting. American and state flags alternated on the light poles in town, and Old Glory bunting festooned the boxwood hedge surrounding the town square and the railings of the white gazebo bandstand in the center of it. Wreaths had been laid at the foot of the war memorial and below the town hall's stained-glass window depicting the founding father, Jim "Mountain Man" Erskine's, rescue of the Indian maidens.

The celebration was planned by the Erskine Celebration Committee, and kicked off around noon with a speech by the mayor, which Janey made as short as possible, omitting any mention of Megamart. Noah wasn't there to hear it, anyway, so why bring down the mood?

Everyone who lived in or near the town spread blankets in the square and picnicked with their families, fueling up for the afternoon round of potato-sack races, egg tosses and the hotly contested race for Miss Fourth of July, which ended with Emma Lee Hastings donning the red-and-white-striped sash and blue enamel crown of stars for the second year running. In the early evening, potluck began, beer kegs were tapped and Big Ed's Rhythm Method tuned up—more or less—in the bandstand.

As twilight fell and the mosquitoes came out, Janey spritzed Jessie with insect repellent, thinking that all in all it had been a pretty peaceful day. Noah still hadn't put in an appearance, and while Jessie didn't seem too happy about that, it had been a considerable relief for Janey to enjoy herself without worrying that everyone in town was watching her. Or that he was.

When Noah looked at her… She could feel herself heating up just thinking about it. She'd thought that staying away from him would be the best thing for them both. Out of sight, out of mind. It seemed, though, that the less she saw of him, the more she dreaded the next time.

"Your dad didn't say whether or not he was coming tonight, did he?" she asked Jessie.

"He said he'd try." Jessie made a face as her mom rubbed insect repellent on her cheeks and forehead.

"What else has he got to do today?"

"I don't know," Jessie said, "but he's on the phone a lot when I'm at his house, and when I asked him who Barbara is, he said it's about work and not to worry about it. Are you done?"

Janey nodded and Jessie took off, yelling over her shoulder, "I'm gonna go find Joey and get a good seat for the fireworks."

"Fine," Janey said absently. *So much for relieving the tension.* Now instead of worrying about her reaction to Noah, she could worry about what he had up his sleeve. Or who. The idea that he had a girlfriend back in Los Angeles hadn't occurred to her, but now it made perfect sense.

She rubbed lotion on her arms and the back of her neck, trying not to feel like too much of a fool for taking it for granted that he was unattached. Just because she'd chosen not to prolong any relationship past the salad course of the first date didn't mean he was that choosy. Of course, this was Erskine; there wasn't a whole lot of husband material out there. Noah lived in Los Angeles; chances were slim to nonexistent that he hadn't found a steady girlfriend in the blond-nymphet capital of the world.

Janey rotated her head to loosen up her neck muscles, then worked her jaw back and forth, thinking it was just as well he wasn't there because she needed some time to convince herself that the idea of Noah with another woman didn't bother her in the least. A woman he might consider marriage material, which would make her Jessie's stepmother—

"I know everyone's anxious for the fireworks and dancing," came a voice over Big Ed's microphone. Noah's voice.

Janey turned slowly, saw him on the raised platform of the bandstand, staring at the microphone while he waited for the screech of the feedback to fade before he added, "So I'll keep my comments brief."

A rumble of general disgruntlement rolled through the crowd, and a couple of the elementary-school boys acted out their disgust at the delay by slapping themselves on the forehead and collapsing theatrically to the ground.

Janey would've liked to smack herself in the head, too— for an entirely different reason.

"I just want to announce that Megamart has generously agreed to sponsor all the sports teams in Plains City and Erskine, starting with giving them brand-new equipment." He was looking right at her when he said it.

Even from where she stood, she could see the light of battle in his eyes.

It really shouldn't have made her want him so much, but everything, it seemed, made her want him. And she couldn't let that change the fact that he had to be stopped.

Unfortunately, the rest of the town wasn't as stalwart in their opposition.

Noah made a few more promises, the right promises, and before he stepped down from the bandstand, the same people who'd refused to even talk to him this morning were falling all over themselves to compliment him tonight. And those who weren't congratulating Noah gravitated to Janey, guilt-induced arguments at the ready.

Ted Delancey was the first, coming to stand beside her where she stood watching Noah make his way through the crowd, pressing the flesh like a politician running for office. A politician who could smell victory.

"I know the two of you have had your differences," Ted said, "but he was a good kid overall." Ted had gone to school with her and Noah, and while there'd never been any friction between them, he hadn't exactly gone out of his way to make Noah feel welcome, either. Apparently he was prepared to atone for it.

"He was good, period," Mr. Tilford said. "Boy used to come down and help me unload deliveries when he got done working at the General Store. Wouldn't take a dime, either."

Yeah, he was good all right, Janey thought, good at making her life difficult.

"I never saw him try his hand at anything he didn't excel at," Ted said.

Except relationships. Janey clamped her mouth shut, in case she got the urge to say something that provocative out loud.

"He's only bribing us because he wants to win the pool down at the Ersk Inn," George Donaldson piped up.

"Right," Ted said. "Noah probably makes more than all of us put together, but he's doing this for the couple hundred bucks in the pool."

"Bryant don't like normal people," George said. "Do you remember when he bobbled that touchdown pass in the game against Eagleton? There was folks said he done it on purpose—'specially since it was the first time the Plains City Patriots lost to the team in fifteen years."

"What if he did?" Lisa Delaney shot back. "It was the Eagles' homecoming game, remember? How do you think we'd felt it we lost our homecoming game every year for fifteen years?"

A murmur went through the small group that had gathered around Janey, as people acknowledged that Noah might've done the right thing."

Even George was swayed, muttering, "I s'pose he had a good reason for doing it."

Janey managed not to roll her eyes, or make an unflattering noise, or call anyone a hypocrite. Noah had been kicked off the team for that mistake, and he'd never taken the field for Plains City High again. One or two sheepish glances came her way, but no one would own up to the truth out loud, and neither could she.

"He's going to buy the football team all new uniforms and equipment," someone contributed from the back of the group.

"And band instruments for the grade-schoolers."

So they'd already embellished the promises he'd made. With a small sigh of resignation, Janey listened as the stories of Megamart's largesse grew.

"Didn't he say he was getting band uniforms for the high-school kids and new equipment for the grade school?"

"He'll probably do both. He seems to be that kind of man."

"Well, somebody ought to tell him both schools need new computers. I'll bet he'd kick in some for such a worthy cause."

"Kick in, hell, he'll probably foot the entire bill. Megamart can afford it."

"That's if Megamart builds that store at all."

That comment, and the voice it came in, perked Janey right up. She raised up onto her toes to look over Ted Delancey's head, and sure enough, there was Max Devlin sauntering over to join the party. He caught her eye and winked.

"I don't know about the rest of you, but Plains City pretty far off the beaten path," Max said, taking his time sipping from a bottle of soda while the sudden silence stretched out and people absorbed the implications of what he'd said. "I'd lay odds they'll decide to put the store in a bigger town."

"But Noah promised," someone said, provoking another chorus of mixed reactions, some outraged at the thought, others chiming up in support of the new hometown hero, certain he wouldn't let such a thing happen.

Max shrugged, impervious to the discord. "Just telling it like I see it," he said. "I'm not really convinced the store would be the best thing for Erskine. Seems to me if it does get built, the schools' uniforms and equipment won't be the only thing getting modernized around here. This town has its faults, but if it's going to change, it should be our decision, not some big conglomerate's whose only real responsibility is to its shareholders."

Janey could've kissed Max. With a few calm, carefully-worded observations he'd managed to go further toward making her point than she could've by screaming at the top of her lungs.

"Well," Ted said at length, "If Megamart decides to build a store here, they'll build it. What can we do against a big corporation like that?"

"We could start a petition." Janey plucked a pen from Ted's shirt pocket and someone else produced a sheet of paper. "I don't know if it'll do any good but it certainly won't do any harm, either." She walked to the end of the table, put the paper and pen down, and waited.

A lot of glances were exchanged but no one moved—until Max came around the table. By the time he'd signed, no less than twenty people had lined up. One by one, they bent over and added their names to the impromptu petition. Janey thanked them sincerely, as much for signing their names as turning on a light to dispel the dark shadow of defeat that had been looming over her.

The last person in line hesitated, so she looked up, her smile dying away altogether.

Edie Macon. The closest thing to an enemy Janey had in

the world. Edie hadn't just had a reputation in high school, she'd earned it. She'd majored in French (as in kissing), animal husbandry, (as in petting) and gymnastics (the backseat variety). And then there was her minor in demolition—of other people's relationships. She'd run through pretty well every boy in high school, including the five graduating classes after her own. Noah had been the only boy Edie had dogged who'd never come to heel, and Edie had never forgotten that, or forgiven Janey for standing in her way.

Janey picked up the petition and a plate, and made her way down the potluck table, tarrying over her food choices as though she might find the answer to the meaning of life buried in Maisie Cunningham's pasta salad.

Unfortunately, it took more than intense concentration and an obvious preference for one's own company to keep people away in Erskine. Hell, it took more than typhoid to keep people away.

"So," Edie said, that single word followed by the inevitable pause while Edie rolled her eyes back in her head, as if she were trying to see the next thought before it was routed to her mouth.

The only explanation Janey could come up with for that annoying habit was that Edie wanted to appear an ingenuous, poor little damsel-in-distress who needed a big strong man to do her thinking for her. Janey could've told her that any man worth having wouldn't be that easily led, but Edie wouldn't have welcomed the advice from someone she'd hated since their school days.

"Everyone saw you and Noah walking through town the other day," Edie said, strolling down the other side of the table, keeping pace with Janey, even though she spent more time staring at the backs of her eyelids than the buffet. But then, she wasn't interested in the food. "You two were pretty cozy from what I hear. All this stuff about you trying to stop Megamart from building that store, that's just a smoke screen so no one will think you're still into him."

"You caught me," Janey said. "I'm making his life difficult in the hopes he'll decide he can't live without me."

That earned Janey a predictably poisonous look. "You already had your shot at him. He wouldn't stay with you even after you slept with him."

That was meant to hurt, and it did, but Janey was a pro at not letting her pain show. "Old news," she said without missing a beat. "But he didn't exactly turn out to be trustworthy, did he?"

"Hell, I don't care if every word that comes out of his mouth is a lie. He's gorgeous and rich, and did you get a load of his car? I'll bet it could fly."

Yeah, Janey nearly said, but what would you possibly do without a back seat?

It would've served Edie right, but there would've been no satisfaction in it, Janey knew. Sure, she and Edie had a sort-of feud going, and Edie had drawn first blood, so no one would have faulted Janey for giving as good as she got. But it would've disappointed her father, and although he was gone now, he'd left Janey his moral compass. She could be sarcastic at times, bitchy even, but she tried not to intentionally hurt anyone. "He's all yours, Edie—unless his girlfriend objects."

"His girlfriend?"

"Her name's Barbara," Janey said, knowing she was getting way too much entertainment out of the situation and not feeling the least repentant about it.

"Well, I don't care if her name is Julia Roberts, he's here and she's not. I can make Noah forget about her."

"Forget who?"

Janey looked over her shoulder and groaned. The only thing that could be worse than letting herself get dragged into a fight with Edie Macon was getting dragged into a fight over Noah—in front of him. And the whole town.

"Barbara," Ted Delancey offered, "your girlfriend."

"What gave you the idea I have a girlfriend, let alone one named Barbara?"

"She did," Edie said, pointing at Janey without even having to check with her brain first.

Noah's mouth curved into a smirk. "Jessie told you I've been on the phone with Barbara all week," he said, "and the truth is, I don't think I could live without her."

Even prepared for it, Janey felt her heart drop into her stomach.

"She's my admin."

Janey's heart shot back up into her throat, and she yanked her gaze away from Noah so he wouldn't see her relief.

"I knew it wasn't true," Edie said, looking seductively up at Noah as she twined both arms around his and pressed her admittedly impressive breasts against his arm. It was no accident his hand ended up all but buried in her crotch.

Noah didn't even have the grace to look uncomfortable, Janey noticed, crossing her arms and pasting a smile on her face. The crowd around them was enjoying the show enough; they didn't need to see her resentment, too.

"The music's starting," Edie said, "dance with me."

"I thought I'd sit down and have something to eat."

"I can get you whatever you want."

Noah glanced over at Janey, a grin flirting with his mouth. "How about a building permit?"

Edie rolled her eyes back in her head for even longer than usual. Clearly she couldn't find an answer for that.

"How about a little bit of everything?" he came out before she fell over backward.

"Don't move a muscle. I'll be back in a jiff," Edie said in a manner that couldn't have been more suggestive.

"What?" Noah asked when he turned back and found Janey watching him watch Edie sashay along the length of the table. "I'm only human."

"You mean you're not Captain Progress today? Sworn to save small towns everywhere from the scourge of stagnation?"

"C'mon, Janey. This is a party. Can't we all be friends?"

"We were more than friends," Janey said. "That's why Edie hates me."

Noah grinned and raised an eyebrow. "This fightin's over me?"

"Get over yourself, Bryant. Edie and I would've found something to disagree about without you in the picture, but… Well, let's just say she got the last laugh after you left town."

Noah's smile faded away. He studied her face, then looked over to where Edie was piling food onto plates and glaring at Janey. "She doesn't miss an opportunity to rub your face in it, does she?"

Janey shrugged. "It's not important."

"It is to me," he said, lowering his voice. "I had no idea leaving town without an explanation would put you in this position. It must've been hell for you all these years."

"Don't beat yourself up about it."

"I didn't think that far ahead—not at eighteen. But I can't, in good conscience, let it go on any longer—"

"Conscience!" She took a step back, her expression leaving no doubt that she thought he didn't have one.

"We need to talk about this," he said, looking as if he wanted to grab her and shake her.

She turned around and walked away. She knew she was being a coward, but what had happened ten years ago was water under the bridge for her. She didn't want to hear him say that he'd left because his career was more important to him than she was.

What frightened her even more was the possibility that he'd tell her he just hadn't wanted to be with her anymore.

Chapter Thirteen

Noah wouldn't say his gambit at the Fourth of July celebration had put him ahead of Janey, but they were even again, at least where the store was concerned. Personally, she had him wound up tighter than a rope swing in a tornado—which, no matter how much he tried to deny it, was why he was lurking at the end of her front porch, letting the mosquitoes feast on him.

Sure enough, Clary was walking Janey home; Noah heard their voices long before he could see them, no more than dark outlines in the pitch black of her unlit street. Even if it had occurred to him to leave them in privacy, he wouldn't have. He knew there was no way Janey would invite the deputy sheriff in for a nightcap—or anything else. But Noah would've lost all respect for Clary if he didn't make a move on her.

He watched as Janey stepped through the gate, leaving Clary on the other side, then found himself shaking his head as Clary stuffed his hands in his pockets and started off down the street. Noah could've sworn he heard him sigh as he rounded the corner.

He understood how Clary must've felt. Janey Walters was the kind of woman who could drive a man crazy without really trying, and then make it impossible to stay mad at her. What was it about her that made her so irresistible? he wondered. And so unforgettable? He'd been gone for ten years and, been with other women—plenty of other women—beautiful, sophisticated women with high-powered careers and stock portfolios, women who didn't want monogamous relationships ending in matrimony, parenthood and anniversaries involving precious metals.

None of them held a candle to Janey.

She'd been his first love, the one woman he'd never been able to get out of his system.

He closed his eyes and smiled, remembering how it had been in high school. All she'd had to do was enter the room and his IQ took a steep drop. It was a wonder he'd ever managed to open a book, let alone absorb enough knowledge to get a passing grade.

He might not be that hormone-crazed kid anymore, but standing there in the dark waiting for her to come to him, he felt like it. Except he was ten years older, and he already knew how she tasted, the warmth and softness of her skin.... "Janey," he said. It was just her name, but the word was weighted with everything inside him at that moment, with emotions he couldn't face, expectations he couldn't name and hopes he didn't dare examine too closely.

She stopped a foot away, in the silvery wash of the full moon that chose that instant to break through the clouds. She didn't shriek and her eyes didn't even widen. She just turned slowly toward him as if she'd known all along that he'd be standing there. And maybe she had, Noah thought. Maybe she could feel his presence, the same way he felt hers.

Before he could follow the path of those maybes to some foolish action, she took a step back. Noah shook his head a little to clear it, and realized that what he was getting from her definitely wasn't I'm-happy-to-see-you. It was more along the lines of why-the-hell-are-you-hiding-in-the-dark-spying-on-me? "Too bad Clary had to go. He could've run interference for you," he said.

"Do you really want to go there after the way Edie was hanging all over you?"

"Barbara," was all Noah said to that, and judging by the defensive tone of Janey's voice she got his point.

"That was an honest mistake."

"And Edie was public relations. I already have you bad-mouthing me to anyone who'll listen. The last thing I need is Edie getting into the act. If the two of you decide to work together, I'll be toast."

Her mouth dropped open, then she laughed, sort of incredulously. "That's probably not something you'll ever have to worry about. Besides, Edie would be your slave if you asked her to."

"And you never would." Noah felt as if he was about to burst into flames. He'd come there to put the past to rest, to prove to her that the contention between them wasn't all about the store. Suddenly that didn't seem like such a good strategy. The store was a safe topic, he reminded himself. It was a hell of a lot safer than thinking about how she'd feel in his arms, and how much he'd give to have her there. And if he really wanted to stay on the safe side of the front door, he'd think about— Damn.

"Where's Jessie?" he asked. When Janey didn't answer right away, he said, "Let me guess, she's at the Devlins'."

"And that makes you angry."

"It feels as if you're using her against me."

"Stop thinking about yourself and think about what it's like for her."

"I haven't put her in the middle."

"Neither have I, but she's in the middle, anyway. She saw us arguing in town and asked if she could stay with Max and Sara for a couple of days."

"I'll just go and talk to her—"

"She doesn't want to be here, Noah."

He could see that hurt her as much as it hurt him, which took all the hot air out of his anger. "Do you have any objections to me going out there to see her?"

"No," Janey said, "but that doesn't solve the real problem, does it?"

"No," he echoed, sitting down on the porch swing. "She let me have it on the way to the movies the other day." He looked up at her, but her face was unreadable in the meager starlight. "I could've used some help, you know. Maybe you could put aside your objections to the store and the three of us could, I don't know, do something together."

Janey propped a hip up on the porch railing. "Why is it that when things are going well between you and Jessie I'm not needed, and when there's the least bit of trouble, you beg for help?"

"Because you're so good at trouble."

"Maybe that's because of all the practice I've had."

"You're the one who's causing the problem here, Janey. If you'd just get out of my way—"

"I did that ten years ago," she reminded him.

"This isn't the same thing."

"Isn't it?"

"No." But the two issues were getting so muddled up that he didn't know himself what they were fighting about anymore.

"You changed my life in a big way, Noah."

"I didn't do it alone."

"I won't deny that. But what you're planning now will change Jessie's life, and not necessarily for the better."

"I'm sorry, Janey. I'm sorry for all of it, but…" he shook his head. "We're both adults. I don't see why we can't separate our personal lives from our public rivalry."

Because, Janey thought, she wasn't entirely sure she could trust him. He'd made no secret of the fact that he'd sacrifice anything to accomplish his goal, including, she was afraid, their daughter. But she was just too tired to argue about it.

"I think it's time we cleared up—"

"No," she said tightly.

He stood and came over to her. She held her ground, but when he wrapped an arm around her shoulder and pulled her against his side, tears formed in her eyes. If she let her guard down in private, how could she keep it up in public? She moved away when she risked a glance at his face, she could tell he understood why. That it bothered him was something she couldn't let herself dwell on.

"We're going to have to talk about it sooner or later."

"Why?"

"Because I don't want to leave town without clearing the air between us."

She met his gaze. "But you will leave town."

Silence was all she got, and silence was all the answer she needed.

"And if I say you're forgiven? No, don't," she said when he started to speak. For ten long years she'd wondered why he'd left her the way he had. Now she wanted it all behind her. "We were both young, Noah, and we both made mistakes."

He turned her to face him. "Don't tell me you've been blaming yourself."

"Maybe if I hadn't been so—I don't know…starry-eyed, naive," she smiled slightly "—spoiled. I was so used to things going the way I wanted that I didn't notice you were unhappy."

Noah caught the first tear as it tracked down her cheek. "Man, I really did a number on you." He leaned against the railing beside her but didn't touch her again. That would have been too much for either of them to handle. "I thought a clean break would be better for both of us."

"You call that a clean break? And I'm not talking about Jessie. By the time I found out I was pregnant, it was a relief to have something else to think about." Not to mention the fact that she'd been so pathetically grateful to have some part of him—even when he hadn't called her back. She'd had no clue back then how hard it would be to face her parents. They'd been nothing but supportive, but she'd broken a trust and she'd seen how much it had hurt them.

"What did I know? I was eighteen."

"My God, Noah, you slept with me! You were the only one. And then you disappeared. Even at eighteen you could've imagined what was going through my mind."

"I wasn't thinking, and I sure as hell wasn't imagining, Janey. I couldn't let myself. You kept saying you loved me, and I—"

"You didn't love me back."

"I couldn't *say* it back," he corrected. "I felt it, but when it came down to the words, when you were waiting for me to say them to you, watching me with that need in your eyes and the future all mapped out, I couldn't say it."

"I was pushing," Janey said. "I know I was, but as we got closer to graduation, you were pulling away from me, and I didn't understand why. I needed to hear the words, Noah."

"And I left instead," he said. "I was a coward, Janey. I left the way I did because I didn't want to make you choose— No, that's not entirely true." He exhaled heavily. "I was afraid you wouldn't choose me. I had nothing to offer you."

"Nothing but yourself, Noah. It was enough for me."

"I did what I thought was best for both of us. I loved you, Janey."

"Yeah? Well, I loved you, too, and you broke my heart."

"I'm sorry."

"Me, too." She went to her front door, pausing with her hand on the doorknob. Maybe it was what she'd learned about him, maybe remembering how much she'd loved him all those years ago. Whatever it was, she didn't trust herself near him anymore. "Good night, Noah."

"Janey..."

She kept her back to him. His voice was much too close, too intimate in the darkness. "What?"

"Thanks. For everything. As much grief as I've given you since I came back to town, you've given me something incredible. Having a daughter..."

Janey looked over her shoulder. She couldn't see much of his face with only the moon for illumination, but his body language spoke volumes. "I've always been so focused on my career, I didn't even realize how lonely I was until I came back here and found out about her."

Janey faced him, surprised by his admission. "You work for a big corporation a big city."

"You can't imagine how much lonelier lonely is when you're surrounded by thousands of people." And it was so tempting to hold that loneliness at bay with her company. The way Janey hesitated told him she was thinking the same thing, and then she turned again and went inside.

Noah stayed where he was, staring at the door she'd disappeared through. He should have gone home; he'd put Janey through enough already, and he was hurting her more every day. That was what he hadn't counted on when he decided to set things straight—that having the truth out there would be worse than keeping it hidden—and the only way he could think of to fix it was to remind them both of the good times.

He walked into the house and straight through to the kitchen, where Janey was leaning against the counter, sipping from a glass of wine. He took the glass from her and set it down, placed his hands on the counter on either side of her and pressed his body into hers. The blood drained out of his head so fast he went dizzy.

"I don't think this is a good idea," she said.

The rasp of her voice sent Noah's need spiraling up another impossible notch. "We used to love each other, Janey."

"Used to."

Noah cursed himself for his choice of words. "When you look back, that's what I want you to remember."

"I can't remember the love without the pain."

"Then let's make some new memories." He laid his mouth on hers, a kiss that seemed to suck all the oxygen from the room.

"Tonight won't change anything, Noah," she said when he lifted his mouth from hers. Her eyes met his, and although he could see the desire there, she had the strength to fight it off long enough to make sure they both knew where they stood. "I'll still do everything I can to stop you from building that store."

"Do you honestly think you can stop me?"

"Absolutely."

"You can't even stop me from doing this." He kissed her lightly on the lips.

"I could stop you—"

He took her mouth again, the taste and scent of him filling her senses as he moved against her—one long, slow twist that wrung a sound from her, part approval, part denial. Complete desire.

Ages before she was ready, Noah pulled away, resting his forehead on hers. "I thought you could stop me," he said when his breathing slowed sufficiently for coherent speech.

"I could—" she looked deeply into his eyes "—if I wanted to." And on some level, she did, but that little voice of reason was so easily justified into silence. Here was a chance, she told herself, to get him into her bed and out of her system, to get over the attraction that kept her from sleeping and haunted her every waking moment. She took him by the hand, but he wasn't about to be led, at least not very far with his head spinning and his body already hard and demanding.

He pressed her against the wall at the foot of the stairs and filled himself with the taste of her. Pulling his mouth from hers, he flipped the T-shirt over her head in one slick move, peeled one bra strap down and buried his face in her shoulder.

To hell with going slowly, and savoring this moment he'd dreamed about since that one incredible night ten years ago. Janey was right here, a flesh-and-blood woman who wanted him as much as he wanted her. He undid the snap on her shorts and backed her toward the parlor.

A laugh stopped him, a low, throaty purr of sound that was uniquely Janey, both playful and sexy. His blood seemed to catch fire. The fact that she stood there in a white lace bra, white cotton bikini panties just peeking through her unsnapped shorts, didn't hurt either.

He reached for her, but she slipped away and started up the steps. "No walls, no couches, no floors."

Noah grinned. "No backseat of the car?"

"My bed," she whispered.

Noah felt as if he'd swallowed his own tongue. All he could do was follow her, eyes glued to her bottom as she slinked her way up the stairs. He caught up with her at the top and wrapped his arms around her waist, bringing her back against him. His hands slid up to cup her breasts. She groaned, low and deep, and every nerve in his body pulsed.

Janey took him by the hand and tugged him into her bedroom. She shimmied out of her clothes and turned to face him, smoothing her hands down his chest and over his stomach, fascinated by the way his muscles contracted beneath her touch. She tugged his shirt up over his head, then trailed her fingers over his bare skin, down to the waistband of his jeans. She popped the snap, lifting an eyebrow at the silk beneath, black this time.

"I've been thinking about those boxers ever since that morning," she said.

"It's not about the silk," he said, shoving the jeans and boxers down and stepping out of them.

She grinned, and he swept her up, and dumped her on the bed. Before she could begin to catch her breath, Noah's hot mouth was at her breast. She arched against him, didn't realize she was begging, or what she was begging for until his hand glided down, over her stomach and between her legs. And then he was in her, his mouth on hers as he drove deep.

He dropped his head into the crook of her shoulder, his mouth on her neck as he began to move. She met his pace, then—just like Janey—tried to quicken it. Noah took her mouth, and when he felt her body tighten around him, he let himself go with her.

"Wow," Janey managed to get out, sounding stunned and breathless.

That didn't begin to cover it, but it was more than Noah could say with his chest heaving and his ears ringing. He managed to flop to one side, so wrung out his muscles were quivering.

Janey propped her head up with one hand, the other sliding down his body.

Suddenly, impossibly, Noah had all kinds of energy.

"Can we do that again," she asked, "or maybe... I was thinking of trying something else." She snuggled close and whispered in his ear, punctuating the suggestion with her tongue.

The breath whooshed out of him on a slightly incredulous, completely aroused burst of laughter.

"Well?"

"Sure, we can do that, but I'm not sure it's a good idea."

"Really?" She leaned back far enough to meet his eyes, then she ran her tongue over her lips, ever so slowly. "I've heard it feels...amazing."

"If it feels any better than that just did, you may just kill me."

Janey laughed, low and throaty. "That would certainly solve a problem or two."

Chapter Fourteen

Noah didn't spend the night with Janey. He was in her kitchen at the crack of dawn, sipping coffee, but he hadn't spent the night in her bed. At least not all of it.

It had been tempting, more than tempting, to just curl himself around her and drift off. Not only would it have meant the best night's sleep he'd had since he'd come back to town, but he would've gotten to wake up with Janey. Instead, he'd dragged himself away from her—even with that sunrise fantasy playing in his head.

She'd been awake but silent when he got out of bed, watching him while he dressed. The look she'd given him had been sultry, suggestive—inviting. She couldn't possibly have been thinking straight, because if she had, she would've helped him on his way. He had to admit he would have liked as invitation to come from her lips. He wanted to hear her say there were no regrets. The lovemaking last night would have no meaning otherwise.

No meaning. That stopped him. Meaning was another word for feelings, and he preferred to leave his out of it. He remembered how weak and needy he'd felt all those years ago, how scary it had been to know that his happiness depended on one person. He didn't know if he was capable of that kind of emotion anymore.

But one thing was certain. He felt better for having un-packed some of the baggage they'd both been carrying around all this time—it was such a relief, in fact, that during the sleepless hours since he'd left Janey's bed, he'd decided he had to finish the job.

He heard the stairs groaning, and even though he'd pre-pared himself, when she appeared wearing only a waist-length T-shirt and French-cut white panties, he could only think about taking her back upstairs—or in the parlor, or on the kitchen floor. It took him a couple of seconds, but he man-aged to put his desire away.

"Good morning."

She yelped, tugging on the hem of the shirt, then sliding into a chair when she realized it was a wasted effort. "What are you doing in my kitchen?" she asked, closing her eyes and pressing her fingers against her temples.

So, Noah thought, she'd slept as little as he had. "You mean you didn't miss me?"

She opened one eye and peered at him. "I could pretend to miss you, but you're still here."

He chuckled, picking up his cup and sipping from it. He didn't miss the wistful way she eyed the coffee.

"That was a hint."

"Okay," he said, reaching over to pick up the bag he'd left on the floor.

Janey had her hands around his wrist before he'd managed to get all the way to his feet. "Is that what I think it is?"

"It is if you think it's coffee from the diner." She reached for the bag, but he lifted it out of her reach. "And what will you give me for it?"

She blushed, but kept her composure. "Do you think I held anything back last night?"

His shifted his gaze down, to the spot between her breasts. To her heart. "Yes," he said.

"Would you have it another way?" she asked quietly?

Noah turned his head.

Janey took the bag out of his hand and went directly to the microwave, an excuse to keep him from seeing the tears in her eyes. He'd brought up the subject of her heart just so he could make it clear that was one part of her anatomy he considered off-limits. She'd be damned if she let him see how much that hurt.

"Nobody's forcing you to hang around," she said, taking her time retrieving her coffee from the microwave and the cream from the refrigerator.

"True," he replied, but he didn't leave. "Why don't you take a shower and put on some clothes, and I'll pick you up in an hour."

"What?" She spun around, her tears buried under a layer of incredulity—mostly at herself because, despite everything, she wanted to go with him. No questions asked as long as they left Erskine and went where they could be alone with no talk of Megamart to cloud the day.

It was ridiculous, of course. She was way too susceptible to her own fantasies to spend the day alone with Noah. "I'm not going anywhere with you. We've already given this town enough to gossip to keep them happy for the rest of the decade. Why add to it?"

"I was hoping we could spend some time alone, just the two of us."

She took a cautious sip from her cup and told herself it was the warmth of the coffee she felt spreading through her, and nothing more. He might have echoed her thoughts almost exactly, but it would be foolish to hope that the feelings that had prompted them were the same as hers. "Someone's bound to see us. It'll only make people more curious."

"I was under the impression you didn't care what anyone else thought."

"I care what Jessie thinks. And I have a million things I should be doing around here."

"The stuff around here can wait, Janey. Maybe you and I should take the opportunity to see if we can find some common ground so Jessie doesn't want to run away again."

"You learn fast, don't you, Bryant?"

"I'm not using Jessie to get you to do what I want, Janey. It's her happiness I'm thinking about."

"I know." And that was why she could feel herself weakening. It had nothing to do with what they'd shared last night, with what she wanted from him every moment of every day.

But he knew better, damn him. She could see it in his amused little smile, and his eyes boring into hers with a dare she almost took him up on. Right there on the kitchen table. She'd show him the difference between sex and making love.

And wasn't that what he wanted? "I agree we need to make peace for Jessie's sake," she said, "but that's all."

His expression hardened with something like anger, or maybe frustration, before he made his face go blank. "In other words, there won't be a repeat of last night. Is that for Jessie's benefit or is it retaliation?"

Janey set her cup down on the table. "Maybe it's best if you go."

"You agreed to spend the day with me."

She snorted softly. "We can't even get through a cup of coffee without having an argument. Do you really think spending a day together will create peace between us?"

"I think we owe it to Jessie to give it a shot."

HE WAS GOOD, Janey had to give him that. The man drove her every kind of crazy, and here she was riding in his slick, little car, a picnic hamper in the back. She'd agreed to go with Noah for one reason and one reason only. It was time to let go of the past.

She wasn't sure exactly how they were going to accomplish that, but in the meanwhile, she could enjoy the ride. She hated to agree with Edie Macon on anything, but Noah's Porsche was spoiling her for all other cars. It didn't fly, but it hugged the road so tightly she felt as if she was on the smoothest roller-coaster ride ever. The motor thrumming through the leather seat soothed her tension-knotted muscles and, as a bonus, she got to watch Noah drive.

He finessed the steering wheel with one hand, the other resting on the gearshift, tendons flexing as he downshifted through turns and let the car race through the straightaways. Even in worn jeans and a T-shirt, he looked as if he belonged in a car commercial—sophisticated, powerful, desirable. With his chiseled good looks and dark, wind-tousled hair, there wasn't a woman alive who wouldn't want him, or man who wouldn't want to be him.

And wasn't that just the problem?

He glanced at her, a sexy smirk on his face. "Hungry?"

Food was the last thing on her mind. In fact, there wasn't a whole lot on her mind, considering what being around him did to her body. Her stomach lurched whenever she caught sight of him, he smelled way too good and his voice, with its perpetual bedroom edge, seemed to strum across her nerves and keep her at a constant simmer. "I could eat," was all she said.

"Do you mind if we take a detour first?"

Janey glanced over at him again. He sounded cheerful enough, but she could tell he wasn't as relaxed as he'd been a minute ago. His posture was rigid, and his jaw was clenched. He took the next turnoff, so quickly the car fishtailed and he had to fight to keep it on the dirt road, hands and feet operating in a symphony of maneuvers that had the Porsche slowing, straightening, then shooting back up to speed in a rooster-tail of gravel.

"Where are we going?" she asked when she was sure the answer wasn't the nearest ditch.

Noah ignored her. It was the kind of silence that gave her chills.

"We're going to your old farm, aren't we?"

He took that for the rhetorical question it was.

"If you don't want to talk about the past," Janey said, "why do you want to revisit it?"

Noah looked over at her. "I think I need to, Janey. Being with you…makes it easier."

She didn't quite know how to respond to that, so she just sat back. She didn't want to read too much into his wanting her company on what was sure to be a tense and depressing walk down memory lane. But she did.

"Pretty bad, isn't it?" he asked as he eased the car as far as he could up a driveway that was rutted and overgrown with weeds.

The house was weathered gray wood. Every window was broken, the roof sagged and the front door hung on one hinge. The barn had caved in on itself, and the other outbuildings were in even worse shape. The only hopeful note was the real estate sign out front, though it was so old that rust had eaten right through it.

"I wish I could say it used to look better than this," Noah said as he unfolded his long body from the car and came around to her side, "but the truth is, it hasn't changed all that much."

He sounded so unhappy. Janey wanted to wrap her arms around him, but he'd turned inward, locked himself and his pain away where she knew she couldn't reach him with anything but words. "It's no worse than the other places that have gone into foreclosure around here. Beats me why the bank thinks it'll be better off taking them away from people who are trying to get ahead and will eventually make payments. They just wind up with a piece of land nobody else wants."

"The bank did my dad a favor. He never saw it that way but my mom would have…" *If she'd lived long enough.* He stripped off his sunglasses and rubbed a hand over his face. "This place was never going to break even, let alone turn a profit, but my old man just couldn't let go. It killed him when the bank took it away from him."

Literally, Janey recalled. The bank had repossessed the farm in the summer of the year Noah had left town, and his father hadn't made it through Thanksgiving. Noah hadn't come back for the funeral.

"I know it looks horrible now, but was it really *that* bad?"

"Yes."

This time, logic was no match for the bleakness in his eyes. Janey reached for him, twined her fingers with his even though he tried to pull away.

"There's a reason I never brought you here," he said.

"Because I was the daughter of a state senator, and you—"

"I was nobody."

"Not to me," Janey said quietly. "To me you were everything, Noah." She let go of his hand. "You were afraid if I saw this place, I'd dump you. You must've had a pretty low opinion of me if you thought all I cared about was social standing."

"That's not true."

"Then fill me in, why don't you?"

"I had no prospects, no future. Hell, Janey, I worked two jobs just to put myself through college, and there were days I wanted to chuck it all and take a nice simple job like digging ditches to get out from under the pressure."

"Maybe I could've helped you."

"How was I supposed to ask you to give up everything to live in a ratty apartment eating pork and beans for weeks at a time so at the end of it we could get a slightly less ratty apartment while I slaved my way up the corporate ladder?"

"When did I ever tell you I expected to be taken care of the rest of my life?" She closed the distance between them, anger and indignation bringing her nose-to-nose with him. "My family might have been a bit better off than yours, but when did you ever hear me say I wanted to get married and play housewife?" The only reaction she got was a muscle working in his jaw. "That's right," she said, "I didn't."

"And what if I failed at everything, like my father?"

He didn't shout or make a threatening gesture, but there was something in his eyes, in the very restraint of his voice, that made her heart shoot up into her throat. She didn't move because she couldn't.

"You weren't afraid of me," he said, "but I was." He shoved his hands in his pockets and walked a little distance away. When he spoke again she could hardly hear him. The anguish in his voice came through loud and clear, though. "My old man was a mean, angry drunk. He couldn't deal with being a failure and he hated me for being around to see it."

"And he took it out on you," Janey said as evenly as she could.

He flashed her a quick, uncomfortable look. "He'd call me stupid and useless when things were at their worst, maybe give me the back of his hand if I wasn't quick enough to get out of the way. I wouldn't call it abuse."

"I would," she muttered.

"It was no different than how his old man treated him, Janey. I'm not defending him, but he didn't think he was doing anything wrong. It was how he coped with what was happening to him."

"Happening to him?"

"That's how he saw it."

Janey shook her head, but it did nothing to clear her jumbled thoughts or settle her pitching stomach. She wanted to do all the things she would've done for a wounded child, make the assurances and give the hugs and tell him it wasn't his fault. But Noah wasn't a child anymore; he'd disappeared and dealt with the wounds on his own. And left her behind to wonder what she'd done to drive him away.

"I can understand why you had to get away from here, Noah, but—"

"I wasn't afraid you'd dump me, Janey—" he spun to face her "—or that you wouldn't be able to stand a little hardship. I didn't want you to be around if I failed."

She'd already made that leap, already understood, at last, what had really sent him running from Erskine. And from her. "You were never like your father, Noah."

"I'd never raise a hand to Jessie," he said. "Ever. I know how it felt to be treated like that." Noah meant what he said about never raising a hand to Jessie; five minutes after finding out he was a father, he'd known that without a doubt. But his old man was in him somewhere and there were other ways to hurt the people in his life.

And there was another side effect of having revealed the truth about his past: the way Janey was looking at him now. Anger was better than pity any day of the week. He rolled his shoulders to work out some of the tension, and slipped on his sunglasses. "Why don't we go find that picnic area you mentioned?"

"You're running away again."

"Call it whatever you want." He turned on his heel and headed for the Porsche, for the world he'd made for himself. "I didn't bring you here to rehash the past."

"Then why did you bring me here?"

"I wanted you to know why I'm building the store."

"I've always understood that, Noah. You're the one who wants to believe you're serving some sort of noble cause."

His jaw tightened, but he didn't defend himself.

Janey pressed the fingertips of both hands over her mouth, then pushed them into her hair, but she couldn't contain her frustration any longer. "What happened to your plans, Noah?"

"I grew up," he said, his eyes as hard and glittering as green glass.

Janey put her hand on his arm, but he stepped back. She

almost told him not to bother—he was already out of reach. "You were going to be your own man," she said, her voice gentler. "Not subject to the whims of the weather, not in debt to any bank. Now you're taking orders from some guy who sits in an office all day, and he's at the mercy of some other guy in some other office, and they're all answerable to the billionaire who owns the company."

"Every man in this world, whether he works for the establishment or claims to be his own boss, is answerable to somebody or something," Noah said. "That's a fact of life. I learned to accept it, and I'm working my way up the chain of command so I'll be the one in charge someday."

"And then what?"

That stumped him. What would he do when he got to the top of the heap? He'd always focused on the journey, the next step, never thinking about what his life would be like when he crossed the finish line. Until he came back to Erskine. And, until then, he'd never realized how badly he wanted someone to be there with him.

Until Janey.

"I don't know," he said honestly. "I guess I'll figure that out when I get there."

"And if Erskine is one of the casualties? Oh, well."

She started to walk away, but Noah grabbed her arm and swung her around to face him. "Why can't you understand me?"

"Why can't you understand yourself?"

"Dammit, Janey." He moved toward her, and although she knew it wasn't wise, she went into his arms.

She was tired, really tired. Sick to death, actually. Of having the past haunt her and the future make her nervous. It was so nice to be held, just held, while the sun shone and the wind whispered through the tall grasses. But when it became more than comfort, when she began to notice the way he smelled, his body pressed to hers, she pulled away.

His arms tightened briefly, long enough for her heartbeat to spike and a part of her to wish he wouldn't let her go. But he did, and she knew it was for the best.

He studied her face, his eyes boring into hers in a way that made her wonder if she would ever get to a place where she didn't wonder what her life would've been like if she'd shared it with him.

Then he held his hand out to her and smiled. "Let's go have lunch."

"Okay," she said with a slightly watery laugh, "as long as you take me someplace I've never been before."

"I did that last night," he said. "Several times, as I recall."

"Your ego is truly colossal, Bryant." But she didn't deny what he'd said, and she was smiling when she said, "Take me someplace that doesn't involve stripping."

"Okay," he said, walking her to the car. "But you're taking all the fun out of it."

Chapter Fifteen

"Today was nice," Noah said as they sat on the top step of Janey's back porch, snacking on what they hadn't eaten of the picnic lunch.

"It improved," Janey said lazily.

To make up for the sad memories his farm had brought back, Noah had taken her to some of their favorite hangouts in high school, places that recalled happier memories. Gradually the tension between them had melted away, along with the years, and even though they were driving in a car neither of them had dreamed of owning ten years ago, Noah was that lanky boy who had yet to grow into his height, and Janey felt young and full of dreams again.

She knew reality was out there somewhere, waiting to pounce, but at the moment there was only the sun going down in the west, the clouds trailing ribbons of pink and peach over the darkening silhouette of the mountains. Noah was a warm, comforting presence beside her, and the conflict between them seemed a million miles away, like something happening to another woman in another lifetime.

"What did Jessie have to say when you called her?" he asked.

"It was all about Toaster—her horse," she qualified. "He's the color of toast, you know, about five different shades of patchy brown with some white thrown in. He's not really

Jessie's horse, but Max said it was better for her if she rode the same horse all the time so they'd get used to each other. And when she wasn't talking about the horse, she was talking about the cats and dogs and fish and birds. Joey has nearly every kind of domesticated animal there is, several of each, come to think of it."

"Did she ask about me?"

"No." Janey's heart lurched at the miserable expression on his face. "She doesn't know you're here, Noah, and even if she did, she wouldn't bring you up. She thinks we're still angry with each other."

"Are we?"

"I don't know. Everything is..."

"Yeah," he said, his heavy sigh and slight shake of the head summing up her feelings exactly. "Tomorrow there's still going to be the store. But what about tonight?"

"I don't have an answer for that."

"Yes, you do."

She shot him a look. "You won't like it."

"I won't accept it." He slid over and kissed the side of her neck.

"No," Janey said, but she shivered and knew he noticed.

He put a hand on her waist, his mouth inching up to her ear lobe, biting gently. His tongue worked its own magic there while his hand trailed along her ribs and upward to touch her cheek and turn her face to his.

"No," she breathed against his lips, but she let herself give in, and kissed him back, poured herself into it until his breath was short and ragged as hers.

His fingers were at her breast, feathering back and forth across her nipple, in rhythm with their kiss. She placed her hand on top of his and leaned back to say *no* again. But he lowered his mouth to her breast, took her nipple in his teeth, and even through her shirt and bra, the pleasure was so intense her body jerked. The denial caught in the back of her throat, and all that came out was a long, drawn out moan that meant *yes*.

She slipped her hand beneath his shirt, dragging her nails over his stomach, down to the snap of his jeans. He took her wrist, though, and she opened her eyes to find him watching her, his face serious.

"Let's go inside," he said.

It took Janey a minute to come back to herself, to remember that they were still outside on her back porch, and there were lights on in most of the houses on the street behind hers.

It was the perfect opportunity for her to put a stop to something she knew was wrong, and to her credit, she did think about it. Even with her brain clouded by need and her body clamoring for more of Noah's touch, she wrestled with her conscience. And lost the battle.

She stood and went to the back door, and when he didn't follow her, she looked over her shoulder at him and said, "Are you coming?"

He smiled—whether at her inadvertent choice of words or at her decision to invite him in—and got to his feet. But when he reached her side, his smile faded and the emotion she saw on his face, the depth of the desire he felt for her, all but bought her to her knees.

She turned away from him and let him guide her through the door. Whatever Noah was feeling, she couldn't let herself read too much into it. This was only sex.

But that was a lie, and she knew it. Even though the rest of her body could be satisfied with a night or two of physical pleasure, her heart couldn't.

And then her brain went wonderfully silent, and there was only the magic of Noah's hands on her and hers on him. Only the sigh of their breath, the slide of skin over skin and the heat—over her, around her, inside her.

By the time she could think again, he was already sitting on the edge of the bed and she suddenly felt so alone and so empty.

As he began to rise, Janey rolled over and put her hand on his back.

"Stay," she said, her voice no more than a weak, hoarse whisper.

He went still, sat there facing away from her for a long, long moment.

"Just this once, Noah."

She felt some of the tension go out of him then. He climbed back into bed and gathered her into his arms. "Just this once," he said.

JESSIE LOVED STAYING at the Devlins', especially lately. They were a family, a real family, and even if Sara wasn't Joey's actual mother, that didn't matter to any of them. That gave Jessie hope.

Her parents fighting at the Fourth of July celebration was the last straw, as Mrs. Halliwell liked to say. Jessie didn't see what straw had to do with anything, but she got the "last" part. Somebody had to do something about the stupid way her mom and Noah were acting, and that someone was going to have to be her. Except she had no idea *what* to do.

"Quit making all that noise," Joey yelled at her. "I'm trying to sleep over here."

Jessie got up and went into his room, which was right across the hall from the guest bedroom where she slept when she stayed there. "I'm not making any noise," she said from the doorway.

"You're sighing about every two seconds," he said grumpily.

She couldn't think of a snappy come back, so she made a noise in the back of her throat that conveyed her complete and utter lack of appreciation for his comment. She was about to add a dramatic exit when he spoke again.

"What's wrong with you, anyhow?"

Jessie stayed where she was, arguing with herself over whether to tell him about her problem or just go back to bed. Joey Devlin was a year younger than her, just a kid who still slept with a nightlight. But he had experience, she had to admit. His dad and Sara had tortured themselves and everyone else in town for a good long time before they figured out they loved each other and got married. Jessie didn't get what was so great about love, anyway, but grown-ups seemed to get pretty worked up about it.

"If you're not going to answer the question, could you leave?"

"It's my mom and—and Noah." She'd tried to call him Dad, but it felt funny. "Even before my mom found out about the stupid store, they were always mad at each other, and I was thinking that maybe, since you might kind of, maybe, I don't know, understand…" She couldn't quite bring herself to ask him for help, so she let the rest of that thought just hang. Even if he was one of her closest friends, he still got a kick of out torturing her, calling her a dumb girl and stuff like that.

To her surprise, he rolled over onto his side and propped his head up with one hand, his face serious in the dim glow of the nightlight. "They won't figure it out by themselves," he said. "Adults know how to do a lot of stuff, but when it comes to something like this, they're complete losers."

"That's for sure," she said, miserable enough to forget her superiority and come into his room. She sat down on the edge of his bed, curling her toes into his carpet so she didn't slide off with the bedspread that was already straggling half onto the floor. "I know I should be doing something, but what *can* I do? I'm just a kid."

"So am I," Joey pointed out, "but I got in my dad's face and made him straighten things out with Sara."

"You didn't get in his face, you threatened to go live with your mom."

"Well, it worked, didn't it?"

"I already live with my mom," Jessie said, "and I can't threaten to go live with Noah. That would mean he'd win, and I can't do that to my mom." She couldn't even imagine how much it would hurt her mom if she said something like that. Besides, she really didn't want to leave Erskine, and she knew better than to make a threat she wasn't prepared to deliver on. She might be only nine–almost ten—but her mom had taught her that lesson the hard way.

"You gotta do something to get their attention," Joey said with a yawn. "They won't try to fix the problem when they're unhappy, but they sure try when a kid isn't happy."

He flopped back down and pulled the sheets up to his chin, conversation over.

He'd given her a lot to think about, though, and that was what she did all night long. By morning she wasn't any closer to a solution, but she knew that nothing was going to get solved if she kept avoiding the problem. Noah and her mom had been doing that for ten years and look where it had gotten them.

Chapter Sixteen

Janey was gone, the bed beside him empty.

Noah should have been okay with that. How he felt, however, was disappointed. He tossed the covers back and went downstairs, not bothering to dress first. Noises from the kitchen drew him, but any notion of a big, restorative breakfast died a quick, painless death. Or nearly painless.

The sight of Janey, on her hands and knees on the floor, gave him a flashback that made him go weak. She'd been insatiable, curious and just as fearless in her sexuality as she was in every other area of her life. And if he touched her again, neither one of them were going to be able to walk for a week. "What are you doing?" He crossed the room to pour himself a cup of coffee, hoping she'd mistake the reason for the hoarseness in his voice. A man should really be sated after a night like he'd had.

Janey sat back on her heels, peering at him over the kitchen table. "I guess you hadn't noticed I've been refinishing the floor."

Noah realized the floor was sanded bare and smooth as Janey's bottom. It was hardly a comparison designed to give him ease. "I was too busy last night to pay attention to the floor—at least this one." He hunkered down beside her. "Now, if you want to talk about the hallway…"

The sexy smile Janey gave him spurred him on. "There are one or two flat surfaces we haven't christened yet," he said. "And then we can start on my house."

Janey's smile faded and she stared down at her gloved hands. Going outside meant the risk of being seen together, and that made her remember all the reasons why getting involved with Noah had been a bad idea to begin with. "Last night was wonderful, amazing." She looked up at him. "Heroic."

"But?"

Her gaze dropped again. "But it's over."

"Until tonight," Noah said, and then he kissed her.

As always, heat moved through her, but this time, it was accompanied by an infinite sadness—the knowledge that the end had finally come. She curled her fingers around his wrist and pulled his hand away from her cheek before she could lose herself in him.

"What's wrong?" Noah asked. "Janey?"

She took a minute to get her thoughts straight so she didn't say the wrong thing or reveal too much. "We can't keep doing this, Noah. I can't keep sleeping with you and ignoring the reason you're in town."

He went still. "Are you saying it's either you or my job?"

"No." She stood and leaned against the counter, her arms wrapped around herself, feeling a pain she knew well. It had gone away for a little while, two short, delusional days, but now it was back to stay. "I'm not foolish enough to believe you'd give up everything you've worked for to have another night in my bed." But she wanted to, oh, how she wanted to think he'd choose her over anything else in the world.

"I just…" *Love you*, she finished in silence. Again. "I can't be your lover and your enemy, Noah. It's too hard."

"Why do you have to be my enemy?"

She flipped open the newspaper to the real-estate section and handed it to him.

"Halliwell's General Store is for sale." He met her eyes, too shocked to sort out his own thoughts, let alone give them to her. If it had been any other business, it wouldn't have hit him as hard or been nearly as personal. But he couldn't allow it to get to him. "And you think it's because of Megamart?"

"Give me another reason."

"Mrs. Halliwell's in her seventies and it's past time to retire."

"She's been in her seventies for a while, Noah. She didn't suddenly decide she wants to stay home and knit sweaters all day."

"I'm sorry, Janey, it doesn't change anything."

"It already has. Don't you see, Noah? You'll build that store and then you'll leave. But Erskine is my home, and Jessie's. You can't change who you are or why you're here or what it's going to do to this town. And I can't ignore it anymore, no matter how much I'd like to."

She was ending it. It wasn't her words as much as the brittle look in her eyes that told him. So he took her in his arms one last time and kissed her. If it was going to be over then they might as well end it on a high note. Apparently, Janey felt the same way. She pressed the whole curvaceous length of her body against his and kissed him back.

"Mom!"

They froze, their mouths a breath away, staring at each other in mutual terror.

By the time Jessie raced into the kitchen, Noah was in a chair, the kitchen table between his daughter and his boxer-clad backside. She took one look at his bare chest, her mouth falling open as she glanced over at her mother and back at Noah again.

Sara showed up in the kitchen doorway a few seconds later. She did the look-at-Janey, look-at-Noah's-bare-chest, look-at-Janey-thing, too, but the expression on her face could best be described as a smirk. "Jessie insisted on coming home a day early," she said needlessly.

Janey could feel her cheeks burning. Noah wasn't as obviously embarrassed, but he shifted his chair a fraction forward. Any closer to the table and he'd be sitting on the other side.

"Go upstairs and put your stuff away," Janey said to Jessie.

"But Mom—"

"Now, Jessie."

She looked at her father and found no help there, so she went, dragging her feet and muttering about how she got sent to her room whenever anything interesting was going on.

But she wasn't all that upset, Janey noticed, sighing heavily. She could imagine what Jessie must be thinking, finding her father here in his underwear. What Janey didn't know was how she could possibly explain it without hurting her.

"Thanks for bringing her home," Janey said, trying to herd Sara out the door. She had at least four inches and a good twenty pounds on her best friend, but Sara wasn't budging. Instead, she ducked down so she could see beneath the kitchen table.

"Silk," she said, grinning at Noah. "Nice. I wish I could get Max to wear something like that, but he claims boxers bunch up when he rides a horse."

"Okay, that's it," Janey said, taking Sara by the arm and pulling her down the hall toward the front door.

"If you think I'm leaving now, Janey Walters, you can think again. I always have to hear everything secondhand in this town. For once I have a front-row seat and I'm not budging."

"How do you think Max would feel about you sharing his underwear preferences with me?"

"That's not fair."

"Sue me," Janey said, still headed for the front door with 110 pounds of redhead in tow. "I'll call you later. On the phone. You remember the phone, right? That magical device you could've used to call me before you brought Jessie home this morning?"

"Oh, no, you're not blaming this on me." Sara managed to

bring Janey to a halt. "How was I supposed to know you'd be…he'd be…that the two of you were…" she threw her hands up. "Maybe I should take Jessie out for breakfast."

"Yeah, and then she'll *really* wonder what's going on."

"I don't think she's wondering what went on," Sara said.

"No. She's wondering what will come of it. I can't believe I was so stupid."

"If anyone understands that kind of stupid, it's me."

Sara would, too; she'd gone through a similarly wrenching experience with Max. The difference was, there wouldn't be a happy ending to this fairy tale.

"I'm sorry," Sara said.

"It's not your fault." Janey walked Sara to the front door and stepped out onto the porch with her. "I knew better," she said. "I kept telling myself it was wrong, but…" Janey shook her head. "I'm just so tired of it all, Sara—the store, trying to keep up a pleasant front for Jessie. I'm barely sleeping, I can't hold on to a thought for more than a second at a time and I don't seem to have an appetite. I've lost ten pounds."

"Well, you've been complaining about that ten pounds for as long as I've known you."

"But I don't want to lose it because of him."

"You didn't lose it because of him, Janey, you lost it because you're in—"

"Don't say it." Janey paced across the front porch and leaned on the railing, but there was no peace in the familiar view of her town. What kind of woman fell in love with a man who walked in and out of her life so easily? He'd just about destroyed her ten years ago, and still she chose—

But she didn't choose. Love chose and dragged her along for the ride. "The question is what do I do about it? And don't tell me only I can answer that." She whirled to confront Sara as though her friend had thrown out that platitude. "He won't stay in town."

"Are you sure?"

"Yes."

"Janey—" Sara hesitated, clearly wrestling with her conscience "—I don't want you to think I'm defending Noah, but are you positive there are no feelings on his side?"

"He came here to build that Megamart in Plains City. That's more important to him than anything else."

Janey waited for the unquestioning support she needed so badly. Instead, Sara sat down on the swing.

"You know," she said, very nonchalantly, "if you don't block the store, he'll be here longer."

Janey was filled with such a surge of yearning that for a moment she couldn't breathe. She let herself think about how easy it would be to give in to what both Noah and she wanted. There was such a slim chance she'd stop him from building the store, anyway. What difference would it make if she ceded the fight now or lost it later? Wouldn't it be worth it to be with Noah again, to spend her nights lost in him and her days counting the minutes until they could be together again? She wasn't asking for much. A few weeks, a couple of precious months.

And at the end of them she'd be right back where she was now. Only without her self-respect. "He'll still leave once it's built, and I'll hate myself whenever I hear the name Megamart. Not to mention what it'll do to Jessie."

"Don't put too much of this on her, Janey. Jessie's as tough as her mom."

"Her mom's not so tough right now.

"All I'm saying is, Jessie will adapt to whatever happens. She might be a little hurt on the way, but kids are resilient. As long as she knows you love her, she'll be okay. And it won't hurt if you're happy, Janey."

Happy? Janey didn't know what that was, or how she could get it. She'd never stopped loving Noah, even when she'd believed he'd betrayed her ten years ago. She'd love him no matter how things turned out this time. Until she accepted that those feelings had to run their natural course, she would never be at peace.

"So what are you going to do?" Sara asked.

"As far as Noah's concerned? Nothing. As far as that store…" She'd do what she had to, Janey thought, just as Noah would. "I'm not sure," she said, "but it'll take more than a petition."

JANEY HALF EXPECTED Noah to be gone when she returned to the kitchen, but he was still there, sitting at the table, nursing a cup of coffee.

"We have to talk to Jessie," he said.

"What are we going to tell her?"

Noah stared into his cup, so Janey answered him. "Nothing's changed."

"You were always stronger than me, Janey."

"No, I just didn't have anything to prove to myself. I still don't."

He looked up at her, obviously puzzled by the anger in her voice.

"It's a lot easier to live in the present, Noah, when you're not always focused on the future."

"What's that supposed to mean?"

"I'm not speaking in code. You're so concerned about where you're going that you don't notice how you're getting there. And when you get there, you don't take the time to enjoy it—you just set your sights on some other place you want to get to."

"And your way is better? You're so busy living in the present that you don't think about the future at all."

"I think about it."

"When you get there, Janey, will you have accomplished any of your dreams? And if not, are you going to regret it?"

"No one gets through life without regrets, Noah."

"Not me," he said. "If I don't make my goals, at least I'll know I tried."

"And what will you have to show for it?"

That stopped him, and she imagined he was toting up his life and coming up empty, except for the career she didn't respect. And when he said, "I have a daughter," she wanted to cry.

"*I* have a daughter," she said gently. "You have a friend you'll visit now and then. You'll be there for what you think are the important occasions in Jessie's life—graduations, her wedding. But you won't be there for her in the way that's really important, Noah. You won't be there when she breaks up with a boyfriend and she's hurting and needs you to hug her. And you won't be there when she gets all As on her report card and wants to hug you. You're going to be off in Los Angeles working for the next promotion and catching up with her once a week on the phone. If you do that much."

"There's nothing keeping me from getting married and having a family of my own."

"But you won't stop long enough for that, Noah."

"I don't see you rushing to the altar with Barney Fife."

Janey smiled, a curving of her mouth that was unbearably sad. "No," she said. "I wouldn't marry Clary even if he asked me. I'd be all wrong for him."

"Because you don't belong in this backwater."

"Because I don't love him." She got to her feet and walked to the door, pausing with her hand on the door frame to look back at him. "I know what that kind of love feels like, and Clary deserves to find it for himself."

Noah flung himself out of his chair and took his cup to the sink, emptying and rinsing it with sharp, angry movements. He put the cup on the drainboard and turned to head upstairs, wanting only to collect his clothes and go home to lick his wounds.

Jessie was standing in the entrance to the kitchen, the expression on her face so much like her mother's, the pain almost brought him to his knees. He closed his eyes to give himself a chance to think. "How much of that did you hear?" he asked.

But it was Janey who said dismally, "All of it."

Chapter Seventeen

Her mom had tried to talk to her. So had Noah. But Jessie hadn't been ready to hear their excuses, so she'd escaped to the tower room. Her world looked the same as it always had from those windows, the town spread out around the house, the fields and pastures and mountains beyond the same as they'd been her whole life. It didn't seem as if anything could change that. But it would be pretending to think it couldn't *look* the same and still be different. That's how it was with her, right? She hadn't grown an inch but everything that really mattered about her had changed, and it wasn't ever going to change back.

After what happened she hadn't felt like keeping her standing date for Sunday tea with Mrs. Halliwell, but her mom had insisted. She told Jessie it would be good for her to get out of the house for a little while, and Jessie had to admit she did feel better, kind of calmer. Mrs. Halliwell's house, crammed with all sorts of neat stuff and always smelling like chocolate-chip cookies, just did that to a person. But the best thing for her, Jessie thought, would be if her parents stopped fighting with each other.

"You're awfully quiet today," Mrs. Halliwell said. "What have you been up to lately?"

"I went to stay with Sara and Max for a couple of days."

"You've been staying there a lot lately."

Jessie was too young to know what a leading question was, but she felt the pressure to answer it. "Mom and Noah were fighting at the Fourth of July celebration," she said. She liked Mrs. Halliwell; she was an adult and everything, but she never corrected her grammar, or told her to behave herself. And she'd been around a long, long—Jessie glanced up at the white hair and wrinkled face—long time, so maybe she would be able to help. "When I got home today, Noah was there." She stacked the cookies on her plate into a little lopsided tower so she wouldn't have to look at Mrs. H. when she told her the embarrassing stuff. "It was in the morning, and my mom was dressed but Noah was—"

"I think I understand," Mrs. Halliwell said.

"That should mean they're getting back together, shouldn't it? But they had me and they didn't get together." She knocked over her stack of cookies. "Maybe it's me. I don't think Noah wants kids."

"You can stop that right now, young lady." Jessie straightened up, mouth and eyes wide because Mrs. H. never talked to her that way. "What happened between Janey and Noah ten years ago had nothing to do with you, and whether or not they end up together is up to them."

"But I heard them talking—after. My mom sent me upstairs to put my stuff away, and I did that." Mrs. Halliwell's smiling face told Jessie she was busted—but what did it matter now? "When I came down, Sara was gone and my mom and Noah were in the kitchen talking to each other, like, you know, not yelling but mad anyway."

"They probably didn't want to be overheard," Mrs. Halliwell pointed out.

"Why do they think it's better for me if I don't know what's going on?" Jessie demanded, launching herself to her feet. "My mom told Noah he'd never get married and have a family, and she said she doesn't love Clary."

"Then she shouldn't marry him," Mrs. Halliwell said immediately. "It wouldn't be fair to either of them, or to you in the long run."

"That's what my mom said." Jessie dropped into her chair again, rubbing at her middle. Mrs. Halliwell nudged her teacup closer, so Jessie took a drink, thinking it would make Mrs. H. happy, but the warm tea really did help soothe her stomach.

"It's not like Clary's going to leave town, so the two of you will still be friends."

"Yeah," Jessie said.

"The important thing for you to know is that your parents want what's best for you, Jessie. They both love you."

"How do you know my dad loves me?"

"Well, I've known him since he was about your age." Mrs. Halliwell bit into a cookie. It was all Jessie could do to wait until she'd chewed and swallowed, but manners were a very important part of a tea party, and you just didn't ask someone a question while she had food in her mouth.

As soon as Mrs. Halliwell had taken a sip of her tea, though, Jessie pounced. "You knew him when he lived here?" she asked, astonished that she hadn't thought of it before. "What was he like?"

"Very troubled," Mrs. Halliwell said. "He didn't have a good family life, Jessie. His mother died when he was young, and his father...His father didn't think about how his decisions affected Noah."

"He doesn't sound very nice."

"Well," Mrs. Halliwell said. "You have to understand things were different back then. I mean, women weren't exactly what you'd call equal citizens, and Jed Bryant was one of those men who believed women didn't have the brains to make decisions, anyway."

"And Noah was only a kid," Jessie said, slouching down

in her chair and staring miserably at her plate of untouched cookies. "Nobody listens to what a kid wants."

"That's just the self-pity talking," Mrs. Halliwell said firmly. "You know your mother and Noah care about you."

"They sure have a funny way of showing it."

"There's a lot more going on between them than just you, kiddo. They were sweethearts from the second they laid eyes on each other in grade school. Everyone thought they'd get married."

Jessie straightened. "Why didn't they?"

"Your daddy left, and your mom was too proud to go after him."

"That's what they told me."

"And it's the truth."

But Jessie didn't want it to be the truth. "Joey Devlin said I should come up with something to get them to change their minds, like if they knew how unhappy I was, maybe they'd try harder to be nice to each other. But they already know how unhappy I am, and that's not working. I've been trying to come up with a plan, but..." She looked hopefully at Mrs. Halliwell. "I don't have a clue."

"Do you really want to trick them into doing something for your sake?"

Jessie wanted to say yes, but she had a feeling that wasn't the right answer so she just shrugged.

"Let me ask you this," Mrs. Halliwell said. "If you trick them into staying together, and they're not happy, how long will it be before you start to feel guilty?"

Jessie hung her head.

"And then you won't be happy, either."

"But what about the Megamart? My mom thinks it's bad for Erskine. Noah says it's not."

"You should let them sort it out."

"But what do you think? I mean, aren't you worried about your store?"

For the first time Jessie could ever recall, Mrs. Halliwell seemed uncomfortable. "Well, now, I wanted to talk to you about that. It's not easy, Jessie, so I'm going to give it to you straight. I've put the General Store up for sale."

Jessie felt like Toaster had kicked her in the stomach. She set her cookie down, and stared at Mrs. Halliwell, who was wiping tears off her cheeks. "It's not the Megamart or, well…" Mrs. Halliwell took a sip of her tea and spent forever putting the cup back just so on the saucer. "The winters here have been getting harder and harder on me, Jessie. My sister is in Arizona and I've been thinking about moving there for a long while, but it seems… Noah's only doing what he thinks is right for Erskine, I know that. But if the town is going to change, I'd like to remember it the way it is now, so this feels like the best time for me to pick up and go."

Jessie heard a sound at the front door; she turned around and there stood Noah. She was on her feet without realizing it, fists clenched in anger. "It's all your fault!" she yelled at him. He was her dad, but he wouldn't stay in town, her mom wasn't going to marry Clary and she had a feeling it was because of Noah, and now Mrs. Halliwell, whom she'd always secretly thought of as her grandmother, was moving away. "I hate you. I wish you'd never come back here."

She tried to run past him, but he caught her around the middle and hauled her into a hug. She would've fought her way free but all she could do was stay there, wrapped in his arms, bawling.

"Your mom told me you have tea over here every Sunday," he said when her sobs subsided.

He let her pull free and turn away from him to wipe her face. She felt stupid, crying like a baby, but she also felt better—her head was kind of achy, but at least her stomach wasn't all knotted up anymore, and she could breathe without feeling like one of Joey's cats was sitting on her chest.

"With the way things are between your mom and me, I figured it'd be best if I talked to you over here first."

"Mrs. Halliwell is putting her store up for sale," Jessie said.

She looked at him, her tear-stained face just as set, her gaze just as direct and challenging as her mother's. Noah abandoned any plans he might have had to soften the truth. Jessie wanted it straight up, and that was the way he'd give it to her. "And you're blaming me."

"Mrs. Halliwell says you're only doing what you think is right, and so is my mom, and that I should let you guys sort it out."

"Mrs. H. is a pretty smart cookie," Noah said.

"It hurts."

"Yeah," he said, "it does."

"Then why are you doing it?"

Noah ran a hand through his hair, wondering where to start. "You're probably too young to realize how a town like this works."

She rolled her eyes.

"Okay, pretend I didn't say that. Every year when the senior class graduates from Plains City High School, what happens?"

"Some of them go to college," Jessie said.

"And when they graduate from college, they don't come back here—they go somewhere else because they have to in order to find jobs. And the kids who don't go to college join the army, and the ones who don't do either still have to leave town to get jobs."

"Not always."

"Sure, one or two stay in town and work at the bakery or the Five-And-Dime."

"What's wrong with that?" Jessie asked.

"Nothing. And there are times when someone stays to

work at a family ranch, or inherits one, like Sam Tucker and Max Devlin. But anybody who wants another career has to leave town."

"And the Megamart will change that?"

"Well, anyone who wants a career in retail will get that opportunity, and having the store nearby will attract other businesses."

"Why here?"

Trust Jessie to cut right to the heart of the matter. If she'd been an average nine-year-old she wouldn't have picked up on that. But she wasn't an average nine-year-old. She was Janey's daughter. And his. "I grew up here, and I wanted to do something for other kids growing up poor as dirt, like I did. I wanted to bring jobs and progress to the area."

"But there are people, like my mom, who don't think it's going to happen like that."

"Well…I think your mom's still mad about the past and that's part of why she's against the store."

"And that has nothing to do with why you're here."

"No."

"That's bull—" she stopped, snuck a look at his face and wisely chose not to finish that sentiment. "I don't get why you left town in the first place when you were in love with my mom—Mrs. Halliwell said so. And I don't understand why you won't admit you still love her."

Noah opened his mouth, but nothing came out. Even if there'd been a thought in his head, there wasn't any air in his lungs. "That's just wishful thinking," he said after he'd managed to draw breath. "I'll always be around, we'll be a family, but we won't live together."

"You're just being stupid," Jessie snapped. "You and Mom are both being stupid. You love her, she loves you and you're letting this stupid store get in the way."

"Jessie—"

"No." She slapped his hand away. "You're just like your dad."

"Mrs. Halliwell has been doing a lot of talking," he muttered.

"She doesn't treat me like a kid. She explains things like how your dad got to make all the decisions and you and your mom just had to go along with them. That's what you're doing. You decided what's good for us, and what we want doesn't matter. You're just like your father."

"That's not true, Jessie." But maybe it was, he realized in horrified fascination.

He'd left town without a backward glance, gone as far away from Jed Bryant as he could get so he could be his own man and make his own decisions. But everything he'd done, every choice he'd made, was because of his father. He'd been in love with Janey, but he'd left her because he was afraid that if he didn't, he'd drag her down. When that hadn't been enough, he'd worked himself half to death getting through college, then attacked his career with an almost maniacal need to be successful. This store was his last-ditch effort to prove he wasn't a failure, but who was he proving it to? A man who'd been dead for the better part of a decade and who wouldn't care, anyway?

Noah looked at Jessie, so proud of her he felt as if his heart would burst apart. She had the courage he'd never had, to speak up to her father and tell him how she felt. If he'd done that, his old man would have smacked him down—but he could hurt Jessie just as effectively without violence. All he had to do was ignore her.

He'd be damned, he thought, if he'd be like his father where she was concerned. "You're right about my old—about my father. Because of the way he treated me, I couldn't wait to get out of this town." He knelt down so he was at eye level with her. "And now he's dead and it's too late for me to change the bad feelings between him and me. I don't want it to be the same with us, Jessie."

"Me neither, but the store—"

"What do you say we just work on us and leave my job out of it?"

She stared down at her shoes, her teeth sunk in her bottom lip. She mulled it over for what seemed like an eternity, then said, "Okay."

Noah caught her up into a hug, and after a minute, she threw her arms around his neck and hugged him back. Nothing in the world could have rivaled that feeling—not getting the store built, not patching things up once and for all with Janey, not getting elected president of the United States. There was no comparison. Having the trust of someone so honest and innocent was scary and incredible all at once.

And so help him, he'd wrap up his business and find a way to make peace with Janey. He wasn't promising Jessie anything, but he couldn't stand to see her hurt and upset anymore.

"I love you, Jessie," he said.

She pulled back and looked into his face. "I love you, too. Dad."

And a heart that had been empty for so long discovered again how it felt to love and be loved.

And it wanted more.

Chapter Eighteen

Noah hadn't had a good night's sleep in more than a week, two if he counted the nights he and Janey had spent together, and he might as well; she was equally responsible for keeping him up, whether she was in his bed or not.

He'd been anything but ready to end their involvement. Even if two nights had been enough to satisfy the fantasies about her that had plagued him forever, she'd only whetted his appetite for more.

Then Jessie had caught them together that last morning and all hell had broken loose. Janey refused to even talk to him, and the one conversation he'd had with Jessie hadn't exactly filled him with peace. But the look in her eyes when she said "I love you," when she'd called him "Dad"... There weren't words for what he felt.

He didn't know what he found more troubling—the faith he'd seen shining on his daughter's face, or the thought that she was still hoping he'd call off the store. All he knew was that his conscience was kicking up a storm, and he didn't like it. And when he didn't like something, he generally found that burying himself in work was the answer; either he'd find a way to fix his problem, or he'd forget about it.

He'd decided the best thing to do was to take a trip back to Megamart's California office. His boss had been bugging him for a progress report, and it didn't take a genius to figure out he wasn't happy with Noah's progress—or lack of it. Noah could have called him on the phone or e-mailed his report, but his personality was one of the things that had gotten him where he was. It wasn't something he could use at a distance.

Of course, he'd arrived at the office in L.A. with the deck stacked in his favor. With town sentiment mostly on his side, it had been easy to complete the survey and turn it in to the Plains City town council. He'd managed to convince his boss that the building permit was only a formality, which got him off the hook for the moment. He should have gone back to Montana right away. He had a meeting with the Plains City town council the next day.

But he'd felt a pressing need to be back in his own house with its astounding view, its perfect landscaping and climate-controlled comforts. There was no food in the refrigerator; there rarely was. But if he'd been hungry he could've picked up the phone and had anything from pizza to a gourmet meal delivered in a matter of minutes.

This house and everything it represented had been his choice. He hadn't been saddled with some big old Victorian with small rooms, narrow staircases and a huge maintenance bill that he was bound to out of love and nostalgia. He was free. If his father had given him nothing else, he'd at least given Noah that.

But he didn't feel free. He was uncertain and confused. When he'd pitched the idea of building a Megamart in Plains City, his reasons had been so simple and clear-cut. The company would make money, and his career would get a boost. The benefits to Plains City and Erskine—and he'd been so sure there would be benefits—would be frosting on the cake.

The cake had turned to sawdust, though, and the only thing he was so sure of now was that he wanted a place in his daughter's life. Being back in Los Angeles, amid all the trappings of his success, wasn't helping him sort out anything else—especially what to do about Janey. If anything.

He'd stripped and climbed in between cool sheets on his king-size bed, and stared at the ceiling all night. He'd finally managed to doze off just before dawn, only to miss his plane and have to take a later flight. He'd gone straight from the airport to Plains City, and almost missed his meeting with the town council to review the survey, now that they'd had a chance to read it. It might have been better if he had missed the meeting.

"Your task was to convince us that the Megamart would not harm the businesses in the surrounding communities."

Noah jerked upright, cursing himself for letting his mind wander yet again. He looked into the face of Mrs. Bannock, head of the town council. "I believe I've shown that," he said, "but you can check out my facts and figures for yourself."

"Oh, we intend to."

Noah got to his feet, but he wasn't about to be dismissed so easily. "Can you give me an idea when you're going to issue the building permit? A few weeks ago it was a formality. Now you've got me jumping through hoops."

The other council members all looked to Mrs. Bannock, who didn't seem inclined to answer at first. Then she seemed to relent a little. "We need to tread carefully, Mr. Bryant. Once we're sure all the ramifications have been considered, we'll proceed."

"Proceed how?" Noah asked. Proceed to give him a permit, or proceed to shut him down? But this time the dismissal was final. The Plains City Five filed out of the room, leaving him, yet again, to make the drive between Plains City and Erskine empty-handed.

And it was all Janey's fault. All of it. The sleepless nights, the listless days, his boss's displeasure and the fact that instead of helping him remember what he'd worked so hard for, going home had only made him wonder what he'd expected to find there.

To make matters worse, when he pulled into Erskine, she was the first person he saw, talking to Clary Beeber, her gaze glued to his face as if the sun rose and set there.

Noah had had no intention of stopping, but she put her hand on Clary's arm just then, and every muscle in Noah's body tensed up. The car jerked forward with a screech of rubber, and they both looked over at him, leaving Noah with no choice but to steer over to the curb as if that had been his intent all along. He started to ease up behind Clary's white SUV just as Clary and Janey burst out laughing.

He hit the cruiser. The first foot or two of the Porsche's low, sloping hood slid right under Clary's much higher rear bumper. He didn't even scratch the chrome on the SUV, and it didn't occur to him until later that the damage he'd done to his car should have been his foremost concern. All he could do was wonder why Janey appeared so happy and rested. Where were the dark circles? The signs of strain, confusion and self-doubt he'd been suffering?

He backed his car up and got out. The deputy sheriff stepped forward and in front of Janey. All she had to do was murmur Clary's name and he returned to her side like a dog at heel.

"Didn't take you long," Noah muttered.

"Only ten years," Janey said, a slight quirk to one corner of her mouth.

He turned to Clary, looked him up and down. "Kind of a step down, isn't he?"

"I'm not sure what he's ticked off about," Clary said, "but I know an insult when I hear one." He started for Noah.

Janey got in front of him, planted both hands on his chest and dug her heels in.

"Let him go," Noah growled.

"He's trying to pick a fight because he's angry with me, Clary. If you hit him, you'll only be giving him what he wants."

Clary backed off, but he clearly wasn't happy about it. "Can I put him in jail?"

"For what?"

"Disturbing the peace."

"You're the one who's trying to punch me," Noah pointed out in a tone meant to inflame the other man even more.

"Then how about reckless driving?"

"Just because he's being a horse's ass, Clary, it doesn't mean you have to make it a matched set."

Clary stared at Noah, then nodded tightly. He walked away, shooting Noah a final pitying look—which was more infuriating than if he'd turned around and socked him in the face.

"And you," she said, turning to confront Noah, "you look tired."

"You don't," he replied, glancing over at Clary Beeber's disappearing truck. "Why is that?"

He looked back in time to see hurt flash across her face, but she banished it almost before he could feel guilty for putting it there. "Jessie told me you were going out of town for a few days."

Five, and they'd been hell. Noah wanted to yell at her, take her by the shoulders and kiss some sense into her—but neither of those things would make one bit of difference. She'd still be on the opposite side of a line neither of them would cross.

"I went home." He made it sound as casual as he could while putting the emphasis on that last word. "There was stuff I couldn't handle over the phone, people I wanted to see in person. You're not the only one who has friends."

Janey shook her head, and in her eyes he suddenly saw the weariness he felt. Odd, Noah thought, how it didn't make him feel any better.

"I'm sorry you don't understand why I had to take a stand," she said, "and I'm sorry you could think— Oh, the hell with you. Think whatever you want. Whatever makes it easy for you. Isn't that how you always deal with difficult situations?"

She started to walk away.

"I'm sorry, Janey," Noah called after her. He didn't really believe she'd move on so quickly and easily, but the idea of her with another man... It killed him—there was no other way to put it—but that didn't give him the right to make her suffer, too. "I'm in a foul mood. I probably shouldn't be telling you this, but I just came from Plains City."

She whirled around and came back, stopping just out of arms' reach. "I didn't know there was a council meeting today."

"It wasn't an official meeting. They wanted to check out the study. I didn't do a very good job of presenting it." His gaze met hers, held. "I guess my mind wasn't entirely on business."

She set off down the boardwalk again, not surprised when he followed her. "I don't know what you said to Jessie last Sunday, but she seems happier."

"At least one of us is," Noah muttered.

Janey refused to let him drag her back into an argument that would end with both of them losing. "I wanted to thank you for setting her mind at rest, Noah. She's even coming to terms with Mrs. Halliwell's decision to sell the store, although I'm not so sure that's going to happen, anyway. If the Megamart deal goes though, it's unlikely she'll find a buyer."

Noah's jaw worked for a second. "She may not be able to sell it as is, but let's face it, Janey, that kind of store has been obsolete for at least fifty years. I'll make sure she sees some money out of it, if nothing else."

"And the rest of the people around here who suffer because of Megamart, are you going to take a personal interest in them, as well?"

"You know I can't."

"You could call off the store."

"It's too late for that," Noah said. "Property's been bought, Megamart is committed, and there are events in motion that can't be stopped." Even if a part of him wished otherwise... "But when it's all over—"

"Don't make promises you can't keep. Or may not want to."

That brought a slight smile to his face. "Still think you can stop me?"

"I have to try."

"Janey..." He pulled her with him beneath an awning, and brought her close.

She stepped back. "I wish things were different, Noah."

He took a deep breath, and when that failed to cool him down, took another and another, finally dropping his hand back to his side. There was only one course open to him. He'd get this settled once and for all, and when it was over, and he'd won...Janey wouldn't want anything to do with him. He'd be the father of her daughter, nothing else.

That hurt, more than he'd imagined possible. The depth of his hurt scared him, enough to send him scurrying back from the edge of the precipice that yawned before him.

He'd had a goal when he came to town; that goal hadn't changed, and it was time to be ruthless. He took one last look at Janey. "Watch *Montana In The Morning* tomorrow," he said. Then he turned his back on her and walked away.

WITH EVERYONE CALLING to tell her Noah was on the most popular morning show in the state, Janey and Jessie could hardly have missed *Montana In The Morning*—or the bouncy blond hostess who was flirting with him. And the way he was flirting right back.

It took Janey a moment to remember that their behavior was not the issue. She needed to focus on the way he answered the questions, and when the hostess stopped giggling and flipping her hair long enough to ask one, Janey finally understood how Noah had gotten where he was at such a young age.

He was good. He was slicker at laying out Megamart's case than a grifter finessing a little old lady out of her life's savings. First he mentioned the downside, the possible effects of a big store on a small community—so the listeners would have plenty of time to forget there even was a downside. And why would they want to remember after he got done talking about jobs, tax benefits, prosperity and progress? He couldn't have made it look any better if he'd personally handed out a pair of rose-colored glasses to everyone in the viewing audience.

He had no idea why he hadn't been allowed to break ground yet, he said with the perfect mixture of puzzlement and sadness. And then he turned up the heat. He stopped just short of accusing the Plains City town council of giving him the go-ahead, then dragging their feet over the building permit. And for the final coup de grâce, he let on that he might, just might, have to entertain other locations.

He did it all with a smile sure to charm the women and an expression of sincerity guaranteed to reassure the men. By the time the show wrapped, there must've been dozens of small communities clamoring for a chance to meet with him, and thousands of people counting on money they hadn't even earned yet.

The Plains City Five had to be sweating in their support hose, worried their nice, new tax revenue was about to fly the coop.

"So," Jessie said, turning away from the television screen. "Was that good?"

"For Noah," Janey replied. "He probably had the building permit before he left the studio."

"Does that mean he wins?"

"Not if I have anything to say about it."

"Oh." Jessie stared at her hands for a minute, then looked up, her face filled with uncertainty. "Do you…If it wasn't for the store, would you want to… The other morning when I came home from Sara and Max's—"

"I still love him," Janey said, and although Jessie rolled her eyes and scrunched up her face, it was clear that was exactly what she'd been trying to ask. Janey hated that she had to qualify her answer, but it was necessary for Jessie to understand everything. "The store has nothing to do with why we won't end up together, Jessie. My life is here, and your father's life is in Los Angeles." It hurt her still to say it. "I'm sorry about all of this, kiddo, but whether or not the Megamart gets built in Plains City, Noah won't stay in town. I'm sure he'll call you and write and visit you whenever he can."

"He said he would. He asked if we could just work on us and leave the store out of it."

"Pretty smart," Janey said, and meant it. "The store isn't a problem for you and me, so it shouldn't be one for you and your dad."

"Yeah." Jessie heaved a truly enormous sigh.

"It'll be over one way or the other soon."

"I know, and I want it to be over. I promised Dad I'd stay out of it, but Mom…" She looked up and the slight pang Janey had felt at hearing her call Noah "Dad" was replaced by a flood of love and pride almost too big to contain. "Do what you have to do," Jessie finished.

Janey laughed, somewhat bemused. "Are you taking sides?"

"No, but if something was this important to me, you'd be all for it, even if you didn't agree with me."

Janey gathered Jessie into her arms, thankful she didn't resist. They both needed the comfort. Janey could have used some inspiration about then, too, but she'd settle for a hug from her daughter.

Chapter Nineteen

Janey walked out the back door of her house, crossed from her fenceless backyard to Noah's and settled down beside him on the back stoop of his rented house, which was kitty-corner behind hers. She was careful not to touch him, and he didn't touch her.

She knew he expected her to retaliate for his appearance on *Mountain In The Morning,* and she would. But not tonight.

"You've been busy," she said.

"You haven't?"

She shrugged. "I had dinner at Sara and Max's. Jessie's spending the night with Mrs. Halliwell…" And she'd put the basics of her plan in motion. Noah figured that store was a sure thing, but he underestimated the Erskine gossip machine. This time tomorrow, if everything went how she wanted, the Plains City Megamart would be history. And so would Noah.

"Janey, I just came back from Plains City. I got the permit."

"You didn't give the town council much choice."

"You're right, I didn't."

She looked over at him, surprised. "You sound disappointed."

He straightened, and when he met her eyes, there was nothing but conviction there. "Why would I be disappointed about the permit?"

"Okay, then you're disappointed because you're not with that flirty blond hostess."

"I could have been," Noah said. He would have been, before Janey. Now he found that kind of obvious come-on ridiculous instead of flattering. "Why aren't you out with Clary?"

"Could have been," she parroted with a slight smile. "I could've had you arrested before your interview, for that matter."

"I wonder how you restrained yourself."

"It wasn't easy." None of this had been easy.

Silence fell. Well, not silence, really—crickets chirped, a plane flew overhead, dogs barked at each other and night fell with something like a sigh. The sky gradually grew dark except for a narrowing band of rainbow colors in the west, and the mosquitoes started to come out.

Janey got to her feet. "Tomorrow's going to decide it all."

"Still trying to stop me?"

"Yes." She scratched absently at a mosquito bite while she got her mind in order. "I've thought long and hard about *why* the last few days, Noah. You know, wondering if the reason I'm so against this store is because of what happened ten years ago."

He frowned.

"It hurt, the way you left me, but I think what's worse is what I did to myself."

"Janey—"

"No, I need to say this. You rejected me when you left, Noah, whether you intended to or not. But I knew all along that it was Erskine you were rejecting, as well. I guess I kind of felt like we belonged together, me and Jessie and this town. Now I realize I was only hiding here, afraid to take the chance of being hurt again, while you went off and chased your dreams."

Was that what he'd been doing? Noah found himself wondering. Chasing his dreams? Sometimes it felt more like they were chasing him, constantly pushing him higher and faster so he never got a chance to enjoy what he'd earned. Ten years ago he'd made a decision to leave Erskine. He'd spent every moment since trying to justify that decision, he realized, and trying not to imagine what his life might've been like if he'd made other choices.

The answer stood in front of him, but he'd found out too late. He'd come back to town with an agenda that put an insurmountable wall between himself and the only woman he'd ever love.

"Noah…"

He looked up at her, struck by the uncertainty in her eyes.

"You'll be leaving tomorrow."

"I think I should."

"Then tonight… I know I said it made me feel like a hypocrite, but—"

Noah was on his feet, his mouth silencing her before she could change her mind.

Before, they'd always come together in a flash of physical desire that seared away emotion. Janey had told herself it was better that way; she could afford to enjoy what he did to her body, so long as she protected her heart.

This time she let love lead the way. She spared herself nothing, gave herself to him in every way possible and filled herself with what he gave in return. And if his was only a physical giving, if his feelings remained untouched, perhaps it was for the best. It would only hurt more to know that he loved her, and that it wasn't enough for him.

JANEY LEFT IN THE NIGHT, thinking him asleep.

Noah let her go. It would be easier.

It wasn't how he always justified his most difficult decisions. He'd left Janey with no goodbye ten years ago and told himself it was easier for her, but he admitted now that he simply hadn't been strong enough to face her. He'd give the news conference today and leave Erskine behind forever because it was easier to follow that course than to throw away everything he'd worked so long to achieve.

He rose, showered, packed and watched Erskine disappear in his rearview mirror for the last time. It made no sense to change his entire life for the chance at a relationship with a woman who might not even want him. She hadn't said she loved him, after all....

But she did. Noah knew it, yet still he let her walk away.

He stepped up to the podium in front of the Johnson County Courthouse and surveyed the motley assortment of people arrayed in front of him. He could have held the press conference in Plains City, but he'd hoped that going to the county seat, with its government buildings and larger population, would net him more of a turnout from the media. Instead he got fledgling newspaper reporters and government workers who would've happily watched grass grow rather than sit at their government-issue desks and speak to disgruntled taxpayers. The construction of the Megamart store being built in Plains City was obviously such a minor issue that only one camera crew had been dispatched to record the event for posterity. This, then, was his greatest weapon, Noah realized, the unbeatable force he'd had no hand in bringing to bear and Janey had no hope of beating. Apathy.

It didn't really matter what he said, or how he said it, but he launched into his prepared speech, anyway. It went pretty well, too. Noah knew he was good at this sort of thing—giving speeches, swaying a crowd. The reporters perked up and a few of them even bothered to jot down a quote to use in their article or newscast.

And then he lost them, just one or two at first. Those on

the outer edge swiveled at the sound of screeching brakes, followed by the sound of what Noah mistook for thunder rumbling in the distance. It rumbled on long after it should have stopped, getting louder and acquiring some tinny-sounding sort of accompaniment.

Instead of tuning in to his speech again, the reporters began moving across the raised concrete landing, so preoccupied with what was happening on the road below that one of the men went too far and tumbled down the steps. Noah watched him get up, absently dusting himself off without ever looking away from whatever was going on. Horns honked and traffic in front of the courthouse slowed, then ground to a halt altogether.

By then Noah had long since given up on his speech. When the camera crew turned away from him and started filming the activity on the street, he surrendered what little pride he had left and joined the crowd. And found himself staring and gaping, as incredulous as everyone else.

A woman walked sedately up the center of the street, traffic behind her stopped dead. She wore a white blouse buttoned to the neck over the voluminous black skirts of an era a century gone, and in her hands she carried a hatchet—the trademark weapon of Carry Nation, the famed temperance leader and saloon-wrecker. It was Janey Walters, come to smash the modern version of the community-destroying saloon. The Megamart store.

Behind Janey marched a phalanx of other women, most of them faces he recognized from Erskine. Some of them were dressed as she was, others in jeans and T-shirts. Big Ed and a couple of his boys were at the back of the small parade, one of them beating relentlessly on a snare drum while the others picked out a reedy unrecognizable tune. Unrecognizable partly because they weren't very good, but mostly because the women in front of them were chanting "Down With Megamart," and nothing much was audible over their strident voices.

Noah should've been angry. Instead a slow smile curved ̱ ̱ ꜱ mouth, respect and admiration unfurling warmly inside him.

Here was a woman who'd settled quietly into small-town life, a woman who'd dedicated her life to raising her daughter and making sure that daughter knew she was loved and wanted, despite the circumstances of her birth. Yet she believed in her cause so deeply that she had the courage to cause a public controversy and risk a very public defeat, not to mention embarrassing Jessie.

There was something else Noah couldn't ignore. He loved her. It should've brought him joy instead of a dull ache just below his ribs. It would've brought him happiness, if he hadn't already made it impossible for them to be together.

When Janey arrived at the Johnson County Courthouse, she led her little parade up the steps. The pack of reporters closed in, shouting questions and preventing her from getting to the top where the podium had been set up. Noah picked up the microphone and made a brief request that she be let through. If nothing else, she deserved to have her say.

It was her bad luck that county courthouses nearly always had a police station close by—in this case right next door. As she made her way across the wide concrete landing where the press conference had been held, four police officers burst through the growing crowd, reaching for her. Noah positioned himself between Janey and the cops, his hands in the air.

"Step aside, sir," an officer commanded.

"You don't need to arrest her," Noah said, aware of the reporters pressing in. Every single one of them was writing frantically in a pad, one of them mumbling a curse that he hadn't brought a tape recorder. Noah remembered the camera crew and looked around frantically, hissing out a breath when he found the cameraman standing on the raised wall a few feet away, tape rolling. A further search located a hand jammed between two of the reporters at the front of the crowd. He couldn't for the life of him tell who it belonged to, but all that mattered to him was the black knob of the microphone clutched in the white-knuckled fingers.

He should've been searching for a way to spin this in Megamart's favor, but he was so torn. The thought of losing his job was something he'd never been able to stand, but losing Janey—

The cops reached for her again and he made the only decision he could. "Miss Walters is staging a peaceful demonstration—and a very bold and creative one," he said, loud enough for everyone to hear. As he'd intended, laughter rippled through the crowd.

"I'm sorry, sir, but she's breaking about five laws," an officer said. "Disturbing the peace, to begin with."

"Let her speak!" one of her supporters yelled out, and the chant of "Speech, speech, speech," was taken up by the rest of them—with the reporters joining in.

Janey turned to face the crowd, her eyes sparkling with the light of battle as she lifted the hatchet over her head to acknowledge the support. In the press of people she accidentally elbowed one of the police officers and narrowly missed taking another's ear off with the hatchet.

One of the officers took it away from her and two others took hold of her.

"Just give me a few minutes," she said, beginning to struggle.

The cops only held on tighter, one of them pulling his handcuffs out. Noah caught the guy's wrist before he could slap them on Janey. "Maybe you should go with them and get this straightened out," he said to her.

"I have something to say. I did this so people would listen to me."

"And they will, just not now."

The police closed in around her and began herding her—respectfully, Noah was glad to see—toward the jail.

Janey, of course, resisted. She turned around suddenly, and tried to get the microphone. One of the officers stepped in front of her, they collided, and Janey, being by far the lighter of the two, wound up on her backside.

"Let her talk," one of the reporters called. Again the chant of "Speech" was picked up until everyone was saying that single word over and over.

Noah approached Janey, who was on her feet again, and gave her a long look. "You might as well let her say her piece," he said to the cop in charge. "It's that or you're going to have a riot on your hands."

The older police officer grinned, taking in the hodgepodge of lunching office workers, reporters and parade participants. "You're joking, right?"

"There won't be a riot," Janey said, sending her contingent of the crowd a quelling glare—because you could take the ladies out of Erskine but, well, the rest of it went without saying. "Just give me a couple of minutes, and then you can cart me off to a nice, quiet, peaceful jail cell."

Noah stepped back as Janey was led to the podium. He had to give her credit. There she stood in her pioneer garb on a day that had to be ninety degrees in the shade and she couldn't have appeared more cool and composed.

"I don't really have a prepared speech," she began, reaching up to adjust the microphone. "I'm only following in the footsteps of other women who have had no real power and still worked to create societal change, women like Carry Nation, Susan B. Anthony, even Lady Godiva."

"Lady Godiva," a man shouted from the back of the crowd. "Now there's someone I'd be happy to, uh, listen to."

"And that's the problem," Janey fired back as the laughter died away. "In order to get attention these days, there has to be sex or violence involved. What does that say about our society? What does it say when a community— your friends and neighbors—are in trouble and you don't pay attention?"

"Pardon me," a female reporter said from the front of the crowd, "but this isn't exactly a new problem, and neither is your solution."

"And that's even sadder. Have we made so little progress in a hundred years? Or a thousand?" Janey let her gaze pan over the crowd. More than one person who felt the weight of it shifted in place. "I live in a small town, like any other small town in this country. There are a lot of advantages to our kind of life, but we have our share of problems, too. There aren't many jobs, that's for sure. Most of our young people have to move to a big city or join the armed forces because there aren't many opportunities at home.

"Megamart claims they'll change all that," she continued, "but building that store in any small community would be like dynamiting it."

Noah started to protest but she held up a hand. "Indiscriminate change is the same as indiscriminate destruction. We have to change," she said with such conviction that more than one voice was raised in affirmation, "that's a certainty. But how and when should be our decision, not some corporations that cares only about profits, not people."

The crowd erupted—people applauding, and reporters yelling questions to her and Noah, one with a frequency that couldn't be ignored.

Janey looked at Noah, one slim eyebrow raised as she moved aside and gestured to the microphone.

Noah took a deep breath, bent over the microphone and made the only comment he could. "Megamart's position hasn't changed."

Chaos ensued as the throng took up the debate. The reporters turned to take the pulse of the people, almost equally split, Noah saw, between support for Janey and support for Megamart.

The police closed in around Janey and she started off without objection, looking over her shoulder at Noah. "Will you…?

He shook his head. No, he wouldn't be there when she got out. He'd be back in Los Angeles, trying to figure out how to deal with her ingenious publicity stunt, and the even more damaging remarks she was sure to make that the entire nation was now sure to listen to.

It would, he was certain, have no effect on Megamart's plans. They'd still want to put the store in Plains City. And they'd expect him to see that it happened.

Chapter Twenty

"You have a visitor, Miss Walters."

Janey looked up at the fresh-faced cop who was unlocking her cell door, her heart giving a painful kick as she saw a tall, broad-shouldered silhouette appear in the shadows behind him. When Clary stepped through the door, she managed not to let her face fall.

Noah had left on the first plane out of town. It was foolish to hope otherwise.

"Sara packed this," Clary said, handing her one of her own duffel bags.

"Didn't want me to think you'd been pawing through my underwear, huh?"

He reddened to the tips of his ears.

"Just teasing," Janey said, trying not to think about how Noah would've had some quick and equally sizzling comeback. "Thank you for coming, Clary, and for vouching for me. Did Sara find my checkbook?"

"She didn't have to. The judge is letting you go ROR."

"You personally guaranteed I'd show up in court, right?"

"Wasn't necessary. They know who you are."

"Who my father was, you mean."

He shrugged. "Same difference. Nobody doubts that you'll show up for your court date, and if I'm any judge of these things, you'll get sentenced to community service and probation. It's only disturbing the peace, anyway."

"Darn, I was looking forward to doing a stretch in the big house, making shivs and showering with a hundred other women."

This time Clary smiled. "I guess you'll have to live with the disappointment—but thanks for the visual."

"You're welcome," Janey said as she slid a pair of shorts on and then tugged off the stifling skirts. "Uh... Would you mind?" she asked, holding up the cotton tank Sara had thought to send along.

He hesitated just long enough to give her ego a nice little boost, then turned his back so she could peel out of the old-fashioned blouse and slip on the nice, cool sleeveless cotton. It was such a shame she hadn't fallen for a guy like Clary, a man who wanted what she wanted, who didn't come around once every ten years or so and show her what life could have been like if they could just find a middle ground.

But that was love.

"Janey?"

She shook herself out of the what-ifs, the smile she'd pasted on her face fading when she saw the expression on Clary's. "Have I said thanks yet?" she asked lightly, and moved toward the cell door.

His tall, sturdy body locked her in more effectively than any bars, as he settled his hands on her shoulders and lowered his head toward hers.

Janey turned her face aside in time to take his kiss on her cheek, but she knew she'd hurt him. Before he could step away, she wrapped her arms around his neck and hugged Clary. "You'll never know how much you mean to me," she said, aching for him. He thought he was in love with her, and she knew he must feel as if his heart was breaking. She also knew firsthand how that felt. She hated being the one to cause him that kind of pain, but it would only be worse if she let him harbor false hope. "I wish… I'm sorry it has to be this way. I'd hate to think I've lost your friendship."

"Friends." He laughed slightly. "I'll always be your friend, Janey, and if ever…" He let the rest of that sentence hang, knowing she understood. Clary Beeber was nothing if not patient.

He was also honest and fair, qualities he was obviously wishing he could ignore at the moment. "Bryant called. He asked me to make sure you got home all right." Clary looked as if he was chewing lemons when he said it, "I assured him I'd take care of you," he added, which obviously gave him an immense amount of satisfaction. "You know he's probably not coming back."

She smiled sadly. "It doesn't change the way I feel."

"Then I guess we're both hopeless."

Janey murmured an assent, but to her surprise, hopeless was the last thing she felt. Noah was gone; there was no escaping that. She felt abandoned and alone, but she refused to spend one minute regretting what had passed between them.

He was undoubtedly getting on with his life and she'd get on with hers.

THE TAPE ON HER ANSWERING MACHINE was maxed out by the time Janey got home from jail. There were messages from people she knew, with reactions ranging from scandalized to admiring. There were messages from people she didn't know, newspaper and television reporters, even the governor of Montana.

And then there was the message from Noah. He'd left a phone number. That was it, not even his name. Just, "Call me, Janey, day or night," and his cell phone number. It took her three tries before her hands were steady enough to write it down. He sounded so calm, not a trace of hesitation in that rough-edged voice, while she… It hurt so much to hear his voice. Too much to dial that number. Everything had already been said, anyway; if she called him she'd only be encouraging hope it would be unhealthy to encourage, and denying time its healing chance. She gave the number to Jessie, and urged her to keep in touch with her father, but Janey didn't pump her for information, and she didn't return any of the messages Noah left for her on the answering machine, especially the one about child support. Thank God he hadn't sent her a check, was all she'd been able to think. That would have been the final insult.

Megamart was set to break ground in the spring and she'd lost the only man she would ever love. But Noah had left her with more than a sore heart and an empty feeling; he'd opened her eyes to the truth about herself. Safety was a great thing, but some people weren't meant to be safe all their lives. Janey had had enough of living in a comfortable, predictable rut.

She'd already taken the first shaky steps on her climb out of that rut, but in the meanwhile her house still needed a paint job. Winter in Erskine tended to arrive early and was usually brutal, and there was that damned western work ethic that wouldn't allow her to face the season with a house even mildly compromised by peeling paint.

Pure spite had her back out on the porch one day at the same early evening hour as the time when Noah had first crashed back into her life, she was even wearing the same paint-stained T-shirt and ratty old bandanna. Thumbing her nose at the memories, she was, daring them to get the best of her—

"Mom!"

She slapped her hand over her pounding heart, paintbrush and all. Just hearing her name was enough to push her already-primed brain over the edge.

Jessie didn't wait for a response, clattering up onto the porch and taking the brush out of her hand, then tugging her over to the steps. "You have to come down to the General Store."

"Okay, fine." She really hadn't felt like painting, anyway. "Let me change my clothes," she said, pulling her daughter to a stop and heading for the front door. "You scared me half to death by shouting like that and now my shirt's all sticky—"

"You have to come now. Mrs. Halliwell said to bring you right away." Jessie wrapped both hands around her arm and had dragged her halfway down the front stairs before Janey finished processing the urgency in her daughter's voice and came up with the obvious reason an elderly woman would want help.

"Is she okay?" Janey raced down the rest of the steps, bending down to look into Jessie's eyes when they reached the ground. "How bad is it? Is Doc Tyler there yet?"

"She only wants you," Jessie insisted.

"Nobody sent for Doc? Go get Doc." Janey began to run. She glanced over her shoulder and saw Jessie veer off toward the clinic, then narrowed her focus to getting to Mrs. Halliwell. Just one more street, she thought, as her lungs began to burn and black dots danced in her vision.

She turned the last corner and stopped dead in her tracks. Practically everyone in town was gathered in front of the General Store, all of them deathly still. Her stomach gave a sick lurch and she started forward again, searching the faces of her friends and neighbors, fearing the worst.

But they didn't seem to be sad or grieving. They seemed to be waiting. For her.

A sick sense of foreboding pinned her between curiosity and escape. Little enough happened in Erskine that any new event was a welcome diversion from the sameness of the days. On the other hand, she'd had all the surprises she could stand for one year.

She turned to leave, but there was Jessie, right behind her.

"C'mon, Mom," she said.

"They don't need us, Jess."

"You have to go in the store."

Something in her daughter's voice had Janey forgetting about the crowd and what might be happening in the General Store. She crouched down, gently nudging Jessie's chin when she looked away. "Time for the truth, kiddo," she said. "What's going on?"

"Dad's in there."

Janey's pulse kicked up to a gallop, but she kept her eyes firmly on Jessie's, waiting her out.

"He's been trying to talk to you forever, Mom, but you wouldn't call him back."

"He came back to town just have a conversation with me? Even if he had to trick me into it?"

"That was my idea. I was afraid you wouldn't talk to him if he came to the house."

"So you arranged for me to have an audience that I couldn't back down from, and Mrs. Halliwell went along with it."

Jessie had the good sense to look ashamed, although it wasn't easy, judging by the way her mouth twitched.

Janey took a deep breath, glancing toward the front of the store windows. They were lit brightly against the darkening sky, but she couldn't see anything through the crowd. "What does he want?"

"I guess you'll have to ask him that."

"Jessie…" Janey said in a tone that usually got her instant cooperation.

Jessie set her jaw and crossed her arms, waiting *her* out, and Janey had to admit the kid had the upper hand. As little as she wanted to see Noah before she was ready, and as little as she wanted that meeting to take place in front of the entire town, she wanted to know what had brought him all the way back to Erskine. It was foolish, she knew, but she still loved him and love couldn't exist without hope.

"If I'm going in there, Jessie, so are you." She took her

daughter by the hand and pushed her way through the crowd. They parted long enough to let her pass, closing in behind her in case she changed her mind. The people of Erskine liked to hedge their bets.

Janey had never been one to care if she was the center of attention, but this was different. If she was about to get her heart broken, though, she didn't want the whole town witnessing it. And if she was going to be angry, she'd aim it where it belonged—at Noah for putting her in this position—and she'd save some of that anger for herself, for letting him.

"You all ought to be ashamed of yourselves." Mrs. Halliwell came out of her store, wrapping a motherly arm around Janey's shoulders.

"They don't mean any harm, Mrs. H.," Janey said, but she let the older woman draw her and Jessie out off the street and into the General Store.

"Not for the most part, no." Mrs. Halliwell closed the door firmly behind them, letting down the ancient bamboo shades she used to shut out the morning sun. There was a chorus of muffled groans that only made her smile. "Erskine is a lot like a family. We have our share of eccentrics and sourpusses, and there might be sharp words or hurt feelings every now and then, but if you're alone in the world, it's nice to live in a place where folks still care about each other."

Janey felt as if her mind had been read. But then, she and Loretta Halliwell had a lot in common, despite their forty-year age difference. "Not everyone feels that way."

"It just takes some people longer to figure it out."

Noah's voice, but Janey didn't turn around, even when Jessie tugged at the hem of her shirt and whispered, "Mom, it's Dad."

She knew who it was; she just didn't know what he was really saying. Or maybe she couldn't allow herself to believe he meant it. Hope was one thing, but could she trust the dream to last if it came true?

Janey could feel the crowd outside straining to hear through the walls, but she waited until she felt reasonably sure she could keep her voice from betraying the riot that was going on inside her. "You set me up," she finally said, looking at him.

"I had some help."

"And since we've done our part, Jessie, we should be going." Mrs. Halliwell urged the girl gently toward the back room.

Jessie wasn't moving. "Maybe we should stick around and make sure they don't mess up again."

"You got us here," Noah said to her. "Now you have to trust us to do what's right."

"For all of us," Janey added.

Mrs. Halliwell gave Jessie a little swat on the bottom and after one last glance over her shoulder the girl went without an objection.

Janey sat on a pickle barrel, then stood again. Her legs weren't quite steady but she didn't like having to peer up at Noah. "You're here because of Jessie?"

"No. Yes. I mean, Jessie is a part of it, but…" His eyes inched upward and suddenly filled with humor.

Janey's hand went to her hair, and she tore off the bandanna she'd forgotten she was still wearing, then tried to fluff her hair. Of course, that made her aware of the fact that, once again, Noah belonged on a *GQ* cover while she was dressed in jeans and an old T-shirt. She put her hand over the splotch of paint on her chest, but he took it away, held it until she pulled free and stepped back. She couldn't think with him touching her and she very much needed to think.

"You're beautiful, Janey." His gaze slid over her, a slow lingering caress she could all but feel.

She couldn't think with him looking at her like that, either, it turned out. She gazed longingly at the door, toward escape from him and everything he made her feel. Again hope kept her where she was. "Why are you here?"

"I owe you an explanation."

"No explanation necessary," she said, her eyes glued to a place behind his shoulder. "You were only doing your job."

"Yeah." He sighed. "Just doing my job. That's what I kept telling myself, and you kept arguing with me. And you were right."

She met his eyes then. He saw the pain on her face and it tore at him. "I wasn't chasing my dreams, Janey. I was chasing a bitter teenager's definitions of success. Money, prestige, title."

"Those aren't just your definitions, Noah."

"But the *reason* I was chasing them was that I wanted to be the exact opposite of my father. I wanted it so bad I was willing to do anything. Like make decisions about how other people should live their lives, and then expect them to fall in line."

"You're not like your father."

His mouth twisted into a derisive smile. "But it sounds familiar, doesn't it?"

She didn't say anything, but he could tell she'd begun to soften toward him. If he wasn't very careful now he'd lose her...

Or if was too careful, too afraid to risk, he'd lose her, too. "I love you, Janey."

She stiffened, turned away.

He stepped in front of her, waiting until she looked at him. "I love you," he said again. "I always have."

"What do you expect me to say?"

"How about that you love me, too?"

"I love you. I always have." Janey smiled briefly, sadly. "But you've walked away from me twice."

"And you have every right to be gun-shy. I can plead stupidity for the first time, but the second..." He brushed his fingertips over her cheek. "I'm not leaving again, Janey. Ever."

She looked up at him, and he thought he saw something in her eyes that he had no right to expect from her. Hope. "You say that now, but how do I know I'm enough for you? That Erskine's enough? I mean the Megamart will be close, but—"

"There won't be any Megamart in Plains City."

"—what happens when…huh?"

"There isn't going to be any Megamart in Plains City."

"That's what I thought you said."

"And yet you're not throwing yourself into my arms."

Janey rubbed her forehead, trying desperately to bring some order to the whirling chaos inside her head. "Is that the reason you stopped the store?"

"If you'd returned any of my calls… But you didn't." He held up a hand. "I understand why. It wasn't fair of me to expect you to listen over the phone to what needs to be said face-to-face."

"I'm listening now," she said softly. "Why did you destroy something you'd worked so hard for?"

"Because it was wrong. I was doing it for the wrong reasons. Seeing you march down that street, Janey, knowing how deeply you believed in what you were doing—and how much you were willing to risk—made me understand just how little my so-called career actually meant to me. It definitely wasn't worth what it might do to Erskine." He reached over and took her hand, and this time she let him.

"It was a long shot, but I had to try to stop that store from being built here. That's why I had to leave immediately after the press conference. I knew my face would be plastered all over the news right along with yours, and I had to get back to the office and do some damage control. If they thought I wanted to stop the store because I loved you, and not because it was a bad idea, they would've gone ahead no matter what I said."

"And Megamart gave up just like that?"

"I convinced them there was too much negative publicity from your stunt. Everyone decided the store would be better off somewhere else."

"But after all the work you did. All their money. Weren't they upset?"

"Enough to fire me."

"What?"

"It gets worse than that. I think George Donaldson won the pool down at the Ersk Inn. And I made it double or nothing."

"Talk about adding insult to injury," Janey said.

Noah straddled a pickle barrel, pulled her over to stand between his thighs and laced his fingers at the small of her back.

"I think you should sue them," she said, putting her hands on his shoulders so she could lean back and see his face. "I'll get the whole town to sign a petition stating how hard you worked to get that stupid store built."

He laughed, the sound of it warm and full and wonderful.

"Making a case for myself wasn't all that easy when they were shoving that picture of me defending you from the cops in my face. It's okay," he added hastily, "it was the last nudge I needed to make me see the light." He took both her hands in his and brought them to his mouth, one by one. "There you were, putting everything on the line—your dignity, your reputation, your job—and what was I in it for?"

"Your job was on the line, too," she reminded him. "The store was supposed to put you back at the top of your game, Noah."

"I wasn't off my game, I was tired of it."

The simple way he said that, the conviction in those quiet words, brought tears to her eyes.

"I won, Janey. I got Megamart what they wanted, but to them it was just another store. To Erskine it was so much more. I couldn't forget that, so I convinced them the store would never be successful. And that felt right. Being with you and Jessie felt right.

"Do you remember asking me why I picked Plains City out of all the small towns in America?"

She nodded, squeezing his hands when she couldn't find the words to ease the pain she saw on his face.

"I told myself I was coming back here to help the community, and that's partly true. But it wasn't just the town that needed help, Janey. I did, too. This is home." He cupped her cheek, catching the first tear as it fell. "You're home. You and Jessie."

She threw herself into his arms and buried her face in the crook of his neck. Finally after ten years, she felt the weight lifting from her.

"You drive me crazy half the time," he said, smiling at the shaky laugh that earned him. "But I've felt more alive in the last few months than in the last ten years, and I've had more fun clashing with you than any business opponent I've ever come up against." He held her away from him, just far enough so he could see into her lovely, tear-stained face. "Marry me, Janey."

They heard a muffled shout come from the back room, a scuffle, then Jessie burst out of that door and barreled into them.

Noah and Janey each wrapped an arm around her.

Mrs. Halliwell took one look at the three of them and went back into the storeroom, sniffing loudly.

"Marry me," Noah said again. "Make us a family for real, Janey, and save me from a life of boredom."

She wiped her cheeks and gave him a wobbly smile. "Before I answer that, you should know I won't be able to support you. I'm not teaching anymore."

"What? They didn't fire you over the Carry Nation thing, did they?"

"I wasn't fired—I quit. You're not the only one who learned something this summer. Your childhood drove you from Erskine, Noah, but mine tied me here. This is my comfort zone—and I convinced myself this was the best place to raise Jessie—" Janey looked down at her and smiled "—but a part of the reason I stayed was fear. If I went out into the real world and failed…" She shook her head. "Scary."

"You don't feel that way anymore?"

"I kept preaching to you about your dreams, but I wasn't living mine. I've always wanted to make a difference."

"Teaching does that."

"True, but it was never my dream." She grinned. "My campaign for the state senate kicks off next month."

"Your dad would be so proud of that, Janey."

"Well, it's the family name that convinced his political party to back me—not to mention a certain protest that got me publicity. But it means I won't have a lot of time to be a newlywed, Noah."

"That's okay. I already have plans."

Janey gave him a sideways stare. "Do I want to know?"

He shrugged. "I bought Halliwell's."

That left her speechless.

"It wasn't easy to keep it a secret, but I wanted you to be the first to know—okay, the first after Mrs. H. and Jessie," he amended after Jessie glared at him. "I have big plans to change the place."

"Why do you have to change it?" Janey demanded. "It's been this way for two hundred years."

"The Megamart is wrong for Erskine, but I still think the town needs some progress. Slow, careful, positive changes," he reassured her before she could put words to the indignation on her face. "Besides, a state senator can't be married to a nickel-and-dime man."

"This state senator doesn't care what you do for a living— as long as it's legal—or how much money you make or what kind of car you drive." She couldn't quite stifle the need for reassurance that had her adding, "As long as you love me."

Noah gathered her into his arms, and kissed her gently. "I do, Janey. I always will."

"And I'll always love you." She returned the kiss, then took a step back, reminding herself that their daughter was in the room. "Let's go home."

"Wait, Mom, you never said yes."

"Jessie—"

"She's got a point," Noah said.

"All right, all right. Yes." Noah and Jessie both looked as if they didn't believe her. "What? Do you want it in writing?"

Noah rolled his eyes. "The first thing you need to know if you're going to run for political office is don't put *anything* in writing—hey," he said as a thought occurred to him, "you're going to need a campaign manager, aren't you?"

"No way, Don Corleone." She gazed up into his handsome, beloved face and felt her heart swell with more love and happiness than she'd ever believed possible. "And, anyway, you're going to have your hands full just being my husband and Jessie's father."

He scooped her into his arms, then reached down to close a hand over Jessie's. "I'm counting on it."

* * * * *

Welcome to the world of American Romance!
Turn the page for excerpts from our October 2005 titles.

THE LATE BLOOMER'S BABY by Kaitlyn Rice
SAVING JOE by Laura Marie Altom
THE SECRET WEDDING DRESS by Roz Denny Fox
A FABULOUS HUSBAND by Dianne Castell

We hope you'll enjoy every one of these books!

Kaitlyn Rice knows the heartland of the country—she herself lives in Kansas. This is her first story in a miniseries entitled HEARTLAND SISTERS, *about the Blume girls, Callie, Isabel and Josie. In this story, Callie's estranged husband, Ethan, shows up and is completely unaware that the little boy who goes everywhere with her is his. Callie has no plans to share her secret with the man who once abandoned her. So why can't she sign those divorce papers releasing him—and her—from their vows?*

Available October 2005

"Let's have a look, Miz Blume." The disaster worker's eyes met Callie's briefly before sinking to the stack of papers she'd just handed him.

She wasn't a Blume anymore. Callie frowned, but didn't bother to correct him. The man appeared to be around her age, twenty-nine, so he must remember her from her childhood here in Augusta, Kansas. That would explain the vague familiarity of his features, as well as the dull greeting he'd offered when she'd sat down across the table from him.

Local folks would probably always think of Callie as one of the Blume girls, and that was fine. Although she signed legal documents as Calliope Taylor now, she hadn't really considered herself a married woman for almost two years. Not since the day Ethan had abandoned her—and their marriage.

As she often did when she thought about her husband, Callie ran her thumb over the back of her wedding band. These days, she wore the ring mostly for convenience. If she didn't have an irresistibly cute, diaper-clad reason to shy away from legal proceedings, Callie would mail the band to Ethan, divorce him and reclaim her maiden name.

But she didn't want to rekindle her husband's interest in her life. He didn't know about the baby. Thanks to a miracle of science, he had actually left before Callie was pregnant.

A spiraling complexity of fertility treatments had failed during the previous twenty-six cycles, so Callie had held little hope for that last set of appointments at the clinic. And, after all, her husband had left her six weeks before.

She had imagined how wonderful life would be if Ethan came home to such happy news, and she'd kept up with every shot and blood test and ultrasound. Miraculously, the procedure had worked—but Ethan had never returned.

Callie hadn't been able to surrender her broken heart to seek him out and tell him. She'd been alone when she made the decision to try one last time. She'd been alone when she nurtured herself through pregnancy and childbirth. She'd gone on with her life. The precious eleven-month-old boy was hers alone.

Welcome to the first book in Laura Marie Altom's U.S. MAR-SHALS miniseries. There are four siblings in the Logue family—and they've all become marshals. Gillian is the only girl, however, and she sometimes wonders whether she's cut out for the job, or whether she should be the traditional woman she thinks her brothers want her to be. This story takes place on a small island off the coast of Oregon—and with Laura's wonderful descriptions, you can almost smell the ocean!

Available October 2005

"Mr. Morgan?" Gillian Logue called above the driving rain.

The man she sought just stood there at the grumbling surf's edge, staring at an angry North Pacific, his expression far more treacherous than any storm. Hands tucked deep in his pockets, broad shoulders braced against the wind, he didn't even look real—more like some mythical sea king surveying all that was rightfully his.

What had him so deep in thought that he hadn't noticed Gillian approach? Two years had passed since his wife's death. Surely by now he'd let his anger go?

Gillian shivered, hunching deeper into her pathetic excuse for a jacket. Even in the rain, the place reeked of fish and seaweed, and all things foreign to her L.A. beat. They were achingly familiar smells, and she could try all she liked to pretend they didn't dredge up matters best left in the past, but there was no denying it—she had issues with coming home to Oregon. Not that this island was home, but the boulder-strewn coastal landscape sure was.

The crashing waves.

The tangy scent of pines flavored with a rich stew of all things living and dead in the sea.

The times she'd played along the shore as a child.

The times she'd cried along the shore as a woman.

Shoot, who was she to judge Joe?

She wasn't on this godforsaken rock to make a new friend. She was here for one simple reason—to do her job. "Mr. Morgan?" she called again.

He shot a look over his shoulder and narrowed his eyes, not bothering to shield them from the rain. "Yeah," he finally shouted. "That's me. Who are you? What do you want?"

The stiff breeze whipped strands of her blondish hair around her face and she took a second to brush them away before stepping close enough to hold out her hand. "Hi," she said. "I'm U.S. Marshal Gillian Logue." Flipping open a black leather wallet, she flashed him her silver star.

"I asked you a question," he said.

"I heard you." She lifted her chin a fraction higher, hoping the slight movement conveyed at least a dozen messages, the loudest of which was that she might be housed in a small, pretty package, but she considered herself tough as any man— especially him. "I'm here on official business. Over a year ago, the drug lord responsible for killing your wife was released on a technicality. Now we have him back and we'd like you to testify."

The man she'd studied quite literally for months eyed her long and hard, delivered a lifeless laugh of his own, then turned his back on her and headed down the beach for the trail leading to his cabin.

"Like it or not, Mr. Morgan, I'm staying!"

Roz Denny Fox, who also writes for Superromance and Harlequin's new Signature imprint, is known for the warmth and realness of her characters and the charm of her writing. Her first American Romance, Too Many Brothers, *was published last year, and now we're delighted to present* The Secret Wedding Dress. *It, too, is an* IN THE FAMILY *story. Roz strongly believes in the importance of family and community, which is reflected in both of these books. So is her irrepressible sense of humor. You'll smile and laugh when you read this book— and you'll feel good.*

Available October 2005

Through an open window in her sewing room, Sylvie Shea heard car doors slamming, followed by men's voices, and very briefly, the voice of a child. She was seated on the floor, busily stitching a final row of seed pearls around the hem of an ivory-satin wedding dress, but the commotion outside enticed her to abandon her project. Her rustic log cabin nestled into the base of the Great Smoky Mountains didn't exactly sit on a high-volume traffic street—nor did any street in her sleepy hamlet of Briarwood, North Carolina. But as her family reminded her often enough, a woman living alone on the fringe of a forest couldn't be too careful. She'd better spare a moment to investigate.

Pushing aside the dress form that held the cream-colored gown, she squeezed her way through six other forms displaying finished bridesmaids' dresses for her good friend Kay Waller's upcoming nuptials.

A tenth headless mannequin stood in a corner. Sylvie automatically straightened the opaque sheet covering *that* dress, making sure the gown remained hidden from prying eyes. Satisfied the cover was secure, she walked to the oversize picture window she'd had installed in what once served as Bill and Mary Shea's sunporch.

The shouts hadn't abated, and Sylvie parted the curtain

she'd sewn from mantilla lace. The filmy weave gave her plenty of light to sew, yet didn't fade any of the fine fabrics stored on bolts along a side wall. Removing the lace filter, a bright shaft of July sun momentarily blinded her.

Blinking several times, at first she couldn't see any reason for the racket. Then as she pressed her nose flat to the sun-kissed glass, Sylvie noticed a large moving van parked in the lane next door.

Iva Whitaker's home had been closed up over a year. At times, Sylvie all but forgot there was a structure beyond her wild-rose covered fence. Iva's land shared a border with Sylvie's, and included a lake fed by a stream running through Sylvie's wooded lot. She often wondered why, when both the Whitakers and the Sheas had owned five acres, they'd built their homes within spitting distance of each other. Iva, though, had been a dear neighbor. If Sylvie was to have new ones, as the moving truck would indicate, she hoped the same could be said of them.

After a moment, she saw a man with straight, honey-blond hair appear, unloading a small pet carrier from a dusty white, seven-passenger van parked to the right of the moving van. He looked thirtyish, was about medium height, and had a wiry build. His only real distinguishing feature was gold, wire-rimmed glasses. Sylvie saw him as sort of a corporate version of country singer Keith Urban.

The man set out several suitcases, slammed the hatch and disappeared behind a thicket of colorful sweet peas. Sylvie was left searching her memory bank for particulars of Iva's will. If she'd heard anything said about relatives, she'd forgotten the specifics.

Sylvie made a point of avoiding gossip, the occupational pastime of too many in Briarwood. Five years ago *she'd* been the prime topic. Sylvie doubted a soul among the town's 3,090 residents gave a second thought to how badly the rumors had hurt. Certainly everyone in town was well aware that becoming a top New York City wedding-gown designer had been Sylvie's lifelong dream. Her best friends and their parents were privy to the fact she imagined prospective brides coveting a Sylvie Shea gown with the same reverence the rich and famous spoke the name of Vera Wang.

So it'd shocked her that people whispered about her—when at twenty-one, she abruptly left New York and returned home to live in the hand-hewn structure she'd inherited from her father's parents. They must have seen her distress over murmurs claiming she'd left Briarwood at eighteen with stars in her eyes and magic in her fingers, only to return at twenty-one with teary eyes and a heart in tatters.

Broken by a man. Or so gossips speculated then and now. What really happened in New York would remain her humiliating secret.

Come back to Whistler's Bend, Montana, in this second book of Dianne Castell's humorous miniseries FORTY & FABU-LOUS. *Dr. Barbara Jean Fairmont and Colonel Flynn Mac-Intire have never gotten along, but now she needs a favor from him. B.J. wants a baby, but the trouble is, she's forty, and hus-bandless, and qualifying for adoption is tough. She has an idea for a perfect arrangement...or does she?*

Available October 2005

Dr. Barbara Jean Fairmont peered across the Cut Loose Saloon to Colonel Flynn MacIntire, the guy who'd ran her panties up the high school flagpole, read her diary over the loudspeaker and called her brainiac. Even if that had happened twenty-two years ago, some things a woman never forgot.

Of course, she also couldn't forget the oatmeal she'd put in his football helmet or her article about jocks running up and down the field because they were lost.

Fairmont and MacIntire, the Brain and the Brawn. They had nothing in common and managed to avoid each other… until now. He was on leave from the army with an injured leg and his grandmother had asked B.J. to help him. He hadn't taken her calls, so tracking him to the saloon was a last-ditch effort.

A country-and-Western singer warbled from the jukebox as B.J. snaked her way through sparsely populated tables and a lung-clogging haze of smoke. Flynn sat alone, cigarette in hand, table littered with longnecks, not doing himself one bit of good. "If you quit swilling beer and puffing cancer sticks, agree to get off your butt and do therapy, maybe I can help you."

He looked up, and she gave his two-day beard, wrinkled clothes and incredible ocean-blue eyes a once-over and shuddered. Because of his appearance or because of those eyes?

Unfortunately, because of his eyes…and broad shoulders, and muscled arms and all the other delicious body parts that had driven her secretly insane for as long as she could remember. Usually, her irrational attraction to the man wasn't a problem because Flynn was not around for her to obsess over. But, oh Lordy, he was here now and likely to stay unless he got better and went back to his army life.

He leaned back and folded his arms across his solid, broad chest. His index finger on his left hand was slightly crooked, as if it had been broken and not set properly; he had a thick scar on his neck, a wider new one on his chin line, and a he was graying at the temples. A soldier. A *fighting* soldier, who'd seen more than his share of combat. She could only imagine what he'd been through and she hated it. But he'd returned alive, and that was something to be hugely thankful for, *though she wished he'd returned somewhere else.*

HARLEQUIN®

AMERICAN *Romance®*

A three-book series by
Kaitlyn Rice

Heartland Sisters

To the folks in Augusta, Kansas, the three sisters are
the Blume girls—a little pitiable, a bit mysterious and
different enough to be feared.

THE LATE BLOOMER'S BABY
(Callie's story)

Callie's infertility treatments paid off more than a year
after she and her husband split up. Now she's racked
by guilt. She's led her ex-husband to believe the toddler
she's caring for is her nephew, not Ethan's son!

Available October 2005

Also look for:
The Runaway Bridesmaid (Isabel's story)
Available February 2006

The Third Daughter's Wish (Josie's story)
Available June 2006

American Romance
Heart, Home and Happiness

Available wherever Harlequin books are sold.

If you enjoyed what you just read,
then we've got an offer you can't resist!

Take 2 bestselling love stories FREE!

Plus get a FREE surprise gift!

HARLEQUIN

AMERICAN Romance

40 & Fabulous

Dianne Castell

presents three very funny books about
three women who have grown up together in
Whistler's Bend, Montana. These friends are
turning forty and are struggling to deal with it.
But who said you can't be forty and fabulous?

A FABULOUS HUSBAND

(#1088, October 2005)

Dr. BJ Fairmont wants a baby, but being forty and
single, her hopes for adoption are fading fast. Until
Colonel Flynn MacIntire proposes that she nurse him
back to active duty in exchange for a marriage
certificate, that is. Is the town's fabulous bachelor
really the answer to her prayers?

Also look for:

A FABULOUS WIFE

(#1077, August 2005)

A FABULOUS WEDDING

(#1095, December 2005)

Available wherever Harlequin books are sold.